DOUBLE-TIME OUT OF TAOS

NASH RUNNING BEAR MYSTERY
BOOK TWO

BAER CHARLTON

Cover design by Roslyn McFarland, Far Lands Publishing

Sketch artist Kelly Eamon

Rogena Mitchell-Jones, Literary Editor
RMJ Manuscript Service, www.rogenamitchell.com

Published by Mordant Media, Portland, Oregon

ISBN: 978-1-949316-27-8 Paperback
ISBN: 978-1-949316-30-8 Ebook

10 9 8 7 6 5 4 3 2 1

CONTENTS

Powder

LETTER

"SIR. I think you'd better see this."

The aide had been stopping and standing in the same doorway for twenty-seven years. His tie persistently snagged to one side. Anyone who worked with him knew the cowlick above his left ear and graying temple was from him pulling at his hair as he read the congressman's mail that made it past the triage. Most might have made fun of his quirkiness, but all knew his manner hid only a seriousness dedicated to his boss and their work.

The congressman didn't even look up from his writing. Instead, his right hand raised a fraction from the paper and curled in, beckoning.

The congressman finished the notes, reviewed the last points, and put the cap back on the pen the governor had given him when he first got elected. Then, placing the notes in a red folder, he looked up. "What do you have, Nathan?"

The aide laid all the documents on the congressman's desk. The man wearing latex gloves and handling security sleeves didn't go unnoticed. The congressman sat back, placing his hands in his lap, and then leaned in.

"We received this yesterday. It's not your usual threat."

The aide spread out the small stack of security sleeves containing five photos and a letter with two brief paragraphs. He straightened as he waited for the reaction.

"Where did it come from?"

The aide placed the envelope secured in its own evidence sleeve on the desk. The congressman looked at the return address in New Mexico.

"Did we check the address?"

The man shifted. "It's Albuquerque's main library address. Even the postage cancellation matches the collection routing."

The congressman leaned back in his chair. Of the thousands of death threats the offices in his home state and D.C. fielded every year, he was still at a loss. "What next, Nathan?"

The man's mouth tightened. "I'll make the call on your say, sir."

Nodding slightly as his eyes closed, Congressman Dwight Wright slowly breathed out through pursed lips and puffed cheeks. His critical day had just hit a land mine larger than the one that blew up his jeep, killing his driver and ejecting him into the national spotlight and eventually congress. Nevertheless, his time in service had been shorter and less harrowing than the first campaign to get him elected.

His war chest desperately needed him to spend long days down the hall in an unmarked office, dialing for dollars from wealthy donors in need of his staying in office. But, unfortunately, today was gone, and the rest of the week looked just as dim. There had been a rumor that they would need him on the floor, but it was just a rumor—for now.

He called out as the aide reached the open door.

"Hey, Nathan?"

The aide turned. "Yes, sir?"

"Who...?"

"Deputy Director Prentice, sir. Anthony, sir."

His mouth opened in a remembered *ah*. "Thanks."

"Certainly, sir." He watched the congressman close his eyes.

They both knew all the other plans had just disappeared from the boards.

"CONGRESSMAN WRIGHT TO SPEAK TO DEPUTY DIRECTOR Prentice, please."

"The deputy director is in a meeting right now. He'll have to get back to the congressman."

Nathan leaned into his desk and the phone. "Please inform the deputy director that this is a matter of life and death."

The secretary's voice took on an arctic edge. "*That* is a term we never use lightly. If there is impending danger, you need to call congressional security or the D.C. police."

"The threat is not to the congressman's life, but a threat directed at him."

The secretary sighed. By Friday afternoon, she suffered nothing with patience. "I have your number. We'll get back to you."

Nathan growled more than mewed. "Thank you. We'll be waiting."

THE SECRETARY TYPED UP THE SMALL MESSAGE AND slipped it into a folder with other papers on her desk. This was not a meeting to interrupt lightly.

Her heels snapped mutedly down the stone hallway. Using stone had once held her younger self in awe. But with the years turning to decades, the number of shoes treading on the stone made sense. Now, she would rather stay in her domain of quiet, wall-to-wall gray carpet. The bureaucrats could keep their marble or granite. The brutal cold simply made her calves ache.

She nodded at the security and quietly slipped through the door. She looked around the large conference table and walked along the wall to the middle of the table. Three-quarters of the eyes were watching her instead of the Senator speaking.

The deputy director leaned away from the table—moving his chair back a foot. The position would allow him to look at the folder without disclosing its contents. His secretary had been using the same out-of-date folder trimmed with the old top-secret markings to bring him important messages for several years. It was their own special code. But it was never trivial.

"What do you have, Eleanor?"

She bowed her head toward the folder as she handed it to him. Her typed transcript of what the congressman's aide had said was as good as a recording.

He glanced at his watch. Then, skimming the length of the long table, he leaned back. "Call them back. Tell them I'll call them in half an hour. If that's too long, they can call the director." He leaned his head—pointing out the man, frowning from across the table.

She took the closed folder and walked out. She could feel the eyes of the Director of the FBI following her the entire way. Four of his predecessors had come and gone during her time with the FBI. The position seemed to always fill and empty with the winds of politics.

She clicked her way back to her office with the folder tucked snuggly against her side. The one without a draft. Wind or political.

2

RELAXATION

A LIGHT BREEZE blew the long gauzy drapes in toward the gigantic bed. The fine mesh of the mosquito netting draped from the single ring twenty feet above belled in toward the naked figure on the bed. The tall louvered doors cut most of the sunshine, but the trade winds passed through the louvers.

For the seventh time, the phone vibrated. The head rolled over. One irritated eye stared at the plastic and metal buzzing on the four-hundred-year-old nightstand. "The old pirate never had to put up with such interruptions."

Mina rolled over across the bed to the nightstand. She picked up the phone. *Office.* She thought about turning the phone off. The phone hadn't dared to ring for three days.

Her thumb tapped the green icon. "This better be earthshaking."

The voice only stumbled for half a second. "The FBI is going nuts. They have been calling your wife. She's not answering."

Mina looked at the silent phone and holstered pistol on the nightstand. "Tell them to keep trying. She'll probably turn her phone back on in two days when we are heading back."

"I don't think the deputy director will wait that long. He mentioned a certain congressman."

Mina didn't want to hear anymore. Her thumb hit the red icon. She turned the phone face down on the bed and slid it under a stack of pillows. It vibrated in her hand. *"Gāisǐ...* I hate redial."

She pulled the phone back as she thumbed the icon. "She's not here, and she won't... excuse me, I miss spoke. We will be incommunicado for fifty-two more hours."

She punched the red icon without listening to the answer, swiped up on the screen, and tapped the airplane. The phone vibrated once and then was silent.

Mina let go of the phone and rolled over, curling into a relaxed ball. Wherever Nash was, it had better be a good long run.

THE TABLE WAS AGAINST THE EXPANSE OF FLOOR-TO-ceiling windows. Jacob smiled as they entered the restaurant. "Your table is waiting."

He delivered the drinks as they got comfortable. As he set them down, he looked up. "Ah, they are warming up the lights."

The three watched as the mile of pink sand glowed and then grew brighter as the four landing lights off a crashed airliner came up to full lighting. Jacob had explained how they pumped water directly from the ocean to cool the large searing lights so they didn't burn up or start a fire. The day-like exposure of the unique pink sand of the beach was more magical than just a modern trick of light and water.

The chef brought out their first appetizer himself. Each course was another small taste of another island of the Caribbean and one of the traditional dishes unique to that island. As the busboy cleared the dishes from the lobster baked in banana leaves from Grenada, Jacob quietly brought another chair to their table.

Mina smiled cynically. "Why, Jacob, are you joining us for dessert?"

He silently shook his head as he turned the chair out.

"No. That pleasure is all mine, I'm afraid."

Mina and Nash looked up at the tall deputy director. Neither moved to stand. Nash dabbed at her mouth and carefully laid her napkin on the table.

Anthony Prentice nodded thanks to Jacob as he sat and pulled up his chair. "What a wonderful view. Is the sand really that pink?"

Nash's rumble clipped as short as her temper. "Yes."

The waiter appeared and held out the small menu. The deputy director glanced at it and shook his head. "I'll have whatever they are having for dessert." He looked back at Mina and Nash. "I'm assuming I missed dinner."

Their glare told him he was correct. He looked around the empty restaurant with only one other couple sitting to the south on the main level. He leaned in. "This place is empty. Did you rent it out for just the two of you?"

Mina's head gently rose back as she watched him down her nose. "It is October. The shoulder season."

His head bobbed as he continued to look around with a soft smile. "Yes, of course. That would explain it." He looked back at Nash. "How was your run today? I heard you ran to the other resort and back. That's almost a marathon, isn't it?"

Nash pulled a small bite of bread from the remaining loaf. "Close." She looked at her wife. "We need better security next time."

Mina stared at the man. She had crossed swords with him often over conference tables and power meetings disguised as cocktail parties.

His head turned and then rose and turned away slightly toward Mina as he remained watching Nash. "Yes?"

"You made good time. I only hung up on your minion, what, five hours ago?"

He wobbled his head as he pursed his lower lip. "Fair. But then, I was already at the airport when things heated up, and Nash's phone went directly to voicemail." He glanced under the table. "Where's Powder?"

Nash's eyes narrowed as she looked at her wife. "Being babysat out at Q. They don't believe she can bomb sniff and do cadavers, too. They're going to find she's even better at figuring out who to trick and embezzle treats from." She looked over at her boss. "But I won't know for another... fifty hours. I have over a month of accrued personal time..." Her threat ended in an edged growl.

The waiter placed the small plates in front of them. The chef had striped the fresh pineapple sherbet, shaped like a nautilus shell, with chocolate sauce

The deputy director nodded at the dessert. "Shall we enjoy this amazing confection before we talk shop?"

Mina put her napkin on the table. "I think I've lost my appetite."

He turned. "Please. The crew is probably still getting their dinner, and they can't refuel the secured jet without the crew there. Please. Enjoy this moment." His having flown sixteen hundred miles for other than a bit of sherbet did not have to be stated.

Nash drew a slow breath through her nose and picked up her napkin. Placing it in her lap, she took the spoon from beside the plate and carved off a nibble of the freshly made confection.

Mina followed her wife.

Anthony breathed a sigh of relief as he took another nibble and marveled at the creamy texture.

The espressos were half gone as Nash pushed her chair an inch back and turned slightly. "Before my wife pulls out the EpiPen full of slow-acting poison... spill."

Anthony almost choked but recovered behind his napkin. "Your wife's friend, Congressman Dwight Wright, has requested your services." He drew his phone out of his breast pocket. Opening it, he found the document and laid the phone on the table. "They delivered this to his office this morning."

Nash looked at the photos.

He cleared his throat. "There's more."

Nash swiped left, left, and left again. She pulled up the phone and pinched open the letter. She swiped left, and the letter bumped but didn't change. She went back to the original photos. "The photographer took these with at least a five-hundred-millimeter lens. My guess is more, and the person was over half a mile away."

"Because of the lack of artifacts, Quantico thinks it was a thousand-millimeter B&L on a Hasselblad H6D and much closer to fifteen hundred yards."

Nash blinked a few times as her face clamped down in thought.

He shifted. "About seventy thousand in equipment. But the photographer was probably more expensive. She's standing in front of a hogan in the middle of the Navaho reservation. South of the border."

Nash tapped the phone in her other hand. "And this stable of a photograph... it wasn't a drone." She looked over at her wife. "Someone spent a long time sneaking over some desolate terrain to take these photos." She held the phone out but looked at the deputy director.

He nodded. "She's in the loop because of the request."

Mina looked at the photos and then read the letter. She thought about the words and read them through a few more times. The other two watched her mouth the words. Finally, she looked up and handed the phone back. "Native English speaker. American. Probably lower Midwest or the Texas and Oklahoma region."

The deputy director pursed his mouth as his head tilted, and he nodded once. "Forensic Language concurs. You never cease to impress me, Mina."

She sat back as she took up her demitasse. "Understanding what people say and how they say it is the core of my job."

His eyes ticked more open. "Anything else?"

She smiled. "Am I sending you a bill for my services?"

"I already paid up the entire bill for the hotel. How much more do you need?"

Nash shied her head as she side-eyed her boss. "That was fast."

He looked over. "How fast can you pack?"

Mina held out her hand. "I don't get a sense that it's a death threat, only that she is vulnerable. Which could mean anything." She gently moved her head back and forth, weighing the possibilities. "Anything from nothing but a threat to kidnap or murder. But murder is only the last stick. If anything, it's a threat of kidnapping. But more disturbing is the strange number: twenty-seven and a half million is an odd number. Why not twenty-five or thirty? People round numbers. The book may cost nineteen dollars and ninety-nine cents, but people will say twenty. Twenty-seven and a half give the allusion of a specific number, only making sense to the congressman. They're showing they know more about his intimate details than they can find in public records."

Anthony scooted his chair back. "We think maybe it's a hidden account of PAC money."

Mina stood. "He wouldn't be the first nor the last to have hidden funds."

Nash stood. "We need to change if we're going to travel. Give us about twenty, and we'll meet you out front."

He stepped out from the end of the table. "Will you need a porter?"

Nash shook her head. "Just two roll-ons."

Jacob met them at the entrance and took Mina's hand. "I'm so sorry to see your time with us cut so short. It's never enough. But you look rested." He glared at Nash. "I pray for your soul. Two marathons in three days are not what Barbados is for. We are here for you to relax."

Nash smirked. "Change your rules and allow my service dog in the old residence, and I promise my runs will turn into casual walks about the gardens with my wife and our daughter."

The man frowned and looked back and forth at Mina. "Daughter?"

Mina laughed softly. "She means her new dog. Change the rules, and we'll bring her next time. She's a legal service dog."

Anthony leaned in. "As well as sniffs out drugs, explosives, and dead bodies."

The man blanched. "We wouldn't have any need for..." He caught the smiles on the three. "Ah, just a joke. Well, if she has her papers, then who are we to stand in the way of you bringing your service dog?"

Mina shook his hand one last time. "Until next time."

Nash took his hand. "Much too short of a stay, but there is always next time."

"Absolutely. Next time."

3

I'M DOING WHAT?

"Is she asleep?"

Slowly lowering into the seat, Nash faced the deputy director. "As close as she gets these days. She refuses to use any sleeping aids, so the doctors now refer to drugs as anesthesia." Nash glanced toward the back of the executive jet. "She's good for about two hours before she'll wake up thirsty."

He studied her as she turned back around. "That predictable?"

Nash shrugged. "We sleep in shifts. Two to three hours, a half-hour up, and then back for another shift."

"Checking emails?"

She twitched her head. "Against the rules. We banned ringers and middle-of-the-night checking before we got married. Haven't you tried to reach us at night?" She watched his face. She had her answer. The stalled machinery inside his head gave his eyes a panicked glaze. She nodded, her chin up. "Ah... staff. They would know. If it's important to reach us... call the doorman. If he thinks it warrants the risk, he rings the bell."

Anthony rolled his lower lip. "Doormen. The formidable first line of defense."

"Chester took a bullet for General Schwarzkopf during Gulf

One. I don't doubt he would do the same for Mina or me." She wiggled her fingers at the file folder.

He drew a deep breath through his nose and let it out in a chest-crushing sigh. "Work…" He peeked up. "Of the worst kind."

He flipped the folder open and turned it around. "These are copies of the photos and letter." He turned them over to reveal the next group of papers and photos. "This is what we have on her."

Nash leaned back, reading the cluster of stapled papers. She mussed distractedly. "It says here Taos Pueblo, but the photo was in Mexico on the Navajo reservation…"

He turned and held up his glass to the steward. "She's a painter. She moves around. She sells through galleries in Taos, Santa Fe, Albuquerque, Phoenix, Southern California, and New York. Sonora West is the name she uses to paint. Usually in the high five figures, but occasionally in the six-figure range for larger pieces."

Nash bobbed her head up but kept reading. "They don't seem to see each other much."

"I think estranged is the proper term here. For a couple of decades or more, one source says."

Nash looked over the top of the papers and studied the man.

"My wife likes her work and has followed her career for longer than we've been married. If I'd let her, she would be your partner on this. She's been to every show in New York but has never met the woman." He took the glass offered by the steward.

Nash studied the bubbles in the tall glass.

He sipped. "Tonic. I hate the stuff, but I hate flying more. The tonic settles my stomach. Or at least I like to think so."

"Try ginger ale next time." Nash thumbed through to a cluster of photos printed with captions. "If she's as popular as you say, I would think she would be as wealthy as her brother, and yet…" She turned the papers around to show him the photo. "She drives a forty-year-old battered death trap."

"More like a sixty-eight-year-old classic C10 Chevy stepside pickup." He smiled at her, squinting a jaundiced eye. "Don't let the looks fool you."

Nash snorted softly as she turned the papers back around, remembering something she had heard recently. "Back in the day, they called it a cowboy Rolls Royce. Only the double R stood for Rodeo Ready."

The man frowned at the term. "Rodeo?"

Nash smirked at the term. "Ugly and beat to shit, but can run hard all day long."

She laid the file on the rest of the folder. "So, what am I supposed to do? I mean, she hasn't been killed... yet. Or kidnapped... yet."

Anthony swallowed at what he was about to ask of a decorated marine who insists she was just administrative shore patrol in Japan and more than a couple of commendations in her FBI file for valor under fire. His lower lip furled, and then he let go. "Go make friends with her. And protect her while we try to sort this all out. We're only on..." He peeked at the date on his watch. "Day three..." He gave her a pleading look. He hoped she would mistake for passively hard-ass enough to quash any flack.

Her look was enough to let him know he hadn't heard the last of this.

He pointed back to where her wife slept. "For her sake. The congressman is a friend of hers. And he made a specific request."

She thought about the assignment and where she would be. "What's my budget?"

The low whistle between his teeth sounded like air escaping from a giant tire. "Well, it's the middle of the desert, so at least it's not Las Vegas or anything..." He gave her a hard, one-eyed look. "Just don't go crazy."

"Okay, but I'll need a good car for the desert."

He harrumphed softly. "How good a car do you think they'll have in Albuquerque?"

"They won't. Which is why I'll fly into Vegas."

"But that's..." His mind stalled again.

She blinked. "About seven or eight hundred miles. Two days for a tourist." She pulled her phone out of her pocket. Thumbing to a text, she typed. She looked up. "What time do we land?"

Anthony glanced at his watch. "About six."

"Helicopter in?"

He nodded slowly. "We can—"

"Charge it to the congressman." She typed some more, hit send, and leaned back. "I'm going to need some sleep."

Her phone vibrated. She looked at the text.

"Just closing doors. BRB in 20 GF."

She leaned back.

The deputy director had watched how fast marines could fall asleep, even while standing up leaning against a wall in the airports. So he quietly got up and moved toward the front. He knew he would need to make accommodations for his agent and her powerful wife. The helicopter would be the least of it all.

***

THE VOICE SOUNDED LIKE IT HAD BEEN UP FOR AT LEAST an hour, with no less than twelve ounces of coffee coursing through the veins. It was West Coast casual—friendly but straight to business.

"This is Rick."

Nash smiled at the guy's voice. A friend of James. "Hi, Rick. This is Nash Running Bear."

He cut in. "Have you landed yet, Agent?"

She only frowned for a second at his knowing she was in the air. "No. Shortly."

"But you'll be in D.C., and I have you flying back out of DCA, Reagan. I've captured your cell, so I'll push all this to you there. Also, there's a link to my app. Load it, and we'll have all your reservations in there no matter who you fly. Don't tell James I let you two-time on him." He hummed a moment as she heard him clicking a keyboard. "When we have time, I'll need to get your information on frequent flier clubs and what credit cards you'll be using for which trips… but for now, I've got you and the dog, a Hell Cat, in Las Vegas. It's white, so it will blend as much as a Hell Cat can. The agent swore it was a full Hemi, so if it isn't, don't take it and call me immediately. It's an open ticket, so the charges will hit your credit card after each rental week. They get a little crazy if you have it longer than thirty thousand miles. Just so you know. Will you need transport out to Reagan?"

She caught up with his firehose stream of information. "No. I think I've got it."

"Okay. I just sent you everything. Please don't lose this number. It's my private cell. So I wake up when you or James think I don't need any more beauty sleep. I'm in the Seattle area just so you know. My husband puts dinner on the table at six o'clock sharp. So, three your time."

She did the time math and realized it was still the middle of the night for him. "Got it. So go back to bed."

"Oh, who are you kidding, sweetheart? London and Paris are up and doing business. I've got almost three hours of arm twisting before I have to compete with New York. Have a great flight." The snip was electronic but was every bit as final as a phone in a cradle.

Her text message pinged. She looked at the information and downloaded the app. Then, as it self-populated the general information, she plugged in the other numbers Rick would need. She hesitated, giving him the power of knowing all her information, but remembered who he was an extension of and continued.

She hung up the phone and looked at the deputy director. He pushed out his chin toward the back of the plane.

Nash got up and walked back to Mina. She glanced at her watch and noticed the sunshine coming through the window with the shade half up.

"You got a nice long rest."

Mina looked up, blinking. "What time?"

Nash sat down next to her on the reclining chair. "Just after five. We land in about twenty. We're taking a helicopter into the office and then livery home. Chester knows we're on our way. He's ordering breakfast from Frankie's."

Mina sat up a bit. "And you?"

"Flight is at one thirty. Best they could do. They're already bringing Powder in from Quantico, so you get at least a hug before we have to go."

4

DESERT TIME

NASH LEANED her hip against the warm hood of the car. The rental agent had been true to his word. As he handed her the keys, the car had just over seven hundred miles on the engine. Rick had warned him that she would log some long, fast miles, so they changed the oil to make her happy and protect the engine.

She watched Powder sniffing at a cactus. "If it's green out here, Powder, don't lick it." The burrito was bad. She knew she'd eaten worse. She just couldn't remember when. "Pee on the sand. Just like we did an hour ago." That reminded her to buy toilet paper in the market part of the gas station.

She looked at the other half of the burrito. Then, rolling her eyes closed, she turned to the market. Maybe just some jerky and coffee.

As she returned with coffee in one hand, a pocket of jerky, and a four-pack of toilet paper under her arm, an Arizona state trooper pulled in front of her. She stopped. The man got out of his patrol SUV. He was watching her as she was watching her.

He pointed back into the market. "They have these things in there called bags."

She thought and turned to show her left hip. "I'm going to take my identification out real slow."

He stopped. His smile grew. "Because packing a load of paper is fairly scary."

Her left hand flipped the thin wallet open to expose her credentials. "No, showing you my other side would have caused some tension, and my dog doesn't like tension." She showed the pistol on her hip as Powder, in her tactical harness, sat down beside the officer.

The man slowly raised his hands. "I know when I'm surrounded and outgunned." Nash smiled. "But you had me with the jerky and the toilet paper. How can I help?"

She slipped the wallet away. "Nash. Nash Running Bear. I'm just passing through, but I must be in Taos by daybreak."

He thought about the distance. "My mother is Laguna. I can get you to the far side of the pueblo. Which puts you just outside ABQ." He looked at his watch. "It's about four hundred miles. Let me get some fuel and coffee." He leaned back and peeked over his shoulder. "Your white car?"

"Rental. But it's what you suspect."

He smiled as he moved toward the gas pump. "Rebel. Rebel Forester. Don't ask. What tribe?"

She smiled at the unusual name. "Paiute. Northern California." She jerked her thumb. "What do you take in your coffee?"

He called over the SUV. "It's already sitting on the counter."

Nash brought it out. "Your wife said not to be late for dinner."

He rolled his eyes. "Her mother is coming over to make tamales. They sell them at the church to raise money for the schools." He lifted the coffee in the black Hydro Flask with a Day of the Dead skull etched into it. "I'm ready if you're ready."

Hours later, the silver with a black striped SUV eased into the gas station. Nash followed. Her gas gauge showed less than an eighth of a tank. Powder had been sitting up for the last ten miles. She knew they needed a bladder break.

The night air was crisp and cool as they got out. Nash stretched with her fists in the small of her back. Powder had stretched when she had woken up.

Nash noted which pumps they were on and headed into the small market. She stopped at the counter and smiled at the large man with the twin braids. She put down her credit card. "Pump two and five. He'll probably need a refill on his flask, and I know I'll also be doing some shopping."

The man looked out at the state trooper's vehicle. "Rebel can't pay for his own?" His mouth pulled back in a small smirk.

She stopped and stepped back as she glanced at the man and SUV. "He just saved me a couple of hours' travel time on a time-sensitive mission. It's the least Uncle Sam can do for a hardworking trooper."

The man held up his hands in front of his chest. "No harm cousin."

She gazed down at the leather binding cuffs on his braids. She waved her hand at them as she moved to more urgent business. "I like the coyotes. They look like my dog."

Rebel stepped in as she came out of the toilet. "I started yours."

She nodded at his Hydro Flask on the counter. "I covered the gas and anything you want to eat."

The large man behind the counter snorted. "Grasshopper is a grass eater."

She scowled at him. He raised his hands with index fingers pointing at Rebel.

Rebel rolled his eyes. "I'm a vegetarian. Grass eater. I hear his fry bread is good but made with lard."

The man laughed in protest. "The cow was vegetarian."

Nash rolled her eyes low as she groaned, looking at Rebel. "I'll get the vehicles. Just don't get any blood on my credit card. When that happens, I'm required to answer to Washington, D.C."

Rebel winked with a smile.

He held a handful of hamburger patties wrapped in wax paper as she hung up the gas pump nozzle. "I figured you didn't have dog food with you, and Junior needed to clean out the night's burgers. The buns I wouldn't feed to a duck or crow. Only desperate tourists eat the dead food. But the burger meat comes from just up the road."

"You can feed her." She looked in the car. "Powder? You want some roadkill?"

The dog came to the door, and then she did her careful crawl of an old woman as she stepped onto the concrete. Rebel approached slowly.

Nash rolled her eyes. "Oh jeez, Indian. He's a nice man, and he's offering you good food. At least act like you're appreciative."

Rebel snickered and squatted. He opened the wax paper and held out the cooked meat. Powder sniffed and looked up at Nash.

Nash growled. "You want to wait until we find a flat bunny on the road? It's food now or starve later." She pulled a jerky stick out of her pocket and held it out. The dog sniffed once and returned to the stack of burgers. Two chokes and they were gone.

Rebel snickered and offered out his hand. Powder shook. "Good enough."

The man stood. "You're ten from ABQ and two hours to Taos. The sky will just be weeping when you make town. You're on your own for breakfast. I haven't been over that way since my honeymoon. I hope you find what you're looking for." He stuck his hand out.

"Thank your wife for the escort." She handed him her card. "Shoot me an email. I've got a bunch of resource information for all the tribes about missing kids. We're trying to build an information center to help with communications between tribes and government agencies."

His lower lip furled as his head bobbed knowingly.

5

TAOS MORNING

NASH DROVE SLOWLY along the four-lane highway leading into Taos. After the winding curves along the river, the town made a teasing start with a fanciful district called Ranchos de Taos. It appeared the developers had sold several lots before the effort had petered out in the hot desert surroundings. The engine rumbled softly through the open window. Against all her defensive training, her left arm rested cocked on the car's windowsill.

In the gray, almost light, she had a strong sense the morning wouldn't be complete unless a mongrel dog ran out and silently chased her into the center of town. She felt let down by the great American storytelling as she passed the Taos Drum outlet store with its display of teepees, and the highway drifted into a two-lane road. No dog. No old man out for a morning constitutional to wave at the strange white car. Nothing but the open high desert soaking up the sound of the massive engine in the morning gray. The warning of impending congestion was the random sun-beaten cheap motels that would never make the chain's glamour magazines.

The engine rumbled against the adobe walls. The original pueblo was now a cramped cluster of tourist shops alluding to waves of Midwestern white legs in too-short shorts who didn't understand the searing nature of the high desert sun.

Across the almost empty morning desert, the red and blue strobing lights were hard to miss. She eased the car to the side of the road, just short of the yellow plastic tape, then carefully stepped out as she held her palm out to Powder and put the window down.

The police officer slowly closed the door he had been opening. Nash wondered, not for the first time, how the white roofs helped in the heat when the bodies of all the vehicles were black. They both approached the crime scene tape cautiously. Nash held up her wallet and let one side fall open to her identification.

"Lieutenant."

The man's voice was low, with a shake of tumbling gravel in the stream of his words. Nash guessed the square box filling his left shirt pocket worsened the husky voice. "You guys are getting a lot faster in your response, Agent. I didn't put in the call until zero o'clock last night."

Nash stashed her wallet and leaned her head over toward her left shoulder. "I was already racing across the top of Arizona when you called it in. Who did you call?"

He tossed his head back toward the house, surrounded by small yellow tents with black numbers. "I was out here, so I told dispatch to call Luecking Park in ABQ. Where are you coming from?"

She put her hand to the tape and paused. He rolled his eyes and nodded his head for her to come ahead. "I left Barbados thirty-nine almost forty hours ago."

The man smiled as he looked at the car. "I knew Dodge made fast cars, but I didn't know they were fast enough to stay on top of the water."

Nash twitched a smile and wiggled her eyebrows. "Jet to D.C. to get my dog. Then, Las Vegas to pick up the right car."

The man looked out the side of his eye. "Get any sleep?"

"Sitting is for sleeping. Same as the service."

The man slid his sleeve up. The Globe and Anchor were greener than any other colors. "Oo-rah."

She smiled with a softer "Oo-rah." She nodded forward. "What are we looking at?"

"Just after moon down last night. Around eleven or a quarter after. Someone pulled up and unloaded a shit-basket of lead into the house. Woke the neighbors who called us. They heard vehicles, but nothing they could identify. By the time they looked, the road was empty."

Nash paused short of the field of marked brass shells. "What about Margaret Wright?"

He closed one eye and took a slow breath through his nose. "Is that why you're here?"

Nash nodded.

"Well, good luck with that. She hates people. But the neighbor said they were coming back from a ride and saw her throw a pack in the back of her truck and take off out the back way." He pointed at the hills rolling out behind. "If you know where you're going, you can catch the valley up Durango way or take the rim road across Apache territory to Navajo country. She's welcome anywhere she would go."

Nash looked over to the road and the brass. "You think she knew this was coming?"

His lower lip furled. "Hard to say. Maggie is her own woman, but she has many people who look out for her. As I said, she's always welcome in any pueblo or land. She regularly floats and paints in Colorado down to the Sonoran Gulf and Baja. Some of her paintings hang in the presidential home in Mexico City."

Nash smiled as she nodded at the meaning. "She's always welcome wherever she goes."

The man shrugged a shoulder. "She also has her enemies because of her work."

Nash frowned as she held out her hand at the road. "Who could hate an artist this much?"

The shake of his head was small. "It's not the art. The art pays for the actual work she does. Like supplying teachers to the pueblo schools. Books. Water. A few years back, she brought in a team of graduating dentists and face surgeons. They spent three months fixing mouths and teeth, and she wiped out half their student debt."

"That's a lot of kids."

His head vibrated. "Not just kids. Anyone who walked in got dental care. Fillings, teeth pulled, bridges, and false teeth. You name it, and they did it. A couple of them are still here with the Bureau of Indian Affairs. Luckily, they fell in love with the region."

Nash looked up at the young officer approaching with a clipboard.

The lieutenant turned. "What do we have, Burns?"

"Three hundred seventy-nine shells."

The lieutenant peeked back at the FBI agent in a starched white shirt with rolled-up sleeves. "You think we found them all?"

The young man let his breath out through tight lips. "With the light, we can make another pass... but..."

The lieutenant turned with a raised eyebrow. Anyone who ever chased brass in the sand knew what kind of hell it was.

Nash smirked lightly. "Want some help?"

The man snorted quietly.

Barely turning, Nash didn't raise her voice. "Powder. Come."

The gray streak didn't come out of the window of the distant car but from behind a nearby large agave plant with dozens of green swords. In a second, the dog was sitting by her side.

Nash knelt and rubbed her hand on Powder's chest under the harness. "This is Burns. He's trying to find all the bullets out there. Just like at the farm. I want you to show him the ones without a yellow marker." She looked up at the man. He hesitated and pulled an evidence tent out of his back pocket. "When he drops a marker, show him the next bullet shell. And if you find them all, we'll get some jerky." She pulled her hand out of the harness. "Go ahead."

Powder ran to the first marker and sniffed the shell. Then she started working the road. She stopped and sat.

Nash smirked at the young officer. "I'd run if I were you. She doesn't take her time when jerky is in the balance."

As they watched the dog and officer work the area, the lieutenant stuck out his hand. "Wes. Wes Walker."

She shook with a smile. "Nash. Nash Running Bear." She pointed. "That's Powder."

"She's good? Are you a CSI team?"

"Special Operations. And this is only one of her tricks. Powder's also a cadaver dog who can sense bones under twenty feet of water."

"Now, that alone is borderline unbelievable. Or just spooky."

Nash shook her head. "The unbelievable was I asked her where the body was when we boarded an empty 737. She went right to row twenty and sat down. The flight attendant gave her an extra chunk of chicken. He was so impressed."

"Was she right?"

Nash nodded. "They were transporting two caskets in sealed boxes."

"Did you know they were transporting on the flight?"

She dodged her head. "Nope. Not my purview."

Wes snorted a laugh. "Have you taken her gambling in Vegas?"

Nash swung her head as she watched the two drop more yellow markers. "Might have to try it on our way out. But right now, I think you have more than a couple of shooters. She's working a whole new throw pattern."

He swung. "Shit."

"What's the interior look like?"

Wes rolled his lower lip up. "Shot to shit. They built the bungalow in nineteen oh six. Two-by-four walls, lathe, and plaster, with no insulation. Not like it would have helped any. The rounds didn't even hesitate to pass through everything. Half the lead is out there in her backyard." He turned back and looked at

Nash. "If there was ever anything of value in there, it's long gone now."

"Got some gloves I can borrow?" She watched Powder leading the young police officer through his crime scene. "She's going to be a while."

As they stepped in under the front overhang, he glanced back. "How much training till you get a dog who steps around the evidence markers like her?"

Nash snorted quietly as she snapped the band of the glove on her right wrist. "Oh. You must be talking about one of those white man dogs." She nudged her chin out at the dog in question. "She's an Indian dog. You're watching her natural talent. She was at Quantico this last week... But she was running the trainers through her paces. They still can't figure out how a dog can sense a skeleton under twenty feet of water, find drugs or cookies in an office, and still sniff out a bomb or who shot their weapon that morning."

She turned to what they left of the front door. Carefully holding the handle, she pushed the shredded lumber in until it stood against the wall. She glanced at Wes and stepped in. As she took in the carnage, she absently continued explaining Powder. "By the time she was a year old, she had already triggered on seven skeletons in a creek. I came along the next year, and she still didn't know the commands of sit or shake. But she will respond if you talk to her like she is intelligent." She waved her hand toward the front yard. "I don't know if she had ever worked with evidence markers. I only asked her to find the shells your officer hadn't found yet. The rest of all that, she's just making up as she goes."

She squatted and carefully lifted the remains of a pottery vase.

Wes carefully stepped over. "What...?"

"It's nothing now. But it was probably a beautiful vase yesterday." She looked up. "Have you found any slugs yet?"

He pointed at the back walls. "Only holes."

She studied the tiny holes where she could stick her little finger or a pencil in. Finally, she nodded and held up the shard of pottery.

"It's the same as we saw in the sandbox. Regular slugs deform after the first wall. The pottery they hit looks like a Babe Ruth hit it for a home run. But jacketed and armor-piercing rounds shatter the vase with no concussion." She stood and looked at the back wall. "This was about sending a message. I think they knew she had already lit out."

She stepped over to the small hallway.

He stood looking at the snowstorm of feather stuffing from what had been an old leather couch. "But what kind of message destroys a house? I mean, even four hundred rounds was overkill."

Nash glanced back. "The message wasn't for Ms. Wright. The message was for me."

Wes frowned as he watched her disappear into the backroom. He followed. "I don't understand…"

He found her standing in a room filled with what had been paintings. The north wall had been all large windows and a modern sliding door.

Nash's offhand waved at the shattered windows. "Northern light. It's softer and truer for her natural paintings." She squinted back over her shoulder. "When did you know I was coming?"

"I didn't. You just showed up."

She nodded, still looking around at the shattered room of destruction. Nothing had stopped the bullets before they left holes in the back wall. "But you called the field office in Albuquerque eight hours before…?" She looked at the officer for confirmation.

"Yeah." He scratched the back of his head. "But they've never been responsive with any urgency. And in the middle of the night…?"

Her lower lip rolled hard against her upper teeth. "I don't run your office, but I was already on the way thirty-some hours before you even reached out." She looked over.

He thought for a moment. "They already knew you were coming."

She passed her hand around. "This, the overkill on the bullets, the number of rounds... This wasn't a quickie drive-by. Four or five people stood out there and spun off hundreds of rounds each. Even with a fully automatic AK-47, that takes time." She looked around with a shake of her head. "This is them talking to me. They know I'm here, and they mean business."

He frowned and glanced back toward the front of the house. "Why do you think AK instead of AR-15s?"

She stepped to the back wall. She pointed at the hole. "This is after three walls and some furniture." She stuck her little finger into the hole in the plaster. Looking back, she held up her finger. "The .223 is faster and more accurate, but when you measure one of those shells out there, I'll bet dinner they will be fifty-one millimeters long instead of thirty-nine. The European 7.6 slug is twice as much kinetic energy. Even with a full metal jacket on the AR, if you can get it, would have been done with that wall." She pointed at the interior wall. "This fat bastard is still going and hasn't cracked a sweat yet."

She pulled her gloves off as she stepped to the opening with shattered glass. "Besides..."

Her hand touched the glass door's handle, and she froze.

The day's heat still hung in the gathering gloom. On any other day, she would have stopped to watch the end of the day. But the phone call from town made her rush. She glanced back at the fresh paint on the new canvas. There would be other days. The dark swallowed the last tip of the mountain to the east. Soon silvery dots would dust the black sky. She threw the large pack in the back of the truck. Climbing in, she touched the coyote fetish hanging from the rearview mirror and started the engine.

"Nash?"

Wes stepped into the shattered glass. "Nash?"

She shook and looked back at him. Slowly the room and man came into view. "She went camping up north."

The lieutenant stood looking at the agent with the long black braid.

6

WHY THERE?

THE SMALL RESTAURANT'S patio was restful. The fountain in the large, brightly tiled tub burbled cheerily. The waitress in a traditional long skirt and bloused embroidered top carried away the menus.

Nash watched the man hold his head down to hide his smirk. Then, he reached for a tortilla chip and dipped it in the salsa.

"What?" She relaxed in the chair. "You're laughing at me."

His neck was more than a sunburn. He looked up coyly. "My mother did that?"

"What?"

"Not use the menu. She always asked the waitress what sounded good. I watched her smile as she ate things she hated. But she couldn't read the menu."

Nash softly harrumphed as she rolled forward to follow his lead with the chip. "I used to be in a rut. But a friend never looks at menus. Every meal he didn't cook was the usual or a surprise. So I don't think he's ever disappointed in what he's served."

"What if he didn't like it?"

She dragged her upper lip through her teeth—thinking. "Have you ever eaten roadkill?"

His head froze as he studied this serious woman. He finally shook his head. "You hear stories... jokes... but no. I just keep driving."

She nodded. "We grew up differently. Sometimes, it was the only meat that week or even a month. Hot dogs and whatever they put in them don't count." She stuck the chip and salsa cruda in her mouth and quietly chewed. "It's probably why there are no Jewish Indians. Which highway is kosher?"

He wobbled his head slightly. "So, anything you get in a restaurant has got to be better?"

Nash raised her eyebrows as she softly nodded. "Just choose your restaurant wisely."

The lieutenant thought about it as he chewed slowly. Finally, he leaned over and looked at Powder lying on the flagstones. "She worked hard today."

Nash leaned slightly and ran her fingers through the fur on the dog's neck. "She had fun. It was a new game. Your officer was the one who worked hard. But I'll bet he never clears a field of fire in the dark again."

"But how did you figure there were five shooters?"

She leaned across the table and pulled a small piece of fry bread from the covered basket. The warmth of home tingled through her hands. As she put the small torn piece in her mouth, she could see her father hanging the stuffed sturgeon between the two deer heads on the west wall. She had been six.

"Have you ever shot an automatic weapon before?"

He shook his head. "I humped the Barrett. One pull, one shot."

"How far did it throw brass?"

He closed one eye as he dipped his head. "About five to seven."

"Always to the right. And if you run through a few hundred rounds?"

"I had a pile of brass and a very sore shoulder."

She pulled at the bread as she leaned back and crossed her legs. Her hand dropped, and the furry mouth sniffed and took the offering. "Even if you're just spraying back and forth, the weapon will spray in a machined pattern. But Powder goes one more. She smells the distinctive scents of the different shooters on the shells. So I just had to ask her to show me where the different shooters stood. From there, I could see the patterns."

"And once you pointed them out to Burns and me, the spray fans became obvious." His face became twisted and conflicted.

Nash looked across the table. "Ask."

He licked his lip with the tip of his tongue. "How does she know what a shooter is if she wasn't trained?"

"You saw her gold shield?"

He nodded.

"It means she took some of the shotgun blast. We both were wearing tactical gear and vests, but... well..." Nash tilted her head to expose the scar on the side of her face and neck. "Her fur grew back, but knocking me back took me out of the direct blast and threw the shooter off. So we both were lucky."

The waitress put down the plates. "The cook said he hopes you aren't allergic to shellfish. It is crab and lobster from his hometown of San Diego. The sauce is special. He said it's what his grandmother won prizes for. There is avocado, Nopales cactus, and a few chilis in the cream sauce. Just enough heat for flavor but not to overcome the seafood. Enjoy."

Wes blinked at the large wet burrito. "Wow. I should have gotten what you got."

The waitress laughed. "Wesley, you haven't changed your order since we were in high school, and you were a busboy here. So have what you ordered or be open to change."

He reeled in mock horror. "Why I never..." He rocked forward, laughing at her face. "Now you're sounding like my wife."

The woman spun on her heel. "And my sister is a smart woman."

He laughed. "Yup, she married me."

"Who sometimes makes mistakes."

Nash laughed. "Sister-in-law?"

The man tossed his head back and forth. "Kind of no. They were in the orphanage together. A kind couple of Americans were vacationing on the coast and met the four girls. They fell in love and adopted all four. It was perfect for a couple in their forties to adopt four twelve-year-old girls. They have a ranchero south of town. They still look after the grandkids as needed. We're all their only family, so holidays and birthdays become noisy."

"When they were in their forties... so that makes them..."

He bobbed his head with a slight chuckle. "Younger than I feel sometimes. But yes, in their eighties. Or something."

The small white lights hanging from the pergola over the patio came on with dusk. It added a special feel to the outside dining.

Wes laid his napkin on the corner of the table. "There's been a Gila monster in the room all day."

Nash smirked on one side of her face. "Why was I on my way thirty hours before the shooting?"

He nodded as he sipped his coffee.

"My last assignment went on for months. Months I probably should have been spending with my wife while she was getting chemotherapy. Instead, after being shot and wrapping things up, the smart doctor, our doorman, Chester, suggested we decompress in Barbados."

Wes leaned a little and looked at where Powder was.

"Nope. She stayed at Quantico. She needed to go teach a master class in searching." She smiled and rolled her eyes into the stretched eyebrows. "Then my boss interrupted our wonderful dinner. So, we finished dinner, packed, and flew back to D.C. I picked up Powder, repacked for work, and caught a hop to Vegas."

"Kind of overshot the target, didn't you?"

She shook her head. "As the guru of all things travel explained, there are seven major cities in the United States. There is a flight leaving every hour from each of those cities to Las Vegas. And the flights are the cheapest. Want to fly in the next hour from New

York to Los Angeles? Fly to Vegas and back out. Also, there was a question of what kind of car I could get in Albuquerque."

"Probably not a fast one."

Her head twitched. "Fast isn't always what it's cracked up to be. A Ferrari was sitting in the lot…"

He laughed.

"My point exactly. In all the times I've been in this area, I've only seen one Porsche. But a white four-door Dodge blends in as another Detroit iron. It also rides well and corners well. Not as well as mine will when it's delivered, but still a solid in the chase department."

"You're buying a Challenger?"

She nodded. "They'll deliver it to a place in the Bay Area where they teach racing and defensive driving. The suspension and engine are being worked over by a company in Los Angeles. They usually work on Chevys but occasionally make an exception. My wife's Mustang is already there."

"Sounds expensive."

"It's not cheap. But your investment only needs to save your life once to pay off."

"You said your boss interrupted your dinner…" He shied his head with a half-shaded eye. "He called… Or…"

"Flew to retrieve me."

"Why you?"

"Ms. Wright's brother specifically requested me."

His forehead wrinkled as she turned his head. "Because you're the only Indigenous people agent?"

She twitched her head. "I'm sure there are others, but he knows my wife and me… so he asked that I come."

Wes studied the table, his eyes searching for an answer he wasn't finding.

Nash held out her palm. "What? When the powerful ask, the minions know it is a command performance."

His head vibrated as he leaned forward. His voice was low.

"Those two haven't talked in decades. I don't think he has ever been here. Or even west of the Mississippi."

Nash leaned back as she pulled her vibrating phone from her pocket. "And yet, when someone threatens his sister's life, he moves the mountain to Mohamad to protect her. So, to speak."

She glanced at the screen and held up her finger as she thumbed the green icon. "Yeah, Muna, what have you got?"

"Hi, this is... Oh yeah. Caller ID. So, I deep-dived the artist. Wow. Some powerful galleries in New York, London, Los Angeles, New Mexico, and Arizona. I finally talked to a gallery owner and close friend in Phoenix. She said that she mostly paints the desert, but when she paints mountains, she goes to Colorado."

Nash nodded. "Yeah, I noticed a couple in her studio. They weren't the worn-down mountains of the Sangre Cristo Range."

"She said something about a Grand Mesa and... wait, I'll have to spell this..."

Nash hit the speaker button.

Wes nodded. "The Uncompahgre Mountains and Gunnison Forest. It's near Grand Mesa."

Nash took the phone off speaker. "Great, Muna. Did you reach Uncle?"

"Alex said he was still hunting. Something about four tags to fill."

"Okay, please keep digging in the other grave for me if you can. Something stinks, and it isn't coming from Denmark."

The young woman cleared her throat. "Wouldn't your wife be a faster resource for that information?"

"It's bad enough she was the intermediary with this. I want to keep her clear of any bones or rotting bodies we dig up."

"Got it. Give Powder a hug for me and watch your six."

Nash rolled her eyes. "You've been watching too much bad TV. Good night." She glanced at the time on the phone. "And go to dinner soon."

The phone snicked with a metallic chirp.

Wes glanced at his watch. "Dinner?"

"She doesn't really have a life and works into the night. Last I heard, she was still in the dorm room above the offices. Of course, a commute separates one's life from the office. But, in this case, it's just downstairs." She slipped the phone back into her pocket and then pulled it back. She texted her wife two purple hearts and slipped it back into her pocket.

Nash looked at the lieutenant. "The Uncampahgre mountains? Beside it meaning the Ute people..."

He nodded. "It's the greater area encompassing the Grand Mesa, Uncompahgre Mountains, and the Gunnison National Forest. It all got expanded and covers about two thousand square miles." He widened his eyes in exasperation. "It's a lot of area to be looking in. But what made you think of there?"

"As opposed to where?"

"No. I was thinking about this afternoon. You stepped through the back door and then stopped. When I asked, you said she went north. How could you know that? The paintings in the studio?"

Nash thought about what she could share with this man she had just met. "Who do you think shot up the place?"

His face twisted as it went through the gyrations of his guesses. "All I can think of is out-of-town muscle. Well, terrorists, really."

She smirked. "So, your gut."

He leaned back in the chair with his cup of coffee. "Touché."

7

NORTH

Nash used her internal GPS more than the unit on the dashboard. She had always preferred maps to get a general sense of direction instead of the new maps feeding you cute pictures four inches at a time.

The scent of pines and junipers mixed with various brushes replaced the faint smell of cactus and yucca. Powder finally woke up and sat looking around.

"Smell like home, girl?"

Powder moved over and stuck her paw on Nash's right thigh. Nash saw the pullout. She leaned over and opened the door, and the dog looked back.

"No, I will not go pee behind a scrawny juniper bush. And don't take all day."

She looked at the clock on her phone. It would be a decent hour in D.C., so she sent a text message.

The message came back with a question mark. She hit the dial.

"I didn't want to wake you if you were sleeping in."

Her wife chuckled. "Because I don't have a six o'clock daughter to get to the door?"

Nash heard the yawn and laughed. "At least your days are more reasonable now."

Mina hummed. "Yeah, been thinking about that. Maybe I'll keep shaving my head and wearing the wigs to keep the meetings short."

"The tyranny of suffering has its perks. Gandhi would disagree, but it does."

"I think he was talking about the tyranny of expectations."

Nash smiled as Powder crawled back into the car and gave her a bored look. She switched the phone to speaker. "Teach your daughter to be more respectful."

"Is my baby Powder not having fun?"

At the sound of Mina's voice, she checked the backseat and then sniffed at the phone. Finally, she gave a soft woof.

"Yes Powder. Mama Mina is here on the phone. Are you being a good girl? I have new treats when you get home."

Powder looked back out the front window.

Nash laughed. "Hah. Treats later aren't as interesting as treats now. Well, the pee-pee break is over. Gotta roll some miles."

"Where are you now?"

"Trying to track down your friend's wayward sister, who he hasn't seen or talked to for a couple of decades—but is now the great savior. Keep him clueless for now, but I'm up in Colorado."

"Hmm, I smell something rotten here. Watch yourself. I need to run. Chester is buzzing. My ride must be here. Talk tonight?"

"We'll see what happens uphill. Have a great day."

"Roasting oligarchs on an open fire. What's not to love?"

"Go get 'em, Princess."

The electronic click was Nash's hand halfway to the second cup holder and her preference for holding her phone on the charging cradle. She always cleared a rental car's hands-free before leaving the rental yard and again when she returned it, if not after each day if she felt the need.

Nash pushed the start button, hooked Powder's restraint, and her own seatbelt. Then, checking the rearview mirror, she goosed the car into the traffic lane—closing the passenger door. She glanced at Powder. "We need to train you to close the door behind you."

Powder moved her left paw onto Nash's knee and applied weight.

Nash snorted softly. "I know. Breakfast is soon."

Her phone rattled in the plastic cupholder. She pushed the green phone icon on the steering wheel, and the caller ID showed on the dashboard. "How's the slow pony?"

"We needed to make a slight detour to pick up a few things."

Nash laughed as she rolled her eyes. "I don't eat those napalm pig bellies. How big a detour?"

Uncle muttered to someone with him. "It only set us back a few hours. But we have a ride-along on this trip."

"Are they trained and licensed to do more than tell lies and drive a bar stool?"

"He said getting out in the world would calm his spirit. Besides, the toilet in his teepee isn't ready yet."

Nash hung her head as she drove, looking through the tops of her eyes. *Thomas fucking Brady.*

"So how far behind?"

"We just left Provo in the dust. We can't hurry much because we're dragging Little Nellie and her twins."

Nash frowned and glanced at Powder, who was bored and lying down. Then, a memory clicked about an old Bond movie. She smirked at another memory in a scorching desert. "Did you pack her twin thirty-caliber lipsticks?"

Uncle snorted. "We all knew we would never get away with the no-no toy. But there's always the Barrett stored in the RV."

Nash reached over and scratched Powder under the vest and neck. "So, what toys did you have to pick up besides Thomas?"

"Little buzzing objects in the air. Where are you at? Your tracker says you made three U-turns while we've been talking. Did you see a yard sale, or are you lost?"

"Your mind is toast, old man. You never put a tracer on this car."

"Did Alex ever touch your phone…?"

She bit down hard on the words, trying to get out. "Alex is going to become Alexa if he doesn't watch out. The gas gauge says Silverton."

She could hear some mumbling. "Alex says the truck stop is at the bottom of the big loops. Food is decent and half the price of downtown and the fancy stores."

She harrumphed. "What's it matter? You won't be here in time to buy a couple of girls' breakfast, anyway."

"We'll just keep watching your tracker. Watch your trail."

Nash spread her hand under the harness and gently kneaded the fur and muscles on the chest behind Powder's front leg. "It looks like us girls are on our own once again."

With her light unmarked jacket, Nash opted for them to sit out on the quieter patio.

The waitress pushed backwards through the door. Her hands loaded with plates and a coffee carafe swinging from her small finger. She put the two plates down and looked around for the other person.

Nash snorted softly as Powder climbed into the seat and waited for Nash to eat. "She's here."

The waitress looked down and chuckled. "Does she need silverware or a mug for coffee?"

"I've never been gutsy enough to see if she'd like coffee. It's bad enough she likes those pork rinds dipped in napalm you sell in the store." She shook her head sorrowfully. "I think she gets it from her father or something. It was an ugly childhood."

"I'll get her a bowl of water. And if you need anything else, just whistle." She turned slightly and then just stood looking around.

Nash frowned. "What?"

The woman flopped her hand at Nash. "Nothing, honey. Some days, I just forget how peaceful it is out here on the patio."

"I'm surprised more people aren't taking advantage of the last of the pleasant weather."

The bottle redhead looked down sadly. "The tourists already think it's cold, and the locals are more interested in seeing friends than the mountain. You see it every day, and then you just forget…" She shoved her hand out at the mountain. "It's right there."

Nash thought for a moment and pulled out her phone. "Speaking of mountains…" She found the painting. "Do you know where this is?"

"Sure. That's the Grand Mesa. Too small to be sure, but it looks like one of Maggie Wright's paintings."

"Do you know where she would be if she was up in this area?"

The woman studied Nash and then glanced at Powder. "Someone trained your dog well to wait like that." She continued to study Nash.

Nash rode up on her hip and pulled out her wallet. She aired her badge. "Ms. Wright's life is in danger."

The waitress chewed on her upper lip for a second and then turned. "You two eat. I'm thinking your dog is better behaved than my husband and kids. I'll be back."

She put the bowl of water down next to Powder, filled Nash's mug with coffee, and drew the map from under her armpit. "I don't think people ever buy these maps anymore. They all have those fancy GPS squawk boxes sending them up logging roads where they die in the snow."

She unfolded the map and then stopped. "You do know how to read a map, don't you?"

Nash smirked as she wiped her mouth on her napkin. "Grew up on them. Then a few years in the Marines. I keep my auto club membership just so I can go in and walk out with a handful of hard copy GPS."

The woman smiled and leaned on the table. With her pen, she circled the mesa. She circled two other areas. "This is the mesa, and this is the side she likes to paint from. Usually, I hear she's staying here or here." Pointing her pen at a tiny circle. "Check in with the Drover's Inn here. If she's around, they'll know." Her finger landed on the other circle. "If she's here. Wait for dusk and hang out on Main Street. She drives a sixty-five—"

Nash interjected with a nod. "Stepside. Looks beat to shit but runs all day."

The woman's mouth pulled up on one side as she jerked her head in agreement. "Rodeo ready."

"Thanks." Nash folded up the map and set it by her plate. "You've been a big help."

The woman straightened and stuck out her hand. "Fish. Tish Fishback. But everyone just calls me Fish. My daddy was big on the Pro Bull Riding circuit until he wasn't. He bought this stick-shack with his winnings and settled down. He was Big Fish. Now, I'm the only Fish in town."

Nash smiled as she shook the warm, friendly hand. "Nash, Nash Running Bear. I appreciate the map and the honest help."

Fish wound her head to one side. "It's a lot of country out there if you don't know where you're going."

Nash bobbed her head in a soft rock. "And the only GPS I like to use in this kind of country, the *P*, stands for Paiute."

"Well, if you ever need anything in this area of the country, give a holler. I'm always around. I live upstairs, so the kids always know where to find me."

"Thanks. Good to know."

Powder moved her feet up and down and finally let out a small moan. Nash smiled. "And this is my daughter, Powder."

"She's a great dog."

Nash smiled proudly. "You have no idea."

8

MAIN STREET MEETING

NASH AND POWDER had driven the circuit. Campgrounds, trailheads, the Drover's Inn, and a few places they had also recommended. It was as if Maggie White was transparent instead. The area was pleasant, but Nash could see how the tourist season could jam the roads with RVs, the sidewalks with meandering tourists, and the restaurants, stores, and accommodations to a bloated overload. Nash fully understood how the locals felt about outsiders by the end of the season and someone who still wanted answers.

They had calmly strolled the short main street as they waited for sundown. Nash had smiled when she spied an old-fashioned park-style bench slightly set back from the sidewalk. At the other end of the block were several men dressed mostly in black. They stood beside an SUV and a commercial van. Neither the vehicles nor the men came close to blending in as tourists.

The older woman came from behind. She quietly slid onto the bench at the other end. Nash and Powder ignored her.

Nash's peripheral vision picked up the mostly salt in the twin braids worn in the plains tribes' style. The soft, faded-blue jean shirt looked well used. The loose-fitting jeans were maybe a few years younger. The silver bracelet was set with red coral, turquoise, and black obsidian. The worn silver matched the chipped and broken stones. It hung loose on the wrist in a permanent dent. It was no tourist trinket.

Nash's smile pulled back on her hidden side. "I was wondering which of us would find the other first."

The woman settled into almost a slouch. "I saw you at Drover's. I was wondering how diligent you would be in your search. So, I waited."

Nash rolled her head over and smiled. "I hadn't expected the Volkswagen with a decent paint job."

The woman kept watching down the street. "Friend's car." Her left hand raised only an inch as she pointed at the men. "Tell me, in your best FBI experience, do the criminals really think the all-black clothes and trucks somehow make them blend in?"

Her knowing Nash was FBI didn't surprise her. Nash had shown her credentials in many places during the day. Nash watched the men still standing around in the gathering gloom. "I'm still waiting for the bad guys to show up in pink and neon lime Ferraris, stickered with those lovebug flowers from the sixties."

The woman harrumphed. "Now there would be a sight. The summer of love was a powerful time in our history."

She leaned closer to Nash. "Have you figured out what they're up to yet?"

Nash rolled up her lower lip into a hard furl. "Well, for starters, your house in Taos is now unlivable."

The woman nodded. "I heard. Something about the ventilation now exceeding the limits of stopping the winter cold. Kind of rude of them if you ask me."

"Full metal jacket armor-piercing is always kind of rude." Nash pushed her chin out at the dark cluster shadowed by the streetlight. "They stood at the street and poured a thousand rounds each through the house. If you don't plow it down, the winter winds will do it for you'."

"Anything untouched?"

Nash wagged her head slightly. "Not that I noticed. Maybe a few of the canvases. But all the beautiful pottery and artifacts were just shards. It looked like some beautiful old Arts and Crafts pottery."

The woman sagged slightly. "Most were from just before or after the turn of the century. Some from Taos, but mainly from back east."

"Any idea what the message is?"

"Someone said you're here because of my brother."

Nash nodded. "He received an envelope with pictures of you at some scattering of pueblos. My guess is it was to show you're an easy target. The demand was for twenty-seven and a half million dollars. It's an interesting number. But the pictures didn't suggest it was about a ransom for kidnapping."

The woman hummed. "Twenty-seven and a half." She finally turned her head. "A very interesting sum of money. And dates back a few years." She looked back at the street. "Where're you parked?"

"Street behind and up a couple."

"Yeah. White car. South side of the street. I thought it was the one." She stood. "I'll meet you there in about ten minutes. I need to go stir a certain pot for their morning's wake-up." She tipped her head toward the men and walked the other way.

Nash slumped on the bench as she watched the slow-moving play down the street.

The elder woman didn't seem as frail or doddering as the photos had suggested. And the mind was fully engaged and running on all cylinders. Nash smirked about keeping up with the older as she reached down to scrunch the fur on the back and neck of the younger.

As she stood, she glanced once more at the men gathered next to the black SUV and van. "Babysitting my ass."

"WHAT KIND OF NAME IS DASH?"

Nash and Powder turned around. "A fast one?"

The woman smiled on one side as she crossed the front yard to the street. "No. What were your parents thinking with your name?"

Nash snorted at not the first time her name was confusing. "They named me after the car they conceived me in. A Nash Rambler. But if they had named me Dash, it would be because my father was in a hurry to get back to work. He worked for the railroads and was always on a schedule. Hence using the car in a dark rail yard." She rolled her eyes. "Or so I've always believed."

"So, it's Nash?" Maggie stood with her hands on her hips, looking up.

Nash nodded. "Just like Nash Graham."

The woman tilted her head and closed one eye. "I think that's Graham Nash."

Nash grinned. She had played this game too many times. "Sure. If you want to believe the propaganda."

Maggie licked her lip and looked down at Powder. "Where are you two staying?"

"Today was about whatever happened."

She bent and held the back of her hand for Powder to smell. "Well, we know they settled the bad guys in at the chain motel. So we can head off and have a nice dinner." She looked up, watching the reaction. "Hamburgers or Rocky Mountain oysters?"

Nash's face was stoic. "I've had worse."

Maggie straightened. "Good. Bison steaks it is."

<hr>

NASH POINTED HER KNIFE AT THE STEAK AS SHE chewed.

Maggie bounced her eyebrows. "Raised about thirty miles from here. A Ute family collective. They sell a few hundred head a year, ending on select plates in New York, Las Vegas, and Los Angeles. If I remembered the names of the restaurants, you probably never heard of them, anyway. All I care about is the tribe does well, and the best stays here local."

Nash looked out on the large backyard fronting against the high desert. "I'm glad we came out here to eat. This reminds me of growing up. Sitting in the backyard, watching the deer grazing out in the pasture. My dad always joked it was dinner on the hoof." She looked over. "There are five large deer heads in the living room. Between each is a large stuffed fish. But he never owned a rifle or learned to fish. The deer were roadkill people brought him to practice taxidermy on. And the fish he bought down in Sacramento. He learned about making molds and painting the fish. The fifty-eight-pound trout was really a sturgeon a friend let go bad in his truck. But they are impressive."

Maggie chuckled softly as she dabbed at her mouth and swallowed. "I think I'm in love with your father."

"He certainly was his own man to the end."

Maggie rested her hands on the table's edge, still holding her knife and fork. "How long?"

Nash narrowed her eyes as she looked out into the evening with the moon peeking over the eastern mountains. "About twenty-some. I was in the Marines and couldn't come home for a few weeks. My mother took a picture of a box of his favorite cereal sitting on the mantel. She wrote he was always waiting for me when I could come home. The box is still there. My sister won't throw it out. It just seems right somehow."

"And the ashes?"

Nash nodded gently. "He enjoyed hunting on Mt. Shasta. So, we got a plane to fly us over. Cold as hell, but worth it."

The woman nodded as she pushed the rest of her plate forward.

Nash picked up the last half of her steak and held it to Powder. It only took a second.

Maggie pointed at her steak. "She can have mine, too. I never was one for reheat for breakfast."

Powder didn't hesitate.

Nash leaned back in the wire chair. "Twenty-seven and a half?"

Maggie's lips furled as her head gently bobbed. "Stashed away somewhere he doesn't dare disclose."

Nash thought for a moment. "I'm guessing an island."

Maggie nodded. "Remember the first oil pipeline coming out of Canada?"

Nash blinked and crossed her eyes. "I think I was more concerned with bunny rabbits growing up to be unicorns or not. Sorry."

Maggie rocked as she nodded. "Yup. And this is the problem. With time, people forget. It's the statute of limited memories. Eventually, with enough time, you can get away with murder."

"Or twenty-seven point five million dollars."

The gray head rocked. "And with compounding interest common in those kinds of banks, more like seventy million now."

"The oil pipeline...?"

"It started as the Trans Canadian Pipeline. British Colombia didn't want a leaky sieve laid across their pristine countryside to an export depot that only the Chinese wanted. Domestically, nobody wanted to clean up tar sand oil to turn it into nothing better than bunker oil. Even trucks can't use it. Just enormous engines, burning a hundred and sixty gallons every mile at sea, can use it."

"So, after British Colombia said no...?"

"They started talking to the Americans. There were already a couple of marginal depots in Louisiana and Texas. So they just needed to get the oil to them and let them load the Chinese ships."

Nash's eyes narrowed. "But your brother represents...?"

She nodded. "Illinois. And if he could also bring some oil to a small refinery in his state... It would be worth getting him elected."

"But you just said only oceangoing..."

"The same tugs pushing mile-long rows of barges up the Mississippi River also push floats of barges across the Caribbean to South and Latin America. So I wouldn't be surprised if they push barges around Florida and up to New York. But I'd think using the Ohio River would be cheaper."

Nash sat, reflecting. "So, we have a leaky pipeline running from Canada to Illinois…"

"And they still want the other part to go down to junk refineries in Houston and Louisiana."

"All because of twenty-seven and a half million dollars."

Maggie sipped on her mug of tea. "Oh, I'm sure they spread more money around. Not just my brother."

"But they paid it…?"

"Outside the country and in secret."

Nash's hand played with one of Powder's ears. "And you know this…"

"I wasn't supposed to. But suddenly, a big to-do gallery in New York wanted to show my paintings. Mind you. This was when selling a painting for five thousand dollars was a big deal for me. And with that show, they listed nothing for under seventy-five."

"Thousand?"

She nodded. "At the pay-up, the owner told me in no uncertain terms he would never deal with me again. He didn't like being strong-armed to hold a sham show. Even though he loved my work."

Nash sensed more to the story. "What did you do?"

Maggie rolled her eyes to one side. "The only thing I could do. I took us out and got us roaring drunk until he told me the entire story. After that, I started piecing together everything else. And as the news came out about the pipeline, it all became crystal clear."

Nash rolled her finger in the air.

"Well, after our three-day bender, we were best friends and recovering from the worst possible hangovers. We were in the East Village and wandered in and out of edgy galleries for four days. We ate good food and awful food. Drank more wine than was called for. But by the end, I had agreed to do a small show a year in his gallery for a closed client list. He introduced me to a few other galleries, and now I'm in nine total, spread across the country to keep it all exclusive."

Nash rocked her head. "And I already know where you spend the money."

The gray hair cocked to one shoulder. "Well... it appears I'll need some of those funds to rebuild my house in Taos."

"Insurance?"

Maggie snorted. "Never enough."

"Ideas?"

The artist smiled and then laughed. "Always a larger studio. Always."

9

OIL AND POLITICS

NASH KNEADED the fur with her fingers as she watched the blush of pink lining the mountain's crest. Dawn had become one of Nash's favorite times of the day. In training, it meant calisthenics, followed by a few miles of double time in a winding route to chow. Later, it meant cold ocean water slurring the mud on the battle fatigues while doing sit-ups with a log across six bodies. In Japan, a monk had told her to stop running and just sit. The single volcano in the distance was her only focus. Later, she would sit and watch dozens of miles of hills to watch for one tiny speck to move and then another. It had brought her peace. Even though the specks were anything but peaceful.

The voice brought her back. "Okay, I've got it. I was in the tenth grade when this all went down."

Nash smiled. She could hear the interest in her wife's voice. "It's why I married an older woman. You know more than me. I was still playing with dolls."

Mina's hum meant her attention was only half there. "I don't think you ever played with dolls." Nash could hear her wife's distinctive typing. For every seventh letter, there was a slight pause, as if a missing letter. But she knew the typing was perfect. The pause was in her mind. A leftover from the first round of cancer. Every surgery, every round of chemo and radiation, would leave its fingerprint. Few were evident, and only Nash had ever commented about the pause.

"Did she say who paid it or how?"

Nash fed another piece of the pre-breakfast frybread to Powder. "She did not. But maybe eventually... I have a gut feeling she knows where they buried all the bodies and how they're dressed."

Mina stopped typing. "Now, that's not a creepy thought. But I think it would help you get a handle on who's gunning for her."

"I was thinking the same. I'll talk to her over breakfast."

"Okay. You stay safe out there. And I'll turn the research trolls loose on this. They've been needing a challenging project lately. This will help them earn what I pay them."

"I love you, Princess. Powder and I are off to work. I'll check in this evening."

"I have a dinner thing. I'll text you when I'm home."

"Don't let D.C. keep you up past your bedtime."

Nash's phone snicked off, and a text message clicked up. She replied with the same purple heart.

She leaned over and buried her nose in Powder's neck. "Let's go get some proper breakfast."

"Senora Wright left before daybreak. I think she go to paint the mesa. She likes sunrise for the back... um...?" The woman was struggling with the right word in English.

Nash remembered something she had heard several times in San Diego. "Fondo?" Back drop?

The woman's face lit up. "Si. Si, si. Fondo. Is very bonito."

Nash nodded. "Yes, I've seen some of her paintings."

"She say you eat, she paint. You meet later."

Nash sank into the chair with her hands and arms spread in resolve. "I guess it's just the two of us."

The woman held her clasped hands in the front of her long skirt. "I no have any dog food."

"Can you make a steak burrito with rice and beans but no sour cream?"

"Si."

Nash smiled. "We'll take two steak burritos in a bowl instead of a tortilla, with two scrambled eggs on top."

The woman pursed her lips and resisted a laugh. "Would your dog also like a coffee?"

Nash's smile grew full. "Not until she grows up. Just a bowl of water would be perfect."

The throat clearing was soft. Nash looked up from her burrito in a bowl as Powder turned from hers. The slight jump at the young man was a happy jump. Nash sat back, chewing on her food, and at the sight of Powder snuggling with the young man with a wild head of curls but no facial hair.

"I'm going to go out on a limb here and say, Felix."

The young man stood with a smile. He laid his cell phone on the table and pointed Powder to her breakfast. Then, looking up, he stuck his hand out. "We thought it was about time we met."

Nash held out her hand at the other chair. "Please. Take a load off. Although… I imagine you've been sitting already this morning."

"I saw a certain truck go past the camp before dawn this morning. I followed. When she parked, I installed the trackers. She's up near the Grand Mesa. Nice view. I'd like to see what she does with the sunrise." He reached into his jacket pocket. "You get to do the dirty work. The little one needs to go in her paint box and anything else she has with her all the time. The larger flat one can go in her wallet or purse. But it needs to be with her all the time."

Nash's smirk grew. "Did Uncle leave anyone back home?"

The kid laughed. "Nobody gets to drive Alex's dune buggy. And the Barrett is mine."

"So, I call Uncle, and Mister DEA brings the whole family of ATF, Homeland, and a sheriff out of his jurisdiction."

"Oh no. You started that one. Once you deputized him, we just figured it would make life easier, so we all deputized him. So now he gets to come play with the rest of us and still be legal."

Nash shook her head as Powder snuck her head into his lap for more hugs and petting. "Would you like some breakfast and coffee?"

"I'd love some."

Nash scooted her chair back and was about to rise when Maria, the owner, came out with a large mug of coffee and a carafe to refill Nash's mug. "Ah, good. Maria, he'll have the same breakfast, please."

Maria put down the mug. As she was topping off Nash's mug, she smiled. "Already cooking. I saw the dog." She turned to Felix. "You are family, no?"

"Sí. Powder es mi hermana."

The woman laughed. "Si, I can tell you are like twins." She fluffed her hand above her head to indicate his curls of hair.

The three watched the woman return to her kitchen.

Felix looked around the yard. "Nice accommodations."

Nash's head vibrated. "I don't think she advertises it as a bed-and-breakfast. I think her clientele is very exclusive."

"Like a certain older painter?"

Nash looked over the edge of her mug. "Maybe a few others... But you get the gist of it. So where are you guys camped?"

Felix put his mug down. "Wow, that's as smooth as one of Uncle's slipping the conversation into an interrogation." He looked up. "A couple of miles out of town. Better to keep a low profile."

Nash's snort echoed in her mug. "Yeah. Low profile. Kind of hard to hide a five-hundred-horse rat engine on a dune buggy."

Felix nodded his head up with a smile as Maria presented the large bowl with warm tortillas on the side. "Alex replaced the Mopar engine and transmission. We went with a transverse job out of a Volvo. Only three-hundred-horsepower, but about half the weight, and it doesn't hang off the back anymore. So, the balance is a lot better. Think less muscle car and more sports car."

"Any strategy, or are you boys just out taking in nature?"

He lowered his mug to the table. "The way I heard it, you called Uncle. What was your strategy?"

Nash snorted. "That one flew out the back end of a shot-up house in Taos. I've been kind of winging it since then."

He pointed at the polybag of trackers and bugs. "That's where we help you keep flapping those wings of yours."

She fingered the two larger trackers in their own bag. "Something new?"

The young man leaned in and looked at them fondly with a smile. "Manufactured by the micro technology wizard himself." He looked up. "Alex stripped a few different trackers and bugs and came up with these. Anywhere in the cabin of your car or her truck is good. The bug side is a dual sideband and picks up almost any conversations above whispers and mutterings. And if this is on your dashboard or in the cup holder, I think even the whispering is a reasonable assumption as well."

She held up the two not-so-discrete chunks of black plastic. "Range and time?"

"The tags we have tested up to fifty miles. And at that, it was still accurate to within thirty feet. So we can find you; we just can't hear you. The bug with the booster is good for a couple of hundred yards, but by three hundred, it gets sketchy. He was working on one slaved into a dash cam that could give us a couple of miles with the extra power and broadcast nature of the electrical network in a car."

She smiled. "Do you guys ever work?"

He playfully rolled his eyes and wetly smacked his lips. "Is it ever work if you love what you're doing and never have to punch a clock?"

Nash studied the bugs as Felix continued. "The dune buggy is more of a research test bed. The old systems of six guys in a Humvee or MRAP with a gunner on top are great when you have a line of vehicles to back you up. But it attracts a lot of attention. The buggy is more for surgical strikes. The Volvo also has proved to be more dependable, and the engine parts are already worldwide. It was also a lot easier to muffle to a quiet purr when you need to go stealth. Any need for quieter, and you go battery-powered only. Like the other motorcycle we made. But it's only good for about eighty miles."

Nash looked over the plastic bags with a raised eyebrow. "And now you're here to install these in my car... But you found me how?"

He pointed at his phone. Picking it up, he swiped through to an app and turned it around for her to see. "Your phone." He pointed at the bugs. "But these will give us more accuracy in real-time." He looked up at the door behind Nash.

Nash smirked. "You're getting old and sloppy, Uncle."

The deeper voice chuckled. "Maybe I should have stopped in the kitchen for some coffee." The man pulled out the last chair and eased down with an enormous smile. "What gave me away?"

Nash pointed at the dog's head in Felix's lap. "Her ears turned a minute ago. But as you came through the kitchen, she never even flinched. Only one other person is Powder like that with, and my wife is busy in D.C."

Uncle tossed his long gray braid back behind his leather-jacketed shoulder. He glared at Powder. "Snitch."

Felix twitched his head up at Uncle.

Uncle shook his head in a vibration. "Nothing. The jocks are arguing about some stupid bowl game played in the ancient past. So, I thought I'd try out your electric bike. It's kind of fun. Not all that fast, but fun."

Nash lifted her coffee to her mouth. "We were just talking about you boys and your toy box."

He rumbled as his mouth pulled back on the left side. "Jealous much?"

She pushed her lower lip out and smirked. "Who has the Hellcat parked out front at the curb?"

"Touché."

10

DIGGING DEEPER

MUNA GLANCED up from the monitor. The last of the afternoon sun turned the rolling west hills of San Francisco into heaps of napalm-encrusted pork rinds. Her left hand absentmindedly pulled open the bottom drawer of the Eisenhower-era oak desk.

She had found it languishing in the basement. A young guy in maintenance offered to strip and refinish it. She had smiled and rubbed it down with the same oil her mother had always used on old, scratched furniture. When she was looking for the right wording or thinking about another avenue of research, her delicate fingers found comfort in the lines of old scars. Someone else had been through worse at the same desk.

She adjusted her hijab around her right ear. Mindlessly, she chewed on the pork rind while reading the reports. Her days had settled gently into a routine lately. Morning ablutions and observances, followed by a hundred rounds of ammo through both pistols before breakfast. Autopsies if there were bodies or sorting and exams if only bones. A light salad followed by typing up reports. Evenings flowed into either hand-to-hand combat or a jog turning to a walk on the paths of Golden Gate Park.

She jumped as the small dialog box appeared in the upper corner of her screen.

The sender was a numbered account in Washington, D.C., but not with the FBI. The cover header said: To help Nash.

Her phone vibrated dully on the desk. A blocked caller's number.

She answered hesitantly. "Special Agent al-Faragi."

"A certain nose says your breath smells like napalm pig bellies. The file you just received. It's safe. Follow wherever you think it leads. Use whatever avenues you need to work your magic."

The voice was female and almost familiar. Muna looked at the time stamp. The call lasted only four seconds. She blinked, staring at the dialog box. The interconnect was within the secure system, but the message was from outside. It was an extensive file approaching the five-gig limit. She smiled about an old cartoon of a delivered box on a porch. The address was to and from Dr. Schrodinger's cat.

She dragged the message into her personal protective sand box and opened it. The document was over two hundred pages long, with photos, maps, and diagrams.

She glanced at the large tumbler on her desk. Less than an inch of the afternoon's tea was left at the bottom. She glanced at the time block on the computer as her stomach growled.

She flipped over her cell phone. The number was one of her most common speed dials. As the man answered, she smiled. "Hi. It's Muna. I need dinner."

The man laughed. "The cook says octopus, but for you, he makes something special."

"Thank you." She hung up as she grabbed the tumbler, and headed for the break room for more tea. It was going to be a long night. Her smile floated lightly on her lips.

The dark had settled. The lights of the city twinkled. A small bank of clouds pushed in from the ocean after the moon had risen above the bay.

The slender, dark fingers automatically picked up the chopsticks, plucked the last sushi from the black plastic tray, dipped the wad in the small cup of soy sauce, and then slid it into her mouth.

Muna bit down on the small ball of soy-tinted wasabi. Her eyes flew open as she looked in horror at the empty double tray. Turning, she looked at the time block on the computer. She slumped in the chair, knowing her alarm clock would go off in four hours. "Ugh. What a rabbit hole."

She put the chopsticks back on the tray and wiggled the empty tumbler. "Et tu Brutus?" She picked up the empty remains of her dinner and the tumbler from the desk.

Looking back at the computer screen. "Maybe no shooting in the morning..." She headed for the break room.

POWDER MOANED AT THE VIBRATION IN NASH'S POCKET. The dog gave Nash a stern look and rolled over the other way.

Nash snorted softly at her partner's afternoon nap being shortened. She thumbed the green icon as she read the caller. "Go."

Uncle grumped. "You've gotten short in your old age, Indian." Only silence responded to his try at levity.

She could almost hear his eyes roll. "We've got a situation here. You and the painter are twenty yards apart and haven't moved in the last five hours."

Nash's voice lowered to the growl she usually reserved for trainees. "Why is it a problem? She's a painter. She's painting. I'm a babysitter. I'm sitting. Where are the cockroaches?"

"Still searching for the truck in the garage. Alex took their tracker and cloned the frequency. Felix tagged the mailman, two cops, three kids on bikes, and a couple of tourists who love to wander about town."

Nash thought about the confusion a split tracker could cause. Her smile pulled back on one side as she watched the elderly woman sixty feet away. The woman put down her painting pallet and brush. Stretched and stepped back from the easel. Nash waited for her to pick up the thermos and drink as she studied the distant mesa and the painting—deciding which was not right. "So, what's the situation?"

"Your little shadow who eats thermal nuclear-tainted pig bellies called."

"And…?"

"She wants a powwow with you."

"She can call me." Nash's eyes narrowed in confused irritation with the phone tree.

"She reached out on the secure network."

The implications of even an innocuous phone call coming over the most secure communication in the field didn't escape Nash. She knew Muna to be by the book when dealing with such protocols. This was not a whim.

"When?"

Uncle grumped at someone in the RV. "How much longer do you think you and the painter will be there?"

Nash glanced toward the west. "Not much longer. This time of day is called the Golden Hour. And it's burning fast. Probably in the next half hour."

"Are you going to have dinner with her?"

The painter stepped to her small stand, holding her paints. Nash could tell she was cleaning her brushes. "She's getting ready now. I'll call you back."

Nash went through a series of muscle flexes in her legs as she watched Maggie wrap up her day. Nash mirrored her as she packed her small day pack. She took a sip of water and poured some into her cupped hand as Powder sat up.

"A good day's work."

Maggie slowly looked back with a smile. "I was wondering when you would come down. I finished what I wanted an hour ago. But nobody will complain about the little extra dabs here and there."

Nash stood looking at the canvas and the distant mountain mesa. She knew it would sell in New York for more than her car. And this morning, it had only been large blocks of bold color. "We didn't want to distract you." She looked at the woman. "What did you have planned for this evening?"

The woman reverently closed her paint box and thumbed the latches. "A light dinner. Maybe some reading. But early to bed. While this weather holds, I'd like to do a few studies from down on that ridge." She turned back. "Why?"

"I need to go to an important meeting."

The woman collapsed her stand and tripod easel. "Well, you have my paint bugged, my truck bugged, the Volkswagen bugged, and…" She pulled the tracker bug out of her pocket. "How much more babysitting did you need to do?"

"I'll follow you back to the house."

Maggie smiled. "I don't know if I should feel like an errant child or a doddering old woman."

Nash looked back at the mesa, now disappearing into the gloom. "Error on the side of the child. I don't think doddering is in your lexicon."

She bent and gathered the paint box and folded the table as Nash picked up the collapsed easel and painting. "It's there. I just try to hold it at a long arms bay. Twisting my ankle while dancing at my seventieth birthday party was a wake-up call. We don't think about our feet, knees, or hips in our youth. We just walk, run, dance, climb, and do or wear whatever we feel like." She turned and started walking back to her car. "And one day, we learn how fragile we really are." She looked back over her shoulder at Nash. "It's a rude alarm clock for our sleeping complacency."

Nash rocked her head. "I can relate."

Maggie put down the box as they reached the car. She stared hard at Nash. "You're what… thirty…"

"Forty-one." She leaned her head to expose her neck and the scars. "Two years ago, I would have told you I was bulletproof. A year ago, we wouldn't be having this conversation if it hadn't been for Powder. It wasn't the same old three days of relaxing and jumping back on the bicycle. It was a steady month of various rehabs. Both for me, for Powder, and my marriage." She stooped to play with the dog's head.

Maggie opened the car and lifted the paint box and table in. Then, turning, she took the easel from Nash. "You don't wear a wedding ring."

"Neither does my wife. Occupational hazards to both careers."

Nash noticed the slight tick of the eyebrows.

She turned back from the car and took the painting. "What does she do if I may be so bold?"

Nash smirked, thinking about how she could describe the unusual brokering her wife wrangled. "She spends her time trying to keep errant children, like your brother, from destroying the country or their careers."

The woman finished securing the painting in the backseat and stood. She stretched her back with her fists pushed against her kidneys. "Now, that sounds like a tough job. Is she any good at it?"

Nash blinked and looked at a movement in the nightfall. Maybe a fluttering bat. "It got me here."

The woman patted Nash on the upper arm. "Then we better work hard at not screwing it up."

THE GOLD AND ORANGE LAY GENTLY ON THE windowsill. The day had started almost as usual. By mid-day, Muna was feeling anything but usual. War, natural disasters, and emanating threats have filled the snippets of news worldwide. Most she scrolled past. One had stopped her scrolling, triggered her to do more research, and now had her sitting in the open window looking out over the city.

She had never questioned her heritage or her faith. Her open secret pleasure at the break with halal was all she really had allowed herself. And now, so many... and it wasn't even a crisis of faith.

She walked back to her workstation. Sitting, she switched to her private zoom account and dialed the only number she had always known.

The woman's face filled the screen. Her smile at seeing her daughter was warm but sad. The long, black hair had the start of silver speckling the wash of night. The hair fell around her shoulders.

Muna nodded. "I had wondered if you had seen the news..." Her right hand reached to the end of the hijab and gently tugged. The long scarf unwound, and she nudged at the loose bun. Her long hair fell to match her mother's.

"Your father had gone to the mosque to talk to the Imam. He is convincing the Imam to support the women and their choice."

Muna's eyes filled as she mouthed her love for both of her parents.

11

DREDGING THE PAST

As a joke, the six in the RV sat poised with pork rinds at their mouths. None had the stomach for the hot coating, so they faked it by shaking unseasoned rinds in a bag of Cheetos. The taste was subdued, but the look passed. They waited for the connection to fill the larger screen.

The connection filled, and they recognized the office space in San Francisco. But the screen didn't fill with their friend, but an old doll. Only Uncle recognized the first action figure, an over-muscled, almost naked blond, and started laughing. The figurine had a small yellow wig from some other doll, and someone had drawn a bikini on with a black marker.

The sign in the altered figure's hand read *technical difficulties*.

Someone walked past the camera. The long, flowing head of hair was not one they recognized. "Be right with you guys. Sorry."

Nash frowned. "Muna?"

The disjointed voice was cheery. "Yeah. Just a minor problem with the translator from my personal sandbox program to the inter-connection server. I thought I had it..." The exasperated face came into the camera. The long hair fell to the desktop. "But obviously,

Master of the Universe, I am not." Her hand held out to the doll. The head disappeared below the desktop.

Nash turned to look at Uncle. "Should we call back at a more convenient time?"

The top of the head rose from under the desk. Muna blinked. "Why? I've almost got it."

The screen flickered and split. A document filled the new panel, and Muna smiled and pumped her right fist and arm in the air. Standing, she then sat, adjusted the camera, and worked her keyboard and mouse.

Looking up, she smiled. "Good evening. Welcome to Muna Talk."

Nash's eyebrows rose as she tilted her head and pulled at the side of her hair.

Muna smiled. "Ah. Yes. I know. I need you to show me how to braid my hair. All I ever knew how to do was wind it into a loose bun and tie it down with a hijab." She looked at one of her other monitors and dragged a document across into the live panel.

"I had to dig back to the nineteen-sixties to find the connections."

Nash leaned back. The elephant in the room would remain in the corner... for now.

"There was a PAC formed in the early eighties. The five reported figures of note have since passed away. Most importantly, the PAC only existed for seven years before being disbanded. Which is no small feat. In fact, it's harder to dissolve the incorporation than to create it. It's like creating Frankenstein's monster. Some stitching together of some spare parts, add a lightning bolt, and voilà, you have a walking, breathing monster. It's the killing that gets ugly."

Uncle growled. "This PAC...?"

Muna pointed at the screen. "Is where the twenty-seven and a half million... well, actually, the one hundred and sixty-five million came from."

"One sixty-five?" Nash leaned forward. "Where are the..."

"Other five shares? Dead. Well, the people are dead. The original people, at least. I'm still trying to track where the money flowed to and where it is now. Only one of the original participants in the scheme is still around."

"Wright."

"Correct."

Thomas pointed at the document on the screen. "That's a high school diploma."

Muna winked. "He's quick. We might keep him around. Yes. To be more exact, it was a boarding school in east Texas near Paris."

Felix frowned. "There's a Paris in Texas?"

Uncle grumped at him. "You can go to Paris, London, Rome, Washington, and Portland and never leave Texas. Texans aren't known for creativity. Now let the teacher teach." He turned back to the screen. "Please. Continue."

"Thank you. As I was saying, it was a boarding school for wealthy children of influential people. Such as those placed high in the oil industries or politics."

Nash raised her hand as she frowned. "Wright fits in how?"

Muna's lips furled in a hard smile as her head rocked. "Scholarship." She pulled in another document. It was a pay record from the Southern Illinois Railroad. "His father was a conductor. But he liked corn lightning. And so did some who rode his train. It was through those..." She made quotation marks in the air. "Customers who gave his smart son a scholarship. I'm sure they constantly reminded him of how his bread was getting buttered." She frowned and cocked her head. "Is that the right phrase?"

She put up another document. It was a contract for bunker oil for the new oil-burning locomotive the railroad purchased. The new train would transport the poor-grade oil from the worn-out oil fields to the new refinery. In exchange, the refinery refined some of the oil to match the locomotive's engine needs. Again, debt showed on the books, but not the profit. "This is where Wright's father shined. I'm sure the rail line showed many years of lost income. Not a loss of income, just not any income showing."

Thomas groused. "It's how the rich get richer."

Nash smiled. "Until they get caught."

Uncle cleared his throat to get the class back on track. "While Wright's father is driving the train, who's greasing the wheels?"

Muna pulled up another document. "Thomas Greeley and Joseph Ivanovic. The two principal figures of the Southern Illinois Oil. Both have sons who will attend the boarding school with Wright."

She looks at her other monitors and drags over another document. Her window shrunk. "Harold Dumont and Dubois. Crockett Abrams and Jonathan Roberts of the Lone Star Oil fame joined them. Both families were more than just Texas oil. Lone Star had holdings reaching west to the oil fields of Los Angeles, south into the Gulf, north through Colorado, and up into Canada."

Thomas squirmed as he looked around for something. "So, the boys are at a boarding school. And I get it's exclusive, but what brings them together? Sports?"

A news clipping pulled onto the screen. The headline didn't make sense with the photo of two boys being led out of a building in handcuffs. Thomas read the headline. "Two arrested for Blood & Bone association. Were they killers? The type is too small to read."

Muna leaned in. "The unrecognized fraternity was where the six formed their bond. The school tried to squash the group over the years, unsuccessfully. But these two took the blood and bones part a little too seriously and were charged with the ritualistic murders of three other students. By the time the trial finished, the school had ceased to exist. Probably to protect the owners from any blow-back suits being filed."

Nash looked up from the paper she had been writing on. "Who's the sixth?"

Muna curled her lip in a sneer. "That's the one thing I haven't figured out. The incorporation of the political action committee shows five people, but only the four officers. The PAC also raises the full one-sixty-five and shows it distributed in six equal shares, but the sixth person is unnamed." The legal form slips into the main window.

Alex stretches his lanky body as he yawns. "Maybe the mystery person is the facilitator."

Nash and Uncle slowly turn around to look at him.

He blinks with another yawn. "What? I'm just spit-balling here. But why else wouldn't they be on the records? And who's threatening the congressman?" He sat up straighter. "First, you have a person reach out from the shadows, and they know of a specific and unusual dollar figure of a large bribe. It was too big to make as a political donation and involved in a shady deal. We're sure the congressman would rather remain buried. So, I think, find the sixth person, and you've found your person in the shadows."

Felix, as the youngest, raised his hand tepidly. The tiny Muna in the corner laughed and pointed.

"Um… or there is another way."

The older five turned on the usually quiet young man. Alex fluffed his hand in the air to encourage more.

"During the early part of the Afghani war, they couldn't find certain people. So, they found their money and hid it. And then they offered it up as a reward to anyone with credible information on their whereabouts. The reward was just a small fraction of the booty, but to a tribe leader, it was a large sum of money—usually more than the tribe could earn in a year with opium."

The tiny Muna in the corner became a blur as she spun toward one of her other monitors. Soon the large screen refreshed, with a tracking form showing a large sum of money moving in and out of a bank. Uncle smiled and touched Nash on the shoulder. She looked at the bank header and laughed. "Our old friends."

Muna's face filled the tiny window. "Yes, but it didn't go to Switzerland or Argentina this time."

"Any idea where?"

"I'm still working on it. But we have a track record of their cooperation, and we can lean on them to help find where it went. I'll reach out to the banking division for help and then make the call tomorrow."

Nash stretched her arms with her fingers interlaced. "Do you have all this in a concise timeline?"

The tiny Muna window flowed into the entire monitor screen. "I will have it in a couple of days. Whoever compiled all this stuff just grabbed and shoved it all in a shoebox, so to speak. Mostly, it's been a grind of sorting it all by dates and seeing where they fit. I have a sizable folder of random documents with no dates and seemingly no connections. But once it has a flow, I'll go back and see where it all fits. Hopefully, there's also some help to track the sixth mystery person."

Uncle leaned back in the camp chair. "Roll the bones."

Muna frowned with a crinkled smile. "There are no bones to this case. At least, I hope there aren't."

He leaned forward. "Of course, there are bones. You're just not seeing them yet. Print out all the documents and throw them on the floor. The same as you did with those skeletons. Spread out, you know the second left hand didn't fit. You have plenty of room in that one room. Spread them out in the timeline. As you get tangential off-shoots, you still have a place to keep them in the timeline, but as a sub-set."

Muna hesitantly scratched at her head and then buried her fingers in her hair. "That can work. Visual filing would give me an overview of the entire sixty years."

Nash smiled. "Now, can you explain where all the hair came from?"

Muna's face grew solemn. She turned to another monitor and typed on the keyboard. The screen split, and there was a video. No sound was needed. The news report was from Iran. A woman with long, flowing hair was dancing toward a makeshift bonfire in the street. She held and swung a long scarf in her hand, which she dropped into the fire and danced away. As she twirled, the long hair floated like a reddish-brown cape behind her. The scene cut to women being beaten in a mob. The last cut was to a picture of a woman wearing her scarf slightly pushed back.

"When my mother was a little girl under the Shah before her parents moved to America. Any head covering was a choice. Most didn't. Tehran was an incredibly progressive city. The same as Bagdad. They were as metropolitan as Paris or Milan. But we follow the decrees of the Imams. But with this, this is no longer about religion but the subjugation of women. And we won't go back this time."

The softly spoken statement of power conveyed the inner struggle of faith and person. The six in the RV knew they would probably never see a hijab on her head again.

Uncle frowned. "When did this happen?"

Felix hung his finger out in the air. "It's been blowing up my news feed all week."

Nash softly snorted as she glanced back at the young man. "Uncle has a flip phone." She turned back toward Muna and raised her right fist.

Muna's hand rose slowly as her smile crept across her face. The fist was tight and firm, showing the whitening in the knuckles. There was a sisterhood.

RUN

"I HAVE NEVER FELT LEFT out by missing a few days of the news. But seeing the news clip... and then having Felix just casually mention he had been seeing it blow up his news feed..."

Mina's voice was soft and comforting. "I was in the bar at the Blue, waiting for my appointment. The bartender turned up the volume. I have never been in the Blue and had it go silent. It was a powerful piece. I'm sure it's not over. I don't think they will ever be able to push the genie back into the bottle a second time."

Nash nodded at the young girl as she put the two plates down. Powder sat in her seat and waited. Nash reached over, took the bacon, and broke it half, holding the half out to the dog. "It just felt like something I should have been aware of but wasn't. I'm not saying the job I'm involved with should have taken second place, but it is a momentous shift in their religion. Not only Muna but her mother has taken off their hijabs. Maybe forever."

"And I'm sure there are still women who, for one reason or another, are still wearing theirs and will continue to do so."

Nash reached over and cut up the omelet with her fork. Powder turned her head and delicately tongued each piece as she watched Nash talk instead of eating. "Um... my breakfast partner is giving me a look about me being rude and talking on the phone instead of eating with her."

Mina laughed. "Give my daughter a hug. We'll talk later."

Nash heard the chirp of the text message as she turned the phone face down. "Your other mother sends her love. Now eat. There are starving puppies somewhere in the world."

Maria stepped out of the kitchen onto the deck. "How was breakfast, senora?"

Nash and Powder looked around. "Ah, Maria." Nash pointed at the dog. "She got most of my bacon, but it was very good. Your fry bread reminds me of my grandmother."

"She was a wonderful cook?"

Nash smiled and shook her head. "I never met her. Or any of my parent's parents." She tapped her head with her finger. "But up here, I always dreamed someone in my family knew how to cook heaven on earth."

"You no cook?"

"My mother taught me how to burn a pot roast or scramble some eggs. Mrs. Fisherman and I can whip up some mean fish sticks in the toaster oven. Or we order delivered. But often, when my wife and I can sneak some time alone, we go out to dinner."

"You can come stay here, and I will teach you how to cook."

Nash chuckled. "I would love that... but by the next month, I would lose the recipe and burn up another pan or two. So it's better if you do the cooking, and I stick to hunting criminals."

The woman's hand dipped into her apron pocket and brought out an old Atlantic Richfield Road map. "Speaking of your work... Maggie left you this." She unfolded the map. "She is here today. It looks like you take this road, but no is possible. The mountain came down last week. So you go this way around."

Nash raised her eyebrows as she smiled. "This is good to know. Did she take a lunch, or should I bring it to her?"

"No. I make a basket. It is by the front door." She stepped around the table and gently petted Powder's head. "I no forget you either. I make you special little cakes yesterday. No azúcar, but much sesame seeds and peanut butter. You will like."

Nash shook her head sadly. "She is so spoiled."

Maria smiled. "She is worth the spoiling. Yes?"

"Si."

Nash pulled her vibrating phone out of her pocket while still laughing. She noticed the caller. "Yes, Alex."

"Get rolling. The bad guys are moving and aren't following kids around the neighborhood. They're moving fast."

Nash stood, and Powder alerted. Maria shooed her with her hands. "Which way are they headed?"

"West toward the mesa. Same as yesterday."

Nash strode through the house. "I'll pick you up in the car."

"I left you an earwig in your center console the other day. It's blue-toothed to your phone, so we can stay in constant contact and be hands-free."

The woven basket was aspen bark and willow. Nash glanced at the packages for a football team. Food never goes to waste, and water is always needed. She grabbed the handles as she opened the door. Then, triggering the trunk, she dropped it in and pulled out Powder's and her tactical vests.

Climbing into the car, Nash checked the console and pushed the earwig into her right ear. If the window was open, the right would always be the quietest. She pushed the start button.

Only a handful of gravel moved as they moved out into the street. The early tourists only walked on the sidewalks as they hunted for caffeine and baked goods.

The phone pinged in Nash's ear and then cleared. By the sound quality, she could tell Alex was using his headphones and boom microphone. "They're about three miles ahead of you and moving at fifty-six."

Nash glanced at the GPS on the dashboard. "They're pushing hard. The canyon is forty for a reason."

"They just dropped to forty-seven. I guess they found out why. I have you closing and now at two miles."

Nash could feel Powder shifting her weight as they muscled through the turns. "In about ten miles, a road breaks off to the left. It goes down and around the mountain where this road goes through the small pass."

"I see it."

Nash grunted with the hard turn. "I need to take that cutoff."

"You won't be able to make up the time and get ahead of them. It's longer and just as winding."

Nash smirked. "A little birdy told me this morning the pass had an acute case of avalanches. When the coyotes find out the train tunnel is just a painting on the mountain, I'll be making like a roadrunner."

Uncle broke in. "We're on the move to back you up. We've got the horsepower, but we're a little top-heavy. Thomas and Felix are out ahead of you with the buggy. They took off when the bad guys started moving. So, they're already out there somewhere. Felix was tracking the painter early this morning, so he would know the track she took."

Alex pinged in. "Nash, you're about two hundred yards from the turn. As you get near them, Thomas and Felix's coms will link with yours to give you sit-reps."

"Got it." Nash eased the heavy car through the turn and gunned it down the straight. She knew she only had a few minutes lead on the bad guys. She pushed the Hellcat through the small canyon. There was no speed limit for life and death matters—only skill and performance.

Once again, the car she had chosen for her personal car performed to her expectations. She could see the mesa in the distance as she dropped into the wider valley.

The ping in her ear was soft. She could tell Alex was watching other moving targets as well. "You're about a mile away. She'll be on your right, but she's a few hundred yards up a dirt road."

Nash pulled the curve in tighter as a tractor-trailer came the other way. She didn't want the driver to react by splattering the produce all over the side of the mountain. "Where's Thomas?"

"They went up the valley to ensure you can exit that way. They're about eight miles ahead of you."

"I just passed a produce truck headed the other way. If he got through, this tinker toy could do it too."

"You're fifty yards from…"

Nash jerked the car onto the dirt road. "Got it."

"You're closing fast. Sorry, I can't give her any warning. She seems to have her phone off or not on her. It just goes to a voice mail that isn't there."

Nash spotted the battered bug. The woman was next to it.

Nash pulled up alongside and toggled the rear window. "Maggie, we need to go right now. Come on."

The woman spun. "Let me—"

Nash cut her off. "No time. They're right behind me. Get in the backseat."

The woman turned and closed her paint box the size of a brief-case. Nash's eyes widened in disbelief. "Maggie. There's no time."

The woman rushed to the car, opened the back door, and set her paint box in the footwell. Climbing along the seat, she looked up. "Go."

Nash hit the gas, and the forward jerk slammed the door. "Lay on the seat and use the middle seat belt to tie yourself in. You can hold on to the other belts."

They fishtailed back onto the blacktopped road as Nash noticed the two black vehicles barreling down on them seconds away. If they didn't recognize the white Challenger, they would gain a larger lead while they detoured to a lonely VW bug and no Maggie…

Nash mashed down the accelerator as the two trucks raced past the turnoff. They had figured it out. One glance at the GPS on the dash told her it was now a race of the largest engines, not skill or cornering. The narrow valley let out onto an alluvial fan millions of years old. The gentle drop gave the heavier SUV and cargo van the advantage over the seven hundred horses under her feet.

A glance in the rearview mirror told her the other drivers had already taken advantage of the slope. The two black grills were feet from her back end and were splitting. Whoever they were, the expertly trained drivers were a coordinated team. The pincer box was an extremely effective tactic.

She peeked in the right mirror. A long gun's nose was out of the window. The view in the left mirror confirmed their tactics. The side cargo door gaped and rolled back. They would position a man with an automatic rifle in the bay. If not two. This is where the deadliest force would come from. This was the brutal club. The SUV would try to take the aimed surgical strike.

Nash grabbed the steering wheel at ten and twelve. Her right hand was palm up. "Powder. Floor. Hold on, it's going to be rough."

As the dog dove into the footwell, Nash stomped on the brake. The two black trucks shot forward. As her front end came even with the open cargo door and window, she hauled down on the steering wheel.

The car slewed violently as automatic gunfire erupted from both sides. Her right nose slammed into and pushed the backend of the SUV. Her rear quarter panel hit the cargo van.

The heavier weight of the SUV pushed the now sideways vehicle over. The automatic gunfire stitched its way across the left side of her car and up into the cargo door and the man thrown in the air.

Nash looked back up the hill as the Challenger continued to spin. Her hand pushed the shifter into reverse as her foot left the brake and mashed back down on the gas pedal. The guttural roar of the big Hemi engine matched the sound coming from her clenched teeth.

The bump of running over the body was satisfying, but the resulting bounce targeted the trunk squarely into the open cargo door, and the second man coming out to take his turn at shooting. The rifle burped once as the trunk smashed his delicate pelvic region into the best metal Detroit could turn out. There was no contest. The van tipped away as it slid into the storm ditch.

The white battered car was barely better than a rolling wreck. Nash knew she wouldn't be getting her deposit back.

She looked in the backseat. "Maggie? Are you okay?"

"Is it over?"

Nash slammed the car in drive and smoked the tires as she spun the rear end around. As she cleared the front of the SUV, she could see the driver and another kicking the front window out.

She hoped her coms were still working. "Thomas. Felix. I could use some serious help here."

"Just keep coming, but stick to your left side. I need the right for a shooting alley."

A moment later, Nash saw the flashes a quarter mile away.

The dune buggy was stationary. Felix had fixed the Barrett on the mount. With the stable platform, the fifty-caliber cannon became a brutal punisher.

Nash glanced in the rearview mirror as the black truck became a ball of orange flame. Only then did she notice the smoke trail from the missile. She smiled. *Don't mess with team Bear.*

The steam was venting out of a dozen finger-sized holes in the hood. As she pulled to the side of the road across from the dune buggy, the soft knock of the engine became more menacing and violent. Nash pushed the start button, and the sound became only steam. She patted the dashboard. "End of the road, but you did good."

The voice was soft from the back. "Kind of hard to get a nap with all the screaming."

Nash released her seat belt and fished her hands at Powder. The dog eased up onto the seat as she looked around and headed into the arms of her mommy.

Nash looked in the back. "Screaming? I don't think anyone had time to scream."

Maggie looked up as she fumbled with the tangled seat belt. "I certainly did." She slowly sat up, leaning on her left arm. "I haven't screamed so much since the twirly ride at the state fair in oh-four. I almost wet myself then too." She looked out the door window. "Oh. Who are the cute boys?"

Nash tried to open her door. Unfortunately, it had crammed into the center post. "See if that door opens, Felix."

They all flinched as another explosion rocked the valley. A second fireball rose from the tipped over cargo van. Maggie stared back through the rear window. "I knew there were bad people in the world, but..."

Felix pulled on the door. The bent metal complained, but the door opened. "So much for that gas tank." He pulled open the back door and reached his hand in for Maggie. "I believe this is your stop, Miss."

Maggie twitched and then focused on the young man. She let him pull her across the seat, but as her legs touched down, she reached for her paint box.

"Those must be precious paints."

She patted the side of his face as she stood. "You haven't any idea."

Nash stood as Powder ran around, sniffing everyone and making sure they were all okay. "How far away are you, Alex?"

"We're the large object in the distance." The voice echoed through the three coms. They all looked back to see the RV nosing its way between the two burning funeral pyres. "Looks like someone might need an auto club."

Nash lowered one eyelid. "I think we'll let the sheriff sort this out."

Thomas smiled with his game-winning smile as he pointed at the white wreck. "They might want to know about this one as well."

Nash glanced back at the now dead car. Her lips furled as she remembered Thomas being deputized by all the alphabet gathered. "Sorry, sweet cheeks, but on the Incident Command System, you're at the top. You'll have to explain this joint operation to your fellow local sheriff."

Alex chirped in their ears as the RV drew to a stop. "I already called it in. They have a patrol on their way. He's about forty-five out."

Felix rolled his eyes and grabbed his narrow waist of youth. "Well, there goes the idea of getting a nice dinner anytime soon."

Nash's stomach growled. She remembered why her breakfast had only been a single bite. Smiling, she snapped her fingers. Stepping to the trunk, she laughed in surprise. The crumpled trunk lid stood open. The picnic basket, looking somewhat rattled, was still sitting where she put it. Lifting it out as the RV pulled to a stop, she called out in her best TV soap opera voice. "Lunch anyone?"

Nash handed the basket to the young, starving waif. She looked back and then stepped over to the woman with her arms wrapped around herself.

Maggie glanced over and then refocused on the two burning pyres. "Do you think my brother wanted to kill me?"

Nash gently grabbed the woman's arm and turned her away from the horror. "No. No, I don't. He sent me here to prevent you from being killed. I don't know what is going on with him or who those men were, but we're still here to make sure you're safe. And right now, it's the only thing that matters."

The woman leaned in for a hug. "Thank you. I guess I needed that."

Nash could feel the gentle shaking. Not usually a hugger. She let her arms settle around the small woman. "We're here."

13

DOWN TIME

The six chairs and two large ice chests lined the side of the RV. Uncle slouched and feigned sleep anytime the state troopers thought about talking to him. The fall sun had crawled its way across the desert sky. The long shadows of morning had shortened, shifted, and grown long from the pinnacles and low sage brush dotting the expanse.

Nash buried her chin in her chest as she mirrored Uncle's slouch in the canvas chairs. The backs of the chairs faced the RV to hide their origins. The movie had never made much of a splash, but the producers had reached out to a few federal agents for authenticity. When the suggestions got ignored or blatantly thrown out, the chairs found a new home. Nash smiled at knowing her's was marked Director. She looked over at Uncle in the Producer chair.

"You know they will eventually work out who the real chain of command is."

Thomas, sitting in the Sound chair, snorted wetly. "Don't bet on it. They still think it was an accident. I guess they regularly riddle car and trucks around here with bullet holes."

Maggie sat primly on the larger red ice chest, sipping on coffee. "It depends on the neighborhood." She looked over at Thomas.

"Tell me; and Nash already told me you have a reservation in your county. Do the vehicles on the reservation have bullet holes in them?"

Thomas blinked several times as he thought.

Uncle rumbled. "Don't strain yourself, Tommy. The answer is a few." He turned toward the woman. "And the other answer is no. The holes didn't come from the reservation. They come from random hunters. Some hunting meat to put on a table, but others just looking to cause trouble."

The woman wobbled her head from side to side. "Ignorance and prejudice usually walk hand in hand. But the answer to the troopers out there..." She waved her mug in the general direction of the wreck and officers. "No, they probably aren't ignorant or blind enough not to see the bullet holes, but they probably don't have the experiences you all have to see the entire panorama of the scene. Even a child finger painting sees the big things. The sun in the sky, the tree in the yard, the mountain in the distance, and their house. It is only with more experience they add the bird in the tree or a dog in a yard with grass... or not."

Powder sat up.

Nash rested her hand on the dog's head. "She wasn't talking about you."

They all looked at Powder and then turned toward where she was looking. A silver car parking the other side of the burned-out hulks. It was missing the usual Colorado State Trooper markings.

Maggie nodded in her mug. "That would be the captain. He's getting slow in his old age. I expected the kid here an hour ago."

Nash rolled her head over. "Friend?"

"Only the last decade or so. He was already a lieutenant by the time I met him at a fund-raiser. He's big on helping kids to read and grow up with an education."

Uncle watched the man with the silver brush cut stop and talk to the troopers working the hulks. The officer stooped and pointed out a few spots on the SUV and a couple of matching marks on the asphalt several yards out in front.

Uncle smirked. "Felix?"

The kid looked over.

"Did you bounce a few of those shots into the SUV?"

The blush grew to the pursed smile. "Maybe...?"

Uncle chuckled as he waved his finger at the kid and then the RV. "You got found out. Now go grab another chair for the man."

The kid glanced back at the man walking their way. The uniform looked fresh, but the man walked with some physical baggage. Felix's voice was low. "Yes, sir."

Uncle studied the man and his cadence. His voice was low. "Nash?"

Her eyes narrowed behind her orange aviator glasses. "I think if he had been Rangers, he would have a more civilian cut by now. Maybe serious marine like an instructor, or possibly a SEAL... hard to say." She raised her eyebrows as she looked over at Uncle. "A flyboy would wave his arms about all goofy and walk duck footed. And Coasties don't know what a brush cut is."

Felix pulled the black chair out of its sleeve and popped it open as the man finally got to them. He waved his hand at the chair. "Coffee's still hot."

Maggie raised her mug. "And good too, Jefferson."

The man blinked one eye as he wound his head in a sweep. "If Maggie approves, who am I to say no? A little cream and a packet of fake sugar if you have it, please."

Felix did a two-finger salute. "Pink or yellow?"

"Yellow, please."

"Got it."

The man studied the line of people as he gently took the seat. He snorted softly. "Permission to address the tribunal?"

Maggie snickered. "Jefferson, if the dog doesn't bite you in the next two minutes, you're probably good to go. They're all just folks."

The man smiled at his friend. "Um, huh? Just like my neighbors. Except the mailman is DEA, the garbage collector is CIA, and the schoolmarm is Homeland."

Uncle laughed softly. "The schoolmarm fetching your coffee is Felix. I don't know how to deliver the mail, but it's pronounced Uncle, just like your mother's brother. No garbage collection on domestic lands, but we have an entomologist to see what's bugging ya. The fuzzy mug is Powder, and her sister is Nash." He waved his finger lazily toward the other two. "Alex would be firearms because he doesn't drink or smoke. And the golden boy is Thomas."

Felix handed him a mug.

The man looked up. "Thanks, Felix." He studied the young man with a slight frown.

Alex smiled. "They recruited him at fifteen. Fresh off his high school graduation stage."

Felix pulled a tall water bottle out of the ice chest and sat down. "They waited until Monday, but they camped across the street from the house. My mother kept taking them food. Dad laughed, saying she was chumming the fish. My pool party went from Friday graduation to Sunday night. It kept my friends off the streets and not drinking."

Jefferson lowered his mug. "Why the Wunderkind treatment?"

Uncle laughed. "His science fair project. He got his hands on the three best bugs and trackers the government uses. His was smaller and more powerful. We use them regularly..." He waved his hand at the still smoldering hulks down the road. "Except they do burn up."

The officer glanced back down the road. "So, you were tracking them?"

Felix nodded. "You'll find a small, melted wad of plastic, silicon, and a rare-earth magnet on the roof of each. Bugs in the wheel well are worthless unless they turn the vehicle off and are sitting somewhere quiet. And I didn't have a chance at getting inside, so only the trackers."

"But putting trackers on the roof is easy?"

Felix cocked his head and nodded. "Yeah, ride by on a bicycle and flip it up on the top. The magnet will stick it either way. If they hear the noise of it landing, they just figure the kid riding by hit the van on the side." He shrugged and smiled broadly. "I'm just a bored kid in the neighborhood."

Jefferson snorted softly. "Dangerous neighborhood."

Nash smirked. "You have no clue how scary these boys can be."

The man nodded as he watched Powder curl up and feign boredom. He turned toward Thomas. "My investigator says you're the top of the Incident Command System."

Thomas rolled his eyes. "I drew the short straw. They told me we were going leaf peeping and maybe squeeze in some dancing girls in Vegas."

The silver brush cut never moved as he rolled his head. "Yeah. Just along for the ride...?"

Thomas held out his left hand to show it rock steady. "But I shoot with this hand." He raised his shaking right hand. "So, what's the question?"

Jefferson smirked at the old joke. He leaned his head down the road. "Who are they?"

Thomas scratched behind his right ear and winced. "Sheriff to sheriff, or the equivalent. We have no clue."

The captain turned to Maggie. "And I hear you have a condemned house in Taos..."

Uncle sat up straighter. "We believe it was these same guys." He pointed at Nash. "The director of the..."

Nash interceded. "Deputy director. My boss assigned me to come out and protect Maggie. Which is kind of like nailing Jell-O to the backside of the barn. I got to her house about five hours after they had been there. The local sheriff said they shot it up around eleven-thirty the night before. Maggie lit out shortly after dark, so they missed her by a few hours."

"Where were you coming from?"

Nash nodded at the white heap. "Vegas. It was the closest rental where I could get a Hellcat. But, if I was going to be in the territories, I wanted a fast pony."

"Vegas is a far piece to come. When did you get the assignment?"

Nash slouched a bit to her right. "About thirty-four hours before we hit Vegas. I had to stop in D.C. to pick up my partner." Her hand could barely touch Powder's head.

The man frowned. "You're not out of the Vegas office...? Where were you coming from?"

"Crane Beach in Barbados."

The man tried to do the math. His finger wavered in the air.

Nash made it easier on him. "The deputy director brought the company plane. It was to underline his point about my not having a choice in the matter. Baby-sit or find a new job."

"Why you?"

Nash smirked lightly. "Do you speak any Athabascan?"

The captain squirmed slightly.

"Well Marine?"

His head snapped up with a hard glint in his eyes. "No. A little, but no."

Nash bobbed her head up as she pointed at Uncle. "Neither do I. And I only speak some northern California Paiute. But he speaks Athabascan, and Powder understands."

The man wound his finger around in the air. "So, you pulled this all together? Why aren't you at the top of the ICS?"

She pointed at Thomas. "Because he's the team captain, and because he drew the short straw. I'm just FBI. Powder and I investigate and baby-sit. But for anything more, it takes a complete village."

"Who made the bounce shots into the SUV?"

She pointed at the kid. "The Wunderkind needed some real-life practice with the Barrett."

Jefferson evaluated the size of the young man. "Kind of an enormous gun for…"

Felix pointed at the mount on the dune buggy. "The mount takes the weight and recoil. It's not as fun as the twin thirty miniguns, but it works for targeted shots."

Realizing he was getting full disclosure all around, and dove in. "So why the skip shots?"

Felix shrugged. "All we had in the buggy was Parabellum rounds. I wanted to get a tumbling distortion and maybe pick up some street shrapnel. The Parabellum round will do the job, but I was a little mad and wanted to tear things up a bit."

Jefferson gazed back down the road and then glanced over his shoulder at the white wreck. He looked back at Nash. "Is that your story, too?"

"They tried a squeeze kill box. In theory and training, it's supposed to be foolproof. As the babysitter, I had a gut feeling. It just kind of worked out better than I expected. I might have to go try to repeat it at Quantico when this is done."

"Judging from the smash on the one nose, you tried a pit maneuver from the side?"

Nash twirled her finger. "Kicked the one with the nose, which drove my back end into the other. Or visa-verse. Things happened a little fast."

Maggie giggled. "Best ride since the twirly ride at the state fair." She pulled a serious face at Jefferson's shocked face. "I almost wet myself."

Jefferson studied the older woman and then chuckled. "Nothing about this is straightforward… is it?" He stared at Nash.

Nash raised her chin toward the early dusk. "As my mother used to say, it's about as straightforward as a pond-soaked ball of yarn."

"And your boss flew down to…?"

"Barbados. It's off the coast of South America."

"… And rushed you back because…?"

Nash pointed at Maggie. "Because her brother is a powerful

congressman, and he had received what we believed was a credible threat to her life."

He glanced back to the pair of tow trucks pulling the hulks onto their flatbed trailers. "I would say extremely credible."

Nash smiled. "I'll make a note of the concurrence when I file my report tonight."

The man stood. "I guess I have everything I'm going to learn here. I doubt if we're going to find anything we can source from the fingerprints…"

Nash stood and fished out one of her business cards. "But if you can share those prints and any photos you get, especially of tattoos. We have sources we can't share, but if we can clear up your accident files…"

He nodded with furled lips. "I'd appreciate it." He nodded at everyone and, last, his friend. "Maggie."

Maggie waited until he was out of earshot. "He's a standup guy. If you can share anything unofficially, tell him over a glass of mescal and pineapple juice."

Nash looked back at Uncle. The man smiled.

He was in.

14

RESEARCH IS THE EVIL OF ALL BANE

THE LIGHT DRIZZLE hung softly in the air. It didn't fall, but more like floating as if waiting to gather enough weight to fall. It was just one of those magical pieces of San Francisco Muna loved.

The large black fingers separated the hair into three and then started weaving. The man softly hummed as he worked. He paused and squirted a small puddle of conditioner in the hand's palm, still holding the braid. He rubbed his palms together and then stroked the long hair.

"If your wife has short hair, and you never had daughters, where did you learn to braid long hair?" Muna's left thumb picked at the nail on her right thumb.

Andy smiled. "Have you ever seen dray horses?"

"I saw a dapple gray one once."

Andy laughed. "No. Dray as in pulling a large wagon full of barrels or goods."

Muna turned her head slightly. "You mean like the Clydesdales?"

Andy straightened her head. "And some are larger. My father bred and raised competition Belgians. They pulled heavy sleds for money." He finished the braid and wound a rubber band on the end. "When they are working or showing, they braid the tails and manes to keep them out of the harness and pull chains. When I was growing up, it was my job. My sister was taller and washed them. And then we both mucked out the stalls. With giant horses, there is giant muck."

Muna turned with a sad smile. "Thanks." She pulled the thick braid over her shoulder. "It's funny. Once I was old enough to wear a hijab, my mother never saw my hair again. I can't remember if she ever braided my hair... even as a little girl." She gazed up at the kind smile on the older man. "And I never remember my father even touching me. Not even to hold my hand..."

Andy rested his hand lightly on her shoulder. "All of us grow up differently. For a while, you wore a hijab. Now you don't. You have beautiful hair, and in a braid, that much hair is more manageable. And I can always braid it for you. Or teach you."

She picked up the bottle of leave-in conditioner. "This is a trick I would never have thought of."

He smiled. "And ask Nash. Lacking any scent means you can add what you want. I think the last time I talked to Nash, she added sagebrush and rabbit droppings. Or something more country."

Muna closed one eye and leaned forward as she gave him a stern look. "I don't think it was rabbit droppings. And besides, she does it for her dog."

Andy waved the air. "Yeah, yeah. She's a fine start of a dog, but I like mine when they hit the two-hundred-pound mark."

Muna slipped her vibrating phone out of her pocket and held it up. "Speaking of work..." She stood and walked into the building. "This is Muna."

THE PHOTOS OF FACES AND FINGERPRINTS WERE OF little help. None of the men had served in the military or had time in jail. But cross-referencing the tattoos took her down the international rabbit hole where Interpol ended.

She laced her fingers and turned her hands backward as she pushed out. The crackle in her slender knuckles reminded her of some of the larger muscle-bound trainees at Quantico. They would flex their large biceps and then slap them in a macho show of testosterone. It might have worked in the military or the gym, but it was a useless display when they were shooting or doing classwork. But to her, limbering her fingers before intensive typing made sense.

She dragged the first man's work into the secure sandbox. Once there, she physically unplugged the connection to any other computer except her private access to the evil side of the internet. The one where the face book was about mercenaries for hire. Cars for sale sites flogged tanks, armored personnel carriers, bullet-proofed limousines, and trucks. She didn't understand boating, so she had no reason to look for surface-effect boats, cigarette drug smugglers, and sub-surface transporters.

If the skull was more frontal and the penetrating weapon was more of a dagger, the tattoo could pass for a Chechen gang who showed up as far south as Afghanistan. But the skull was a quarter view with an Arabian scimitar. The dead rat, smashed by the skull, made no sense to her, but it was another detail to sort out from the other skulls with a knife in them.

Muna leaned back and sipped on her iced green tea. She turned to her other computer and typed in a few searches. Dragging the images she wanted to a comparison window, she glanced back through the doors to the autopsy lab.

"Mike or Oz... anyone got a minute?"

She could hear the distinctive sound of the titanium legs in sneakers. His metallic tone was soft, but a tiny whir of the micro servomotors gave him away to her ears. The rustle of a plastic bag was a bonus.

Oz's voice was soft but filled the room. "Wow. Great braid."

Muna turned around to watch both men entering through the archway. She reached out for the bag of Double-Hot Jerk pork rinds. "Thanks, Oz. Andy did it for me this morning. He grew up braiding horse tails or something."

"Competition dray horses of some kind."

Mike stuck a pork rind in his mouth as he stared at the images of swords on the larger screen. "Belgians." He pointed at the smaller screen. "This is a scimitar. They put a cutting edge on the inside of the curve. Horsemen used it because it would take a head off as they rode past."

Oz pointed at the third sword she had in the comparison window. "That one. This one is more of a Hessian version. But they sharpened the outside, and it's longer. They had taller horses. The thought process of the difference was to slash as you passed, and if you didn't kill the soldier outright, he would tie up a couple of support people taking care of him. So, they would ride through the armies, slashing right and left, and sort it out later."

Mike leaned in as his hand passed into the bag. "Yeah. What he said." He drew three or four rinds from the bag and pointed at the tattoo. "What's with the squished nutria?"

"Rat."

"Nope. Nutria. The nose isn't long enough for a rat. Also, the lower jaw is the prow of a rowboat and comes up to the teeth. Myocastor coypus is also called the coypu. Originally from South America, but has invaded the southern states and subtropic regions of Europe, the Middle East, and northern Africa. Easier to trap than a possum, coon, or gator. Just as greasy to eat."

Muna stared up at the man.

He glanced down as he pushed the last rind into his mouth. He beamed. "Or so I've been told."

Oz shifted as he scratched into his mass of white hair. "He's right. My sister likes the swamp pig, but I'll stick with the farmed gator. How many of these tattoos does this feller have?"

Muna pulled up the full-body photos of the corpse. Front and back. "A few. I'm just getting started."

"Well, throw out the obvious old ones. The ones they got in jail or juvenal hall." He pointed at the cross near the man's crotch. "Like this green cross. How crisp and clean is it?"

She pulled up the detail, and they could see it was old and amateurish.

Mike pointed at the man's neck. "What's on the side here?"

As she pulled up the warthog wearing armor, the two men smiled. "Mockba." They raised their hands and gave a high five.

Oz continued as he pointed. "He was a driver in an armored division. He served in Chechnya or Afghanistan. There was a group from a mean ghetto in Moscow. They called themselves the warthogs. They were notorious for driving over men, women, or children in Afghanistan."

Mike nodded. "I remember the theater in Moscow." He looked down at the confused face of Muna. "One night, about forty Chechen freedom fighters took the audience hostage. It was about eight hundred people. They demanded Russia withdraw its troops from Chechnya. The Spetsnaz were called in. They were all milling around. It was all being covered by the news. The FSB were dressed in their usual dark green tactical gear. And then suddenly, there was a bunch all dressed in black. They pumped fentanyl gas into the church and then had the Spetsnaz breach with gas masks. Many people died, but someone got a closeup of one of the black uniforms and a patch. It was the first time we had seen the warthog in armor. But after that, stories started coming out of the decade of Russian occupation in Afghanistan."

Oz pointed at the computer. "What about the others? Any with the same tattoo?"

"I don't know. I just got started on this one." Muna called up the body shots of the others.

Mike pointed. "Necks. They'll have the same location."

Muna cleared the screen and reset the sort and recall. Eight images of eight left sides of eight different necks. Three matched.

Mike circled a tattoo on one of the necks. "Enlarge, please."

The image was a full-frontal death head. Not really a skull. But the head still crushed the nutria. The sword was a shorter, straight sword. Longer than a dagger but shorter than a medieval great sword. The pommel or hand guard twisted away from the handle on one side and toward the handle on the other.

Muna leaned back in her chair. "Same sentiment, but not the same sword."

Oz pulled up a chair from another desk. "It's too long to be a dirk. It's more like a Roman short sword, but the guard is wrong. They had none or an oblong disk. They didn't believe they needed protection."

Muna looked at one man and then at the other. "If I didn't work with you two, your knowledge of this stuff would creep me out."

Mike snorted. "Swords or tattoos?"

Muna inched her finger into the top of the bag in his hand and peeked in. Mike handed her the bag. There were only two rinds left. "Both. Well, all of it. I don't remember a class on the history of swords and their use and by whom." She looked at Oz.

The older man nodded. "I was a Rhodes scholar and ended up at Oxford. Once I found out there were several universities where the tuition was free... I applied to Munich for my master's. There are nine museums in Germany and Austria with the greatest early arms and armor collections from Phoenicia to the nineteenth century. There was only one war for centuries, more like a game with human pawns. The armorers strived to create the best protection against the weapons of the day. When they succeeded, the weapons makers worked harder to create better weapons."

Muna spun her chair to look at her former teacher at Quantico. "Who won?"

He shrugged. "Nobody, really. In France, well, Normandy, they created a better chain mail. With a padding and leather undercoat, it turned the Roman short sword that had ruled the world for three hundred years. So, the English took the Viking's great sword and cut it down to a three-pound sword about a meter in length. The great sword ruled the world for about four hundred years until the Germans came up with a better plate armor. And so the French invented the musket, and heavy armor became useless. Well… pointless. As did the larger horses, the knights needed to carry the weight. So smaller, faster, more agile breeds became important instead. Which led to expanding the cavalry. Which brings us back to the scimitar and the cavalry-swept saber."

Muna stuck her finger back at the screen and the twisted hand guard. "Why would they have a guard like this?"

"There used to be similar guards once the blades got lighter. They were for trapping the blade, and then you would, in theory, twist it to snap the blade in half. But I never read if it really worked or not."

"And this sword in the head?"

Oz glanced up at Mike. The man winced and shrugged. "I'd say pass for the moment and go look for other tattoos they may have in common. Compile the groups, and see if there's a theme for the group. Right now, you have a group with left neck tattoos with a commonality of sword, skull, and crushed or killed nutria."

Muna hummed as she looked at the tattoo. "Yeah… the nutria. I'm not sure I want any lunch."

Mike snorted as he rubbed his neck and jerked his head. "Forget lunch. Have you looked outside lately?"

She glanced at the dark windows. Her eyes grew wide as she turned to all three time and date blocks on the bottom right of her screens.

UPDATE?

NATHAN ABSENTLY PULLED at his cowlick, his thumb stroking the dot of gray at his temple. The report was brief for so much happening but ran page after page describing the shot-up house and an accident that didn't seem to be an accident. He felt he was missing something. Then, with a deep sigh, he started over.

Seven thousand eight hundred and ninety-one bullet shells were recovered in front of the house. The neighbors reported the barrage lasted for over five minutes. The house was a total loss. But a witness said the resident had reportedly vacated the building several hours before, shortly after dark.

Nathan circled the statement and wrote next to it: Why?

He turned the page and stared at the only slightly grainy photos of the eight men standing next to the black armored SUV and cargo van. Even from two blocks away, Nathan could tell they weren't tourists there for some exhilarating hiking and camping in the awe-inspiring beauty of nature. They were thugs, and they even looked and acted like thugs. He circled the two vehicles and wrote in block letters: Why armored? Who are these thugs?

The young new aide stopped in the doorway. Nathan looked up. The man almost told him to never mind. "Um... Mister

Donner..." His voice was still showing signs of finding its comfortable tenor. "Some of us are going to Sixth Street for a drink..." His nerve faded.

Nathan glanced down at the report. "I'm kind of tied up with this. Maybe another time... um... Robert?"

"Jeff." He waved it off and pointed at the report. "Yeah. Stay on the... whatever. If you're doing it, it must be important."

Nathan leaned forward and refocused on the photos. And then, realizing the young man was still in the door, he focused on the man. "But thanks for thinking of me."

"No problem." The young man nervously waved his thumb back over his shoulder. "They said you never... er... wouldn't. But I had to ask. It's the right thing to do where I'm from."

Nathan put down his pen. "Where's that?"

"Where's what?"

Nathan narrowed his eyes. "Where you're from?"

The kid's face lit up. "Oh. Oh... Springfield. Springfield, Illinois." And then he remembered every staff member was from Illinois. He blushed and just waved as he turned and rushed for the elevator.

Nathan watched the open door and waited for the soft laughter at the sacrificial lamb's expense. It happens almost every year. Go ask the old congressional aide to join us kids.

He picked up his pen and restudied the photo as the sound of others suddenly snapped to silence by the closing of the elevator doors. He softly shook his head. None had ever asked him to join them out of sincerity. Ever.

They took the next set of photos in the late afternoon. The two vehicles were still smoldering. The background was an empty desert. They took one photo from the backend of the cargo van. In the background, an old RV sat parked on the side of the highway. Sitting along the side were several people.

Nathan opened his top drawer. The glass bubble was a magnifying glass. He set the bubble over the one person. The elderly woman sitting prim and proper on the cooler was laughing at something.

He moved the bubble along the row of people. He only knew one person sitting in the chairs.

His pen circled the others. And he wrote: Who are these people?

He looked up and stared through his open door. He knew he was alone in the office. At this hour, he was always alone. It was the nature of his work and the nature of his being.

THE RV PULLED INTO THE SLOT NEXT TO A FANCY NEW bus with a custom paint job. Uncle started laughing as Felix eased the nose to the end of the parking slot.

The kid glanced over with a frown. "What?"

Uncle waved him down as Nash gave a disgusted grunt. "Old age. Don't get old, Felix. When they get this old, they can't remember if the conversation in their mind is an actual conversation or just one they're having with themselves. Either way, it doesn't make sense."

Uncle gave her a foul look. But he brightened as he noticed the man was sitting at the steering wheel of the other bus. He waved his hand toward Felix. "You want I should ask the guy if he wants to race for pink slips?"

Felix frowned and looked first at Nash and then at Uncle. "What's a pink slip?"

Nash exploded in laughter. "See. I warned you."

Felix smirked at her and then winked with a small smile when Uncle turned back out the side window.

Maggie cleared her throat from the small table. "I've seen some big buses whipping down the highways doing eighty and ninety. I don't think a race would be a fair match."

Felix turned off the engine and turned the seat to face in. "If that's all they can do, you're right. Last spring, Alex pulled a twenty-seven-foot fishing trawler up the grapevine at over a hundred. The temperature gauge twitched."

Uncle turned around with a chuckle. "Yeah, it twitched. But it didn't move. Death Valley was a different story. We hit a hundred and twenty-three. Middle of August at high noon."

Maggie waited for the tell that it was a lie. I never came. "Why would you race across Death Valley in the middle of the heat?"

Uncle got up and headed toward the refrigerator with a jerk of a scowl. "We'd been staked out for eight days. I wanted out of the heat. I hate the heat. Besides, the waste tanks were full."

Maggie's head rocked back. "Oh yes. The need for a toilet can be a powerful motivator."

Uncle nodded as the gray braid rode up and down between his shoulder blades. "Slit trenches aren't allowed in a national park anymore. The water tank was also running out. Something about staying hydrated or something." He turned and smiled.

She rocked with a nod. "Most important rule to mind in the desert."

Uncle leaned to one side at the sound of engines. Outside the small kitchen window, he watched as Thomas parked the dune buggy behind where Nash had parked Maggie's bug. "Finally, now we can start dinner." He turned. "Junior. Go help Alex set up the barbeque while Thomas and I prep the steaks."

Nash couldn't resist. She pointed at Maggie. "You remember she's a vegan, didn't you?"

Uncle turned on the older woman. "Portabella or eggplant?"

She shuddered. "I'm surrounded by cretins. Sautéed portabella over my medium rare roadkill. Thank you very much." She smirked and winked.

Uncle faced her with wide eyes of shock. His Scottish brogue was pure Sean Connery. "Are ya single, miss?"

Nash groaned and stood. "Sit, Felix. I'll go help Alex settle in. I can only take so much of this manure pile."

Uncle turned toward the kid and raised his hand alongside his face. "She's always had this kind of delicate nature. Humor gives her the vapors." He frowned. "Or was it gas?"

Nash slugged him in the arm as she passed. "Come on Powder. We need a better grade of humor."

The dog rolled over on her bed. Presenting her back to the lot of them.

Nash rolled her eyes. "Okay. I guess you didn't need a steak either."

The dog flipped over in the air and was out the door before Nash.

Uncle furled his lips as she wagged his head. "Hungriest dog I've ever seen."

Maggie stared at the man. "Food motivates all dogs. Some of those even walk on four legs." She stood and walked to the door. "I'm just going to check what kind of steak we're having."

Felix pointed at the refrigerator. "The steaks are in the…"

She stopped him with a stern look. "But the cook is out here. Coming young'un?"

Felix ejected himself from the driver's seat. He smiled broadly at Uncle as his head followed his body. "Don't have to ask me twice."

Uncle waited until the kid reached the door. His growl dripped with disgust. "Slut."

Felix turned with a larger smile and fell out the door like he was skydiving. His salute was with one finger.

IN THE CORNER OF THE LARGE ROOM, AN ENSEMBLE played quietly. The tuxedos mingled with the dark suits as they all danced the mingle waltz with the ladies in long dresses.

From the creamy shoulders, the blood-red silk crepe sheath draped exquisitely. Mina stood taller than most of the men. Her dress hid her secret weapons. She called them her battle shoes. The custom-built eight-inch heels complemented the two-inch platform toes. She floated through the masses with her new Rachel Welch wig, flirting with six-foot-five. She justified the height by swearing that it allowed her to find her prey easier. She also knew even without her similarly statuesque wife, she could stop conversations, turn heads, and dominate most at any gala.

Standing on the fringe, she scanned who was there. Sipping, or appearing to sip, from her champagne flute. Her eyes swept the room—targeting.

"Have you spoken to your wife in the last few days?"

Her eyes narrowed as they slid to her left. The man was almost as tall as she was. "Deputy Director." Her eyes scanned toward his shoes.

He smiled. "Forget it. Two can play the game. Cowboy boots with three-inch heels and a half-inch lift." He gazed around the room. "Nash was right. You can see a lot more from up here."

Mina smiled and nodded slightly. "Only three inches?"

He nodded. "The full sole is another inch more."

"Hum. Cowboy boots. I'll have to talk to my wife."

"Worth a try. I doubt you would ever convince her to wear a dress."

Mina let her roving eyes stop at his face. "She has one. A dress. I bought it for her. She told me it was Navajo, not Paiute. We'd been dating for a year, and I didn't know the difference."

She could see the glint of surprise flash in his eyes. "So, she never wore it?"

"For about ten minutes. The next day she went and bought a kimono."

He frowned. "But a kimono is…"

"And we've never played dress up again." Her smile was the one almost every woman was wearing at the boring gala. "You had a question, Deputy Director?"

"Please. Anthony, or Tony…"

"Only when my wife and daughter aren't in danger."

"I was asking if you had spoken to her in the last few days."

Mina placed her full champagne flute on the tray floating by. "She sent a text. She was in Taos. It was very early in the morning. I can only guess they had driven straight from Los Vegas. But I haven't heard anything since then." Her eyes dug at him. She understood there were some communications he would share but also some he couldn't.

He shook his head. "Last I got was from her backup staff in San Francisco. She said your wife had assembled her team, and they were chasing the suspects."

Mina's left eyebrow climbed. "She has a team?"

His neck blushed. "I didn't... um... ask."

Mina frowned as she brought her hand up with her index finger hanging in a circular waltz. "Wait. Her backup is in San Francisco. Are we talking about a little black girl named Muna? Wears a hijab. Lives on napalm-encrusted pork rinds and chocolate-covered raisins?"

He frowned as he turned his head slightly. "I didn't know about the chocolate-covered raisins."

Mina snickered softly. "I made the raisin part up." She turned with a shocked face. "Why, Deputy Director Anthony Prentis, you were afraid to ask. Weren't you?"

He cleared his throat in his fist. "Let's just say, with Nash doing her job, it's better if I don't know all the details. It got us in a pickle the last time."

Mina leaned all her height in on the man. Her voice was little more than her chilled breath. "No. It almost got my wife killed. You, sir, were sitting safely in your office three thousand miles away."

He swallowed hard.

"And have you heard anything from the congressman?"

His head barely moved. "Not a peep."

She stared at him, letting the meaning and weight of his statement sink in. "Don't you find it just a bit unusual? He makes a stink big enough for you to fly down and disrupt our time alone because he is supposed to be worried about his sister? And now it's been five days and not a single phone call nudging the FBI for information?"

Anthony cleared his throat as he glanced down and then around the room to see if anyone was watching the two tallest attractions. Mina didn't have to. She already understood they had drawn more than their share of attention.

His lower lip slid past his upper teeth. "Obviously, coming here was a waste of time. I could have been putting it to good use checking on my agent..." He looked up with one eye. "Or the congressman."

She gracefully turned him away from the crowd and slid her arm into his. "Let's see if the hall is a little quieter." She sauntered him out into the large, echoing hallway. She nodded toward the lobby that she realized was still public but had a bar.

16

UPDATE, TOO

THE TWO APPEARED to wander into the hotel bar. To anyone who didn't know them, it would seem like two people escaping the mind-numbing nature of another Washington gala event. The politics and city had subjected everyone above an aide or congressional runner to a version of what was back down the hall or in Dante's imagination.

They took refuge in the furthest booth. The circular nature of the table suggested it was for larger parties, but the open expanse also allowed for them to be seen or, more important, to see anyone coming.

The bartender softly approached the two people he had known for years. He smiled and bowed his head slightly. "Good evening, Miss Smith and Mr. Jones. Your usuals?"

Mina smiled at the man's subterfuges. "Good evening, Ivan." She glanced at Anthony for his nod. "The usuals would be perfect. Oh, but could I get a twist with mine?"

The man with a nametag of Mike nodded. "Certainly, miss." He backed away.

The deputy director chuckled. "Does the entire city know and protect you?"

She nodded with a twitch of her head. "The FBI can't always be here to do the job. And I think the Secret Service is busy elsewhere." She slipped her phone out of the hidden pocket in her dress.

The deputy director harrumphed at the sleight of hand as he stared at the small clutch, barely large enough for a few credit cards and an ID. "I think I'll have my wife get your seamstress's phone number. She's been wondering about hiding pockets in her dresses for years."

Mike approached and moved the two glasses of water on the rocks in Collin's glasses onto the table. Then, with a show, he took a lime rind from the small plate, twisted it, and slid it around the rim of the one glass. He then slid a whole slice onto the edge and placed it in front of Mina.

Anthony smiled. "On my account, Mike."

"Very good, sir." Taking up the tray, he turned and vaporized.

Mina took up her glass of water and held it out. "Here's to talented backup."

The deputy director clinked his glass. "Oh, wholeheartedly..."

Mina turned her phone over and opened the screen. There was one icon the deputy director didn't recognize but suspected. It was merely the stylized footprint of a bear. He watched as the slender finger pressed the icon and then adjusted the volume on the speaker as the phone rang.

"Good evening, Princess. I thought you had a grip-and-grope to go to tonight. Are you okay?"

Mina peeked at the man as she smiled. "Rachel Welch, Vera Wang, stacked on top of Wolfgang's finest. But I'm also here with your boss. So one of us is lying or neither has heard anything for three days..."

The deputy director leaned into the silence on the other end. He knew there was an expected report she would file for work and probably another version she might share at home. "Agent Bear, on this assignment, I think we can proceed with the understanding we read your wife in from the start."

"Yes, sir. Understood, sir. Let me start by saying: report aside, we are safe. The boys are grilling us some steaks and campfire French fries. And Maggie whipped up some biscuits with flour she begged from one of the other campers."

Mina's voice dripped with sarcasm. "How countrified. Where?"

A deep sigh vibrated through the phone. "Well, we are in Colorado. It's an off-the-beaten-path kind of camping area only serious full-time RV people seem to know about."

"I saw a report from Taos of a house shooting…"

Mina frowned at the strange statement.

Nash started and then cleared her throat. "Yes, well. At the time I was still in Arizona, Miss Wright had a sudden urge to decamp. She hasn't explained how she knew to leave. I'm assuming someone in town tipped her off about two vehicles with eight men and over seven thousand rounds of ammunition for AK-47s headed her way. There didn't appear to be anything salvageable when I went through what they left of the structure."

"Even with nine-millimeter rounds…"

She cut him off. "My little finger fit tight in the holes in the front and my ring finger in the holes after three walls. They were using full jacketed armor-piercing seven-six rounds mounted on full NATO fifty-ones, sir. The intent was full penetration."

"Which would account for Colorado?"

"Partially. She came up here to paint an area called the Grand Mesa. There's a national park named for it. The mesa is impressive, but the hit squad still tracked her down even after swapping her known truck for an equally innocuous Volkswagen bug. Luckily, we were already on them as well. So, we were following but two steps ahead."

The deputy director closed his eyes before he dove in. "Yes. Agent al-Faragi mentioned you had… and I quote… assembled your team. I'm assuming there is a can of alphabet soup for this team?"

Mina started laughing. "Say hi to Uncle and the boys for me."

There was laughing on the other end. "My wife says hi, guys."

They could hear the chorus of people saying hello back.

The deputy director coughed in his fist. "So, where is the other team now?"

"I believe they sent them up to Pueblo. Muna can get you the scoop on them. But for now, they're on ice in roll-out beds one through eight. Muna is trying to find out who they are. The locals ran what fingerprints they could, but no hits came up in their usual databases. Muna said the same for the usual Interpol searches, so she went to her sandbox."

"Any headway on the deep web?"

"She's only been at it for less than a day. What have you heard from the congressman?"

Mina frowned. "Why?"

"Because we forwarded a report yesterday. Pictures with circles, arrows, and explanations on the back, Uncle said."

The deputy director bit on his lower lip. He recognized the obscure reference to rural law enforcement. "Tell your uncle he needs to find a better place to eat." He waved down Mina's frown of curiosity.

"Anything else?"

Nash paused. "Um… The rental car isn't returnable this time."

The man shook his head and rolled his eyes. "Company insurance fully covers the car. How are you?"

"Oh, us three girls came through, as in the words of Maggie, like the twirly ride at the state fair. I don't think it's a ride she would want to take again. But I want to work on it at the Q. It was a double pit maneuver out of a pincer."

His eyebrow rose. "At what speed?"

"Probably about ninety before I hit the brakes."

Mina knew the signs of gear heads running down the street on empty. "Has the brain trust come up with any ideas of who the threat is from?"

They could hear someone yelling dinner in the background. "Our best guess is it all goes back to a private school in Texas and the mid-sixties. Other than that, someone with a Texas, Illinois, and oil connection. Or there in Washington. Muna was also trying to figure out where the money landed. And I have five people and a dog staring at me so they can eat. Maybe you can pressure the congressman to come up with all the names of the political action group. We're missing one."

"Ok, tell the wild bunch to dig in. We'll talk tomorrow." Mina's finger feathered the red phone icon, and the screen cleared to the usual forty icons, covering a picture of a dog in her tactical harness. The phone vibrated, and the number over the text icon grew by one.

She stared at the deputy director as she sipped her water.

"What?"

She patted his hand. "Not your fault. I was just wondering why the congressman hasn't reached out. If they had a preliminary report sent, it would have been yesterday." She pulled up her phone and glanced at the incoming log. She switched to her email. Still nothing. "Nothing." She narrowed her eyes while watching the FBI work through the man's brain.

He pulled out his phone and texted a message. He turned his wrist and looked at the slim gold watch his wife had bought him for their twenty-fifth anniversary. His phone pinged, and he typed in more. He put his phone away.

Mina cocked her head as one eye floated closed.

Anthony slightly raised his hand. "He's on his way out. He was here."

They watched as the older gentleman strode through the archway from the lobby. He didn't even look around.

He held out his hand to the bartender to wave him off as he silently slid into the other side of the booth, blocking him from view. "I'm in the bathroom. With this prostate, we have about ten or fifteen minutes. Why haven't I heard from your agent?"

The deputy director shouldered in. "Our question exactly. They sent a full report of the shootings, car crashes, and deaths…" He paused for effect as he watched the man's eyes grow. "Yesterday morning. It should have been on your desk by noon."

"I was in my office all day. Ordered lunch in. I hate the cafeteria." He glared at Mina. "She's your wife…"

Mina leaned in. "Point a finger, Wit, and we are done. I will bury your body with the remaining skeletons wiped from memory. Someone in your office screwed the pooch. The FBI has been doing a hero's journey here. But you haven't been so forthcoming."

The man reddened. "What's that supposed to mean?"

Her finger tapped each point on the white tablecloth. "There were six people in the PAC formed to launch your career. All of you went to a private school in Texas. I want all the names. We already know about the money."

He sat back in the seat like a deflated balloon. He looked around and glanced at his watch. "I don't remember all the details and names. Most are dead by now. They were older."

"Call me direct tomorrow. I don't want the people in your office to be any part of this. They have already proved unreliable. I also want to know where the money went offshore. Not just your share, but all of it."

He frowned. "My share?"

"The twenty-seven and a half million."

"That was all of it."

Mina leaned back in the chair and sipped on her drink. "Dig deeper, Wit. And when you call me tomorrow morning, you had better have all the answers and no more lies." Her little finger flicked out and pointed toward the door and the man standing looking around. "Your minder is here. Give him a minute to look around. I'll let you know when you can escape."

The deputy director covered. "So, the handler was new to the show world. She had been a good groomer, and we were letting her have some experience. But her attention wandered just at the critical moment, and Caster decided the judge's leg looked as close to a fire hydrant as needed..."

Mina's face was a portrait of horror. "And he still took first place?"

Anthony pulled himself up like the proud fur father he was. "Grand Champion."

Mina erupted in a fit of giggles. At the count of four, she stopped and leaned in. "He's gone. Tomorrow at ten. And you better have all the names spelled right, bank account numbers, and routing numbers. You screw me on this, Wit, and we'll pull your sister's protection. As for you... you can pack up and start walking back home. Your life won't be worth a plugged parking meter in Springfield. Now go."

She leaned back as she watched the man sneak out. He never looked back.

"Remind me again why we don't hire you to come work for the FBI?"

She slowly ground her head around. Her index finger drew circles on the tablecloth. "This last ten minutes...?"

He nodded.

"I'd bill more than your annual salary. Maybe even more than your entire compensation package."

"You don't know what I make..."

She only stared at him.

"Shit."

She nodded. "Let's get my girls home. I need to go take my dog for a long walk."

17

DARK WEB RIDER

THE HELLO KITTY pajamas and bare feet stood in front of the expansive wall of rain-washed windows. The drizzle wasn't unexpected, just not wanted—here. The state desperately needed the rain and snow in the mountains. But running in blinding rain was no fun. When the drivers become blinded by even seven drops of anything on their windshield, a real rainstorm could all but freeze San Francisco streets. Even with a large cape of hair, Muna knew she was but a speck in the morning haze of water from the sky.

She traded the mug of coffee into her left hand and flexed her right. The bruising was subsiding, but she knew she wasn't ready for even a light round in the shooting alley. Waking up with the dawn was proving almost a waste. Other than her prayers. She sipped again on the coffee and wondered how she had resisted the earthy taste all those years. She turned at the clicking.

Mike turned the corner at the movement. The smile started softly, but at realizing what the woman was wearing, it turned to laughter. "I had a pair just like that."

Muna looked down and shook her head. Looking up, she cocked her head. "I call bull manure. You're too old for Hello Kitty."

"Not anymore." He smiled and stepped to the coffee service they had moved into what they now called the office. "After the accident, the nurses found a pair my size. I think they were trying anything to make me smile or laugh. They hadn't cut the legs short, so it was where they continued to play their pranks. One day, I would wake up to rubber monster feet; the next would be woolly hooves."

"Did it work?"

"Eventually. I resisted out of principle. Then one day, I woke up, and they had shortened the legs to above knee length. I don't know why, but it was funny."

Muna wrinkled her forehead. "Why would it be funny?"

He turned to glance over his shoulder. "Because it meant they were done. They had given up trying to distract me from reality. I hadn't won or anything, but they had given in."

"How could they do all that and not wake you up?" She peeked around the corner to see what he had looked at.

He glanced at where she was looking. "Oh, I was going to whip up an omelet. Have you eaten yet?"

Muna started toward the breakroom. "No. And I'm starved. What are we putting in the omelet?"

He spun on his one bionic leg. "I stopped for some crab and asparagus. There was still half a block of brie here last night."

She rolled her eyes. "Sounds San Francisco halal enough for me."

He glanced at her. "Really? I mean... If you'd like, I can make yours with just greens and cheese."

"I can try new things." She smiled as she rolled her eyes large. "So, back to sleeping through the shenanigans."

Mike grabbed the carton of eggs out of the refrigerator. "Night terrors. A person can tear up their cardiopulmonary from all the thrashing with violent terrors. So, it was more judicious to knock me out at night. It took me a long time to adjust later. But it got me out on the other side."

Muna rested the large knife on the oval loaf of sourdough bread. "Did the shorter legs help?"

The man grabbed four eggs in his two hands and cracked them on the sides of the bowl. "Unlike autopsy, there's no silver bullet to recovery or adjusting to a new reality." He waved his hands down his two legs. "It's about time. One day you're fighting or resisting, and then another day, you realize you stopped fighting. It's not like you accepted, but more surrendered to reality, and you move forward. Only looking back, you keep trying to find *that* moment. And there really isn't one. It's more of many little things simply coming together."

He looked up with the large chunks of crab in his hand. She nodded, and he dropped them on the cutting board.

Her hand shot out. "Not too small. I want to savor the moment."

His smile pulled to one side. "Did you say your prayers this morning?"

"Yes, daddy."

He held the knife out with a serious look on his face. "Never think you're too big or too old to be turned over someone's knee."

She leaned over and looked at his two shining legs. "I guess I'm safe today."

The knife flashed across the crab and asparagus. "See, when you took off your hijab in solidarity with your sisters in Iran, you didn't stop being a Muslim. You didn't suffer a crisis of faith. Instead, you had a crisis of following a rule, which was just there to be a rule. Have you seen photos from the times under the Shah?"

She nodded as she buttered the bread to be toasted. "Most look like they took them near the beaches of Los Angeles. No hijab, no covered arms and shoulders, and shorts as short as panties."

"Don't forget the bikinis. Nothing like today, but oo-la-la." He rolled his eyes in exaggeration. "But please, if you are going to wear a bikini, keep it to the pool or beach."

"I don't think I'll be wearing any bathing suit any time soon. I'm not a swimmer."

"But what I was getting at…" He poured the eggs into the pan and slurried them around to spread them over the entire surface. "I wasn't surprised when you took off the hijab. You had already started down the path of interpreting your faith to fit your life."

"How so?"

He sprinkled the crab, cheese, and greens on the eggs. "I think this could use some pork rinds to spice it up." He turned to look out of the side of his eyes. "Don't you think?"

She stood back from the oven. She ballooned her lower lip in thought. "Point taken."

He twitched his head. "And yet, you never stopped your morning prayers. Your faith never wavered, just how you fit it into your life. More like a Malik Sunni than a Shia." He flipped the omelet closed and slid it out onto the cutting board. Then, with a flash of the knife, he served them onto the two plates as Muna pulled the toast out of the oven.

"As for the other prayer times, you pray more through your work than I think most imams do in Iran."

She slowly wove her head from side to side as she chewed.

Mike snickered softly through his nose. "Agreeing with me…? Or focusing on the omelet?"

"Praying this isn't the last time you make this omelet."

A SMALL BOX APPEARED ON THE UPPER RIGHT OF HER other screen. Muna moved the chair to get to the secure FBI link. She clicked on the box and smiled.

"Hi stranger. How's D.C.?"

Mina shivered. "Cold and wet. We're getting a couple of inches if it dries enough to stick. What about you?"

"I gave up on running this morning. It's an all-inside day today."

Mina snorted softly. "I like the new uniform."

Muna looked down and then shrugged. "I tried the ballistic vest over it... but it didn't look right. Mike was here earlier. We had breakfast, and then he went down to San Jose. Nobody will be in the rest of the day... so what the hey?" She threw up her arms. And then she realized Mina was on the secure network. "Are you in the D.C. office?"

"She's using my terminal." The voice of the deputy director was distinctive enough that he didn't have to identify himself. But it also labeled the connection with the security level Muna needed.

"Got it. I'm assuming this is about our painter and a bunch of money."

Mina nodded as a second window popped onto Muna's screen. "Supposedly, this is the list of all six of the responsible. The routing numbers and accounts are somewhere in the Cayman Islands. All this information is ancient history, so treat it as such, and you won't be disappointed."

Muna looked at the number. "The country code is still active. It's Grand Cayman. I think the banking numbers are similar and should make the conversion. I can work with this. Anything else?"

Mina dipped her head. "You told me they sent the congressman an update. Do you know who it went to? He swears he never saw it or heard about it."

"Sure. It routed through me." She bounced to her other secure computer and pulled up the folder. "I sent it for his eyes only. It shouldn't have been able to be opened by anyone else..." Her one eye narrowed as she turned back to Mina. "He does seem to have a longtime aide. Long enough to be chief of staff or something, but then, the position would put him in the spotlight."

Mina smirked. "I think you meant limelight. And you know what lime is good for..."

Muna smiled evilly. "One is good for pies, and the other is good for disposing of bodies. Yeah... I smell a rat."

Mina rocked with only pencil lines for eyes. "Find the money. Leave Nathan to me. I never trusted the slimy weasel."

NASH ROLLED OVER ONTO HER RIGHT SIDE. HER LEFT arm reached out and pulled the body into her face and chest. Even in her sleep, she had grown accustomed to the smell that made her feel safe and calm. Even Mina now used the body soap they had sent from California. The earthy scent of the two types of sage, hand-gathered and dried, seemed more natural than anything they could buy at the store marketed as organic.

Powder's groan was the soft one she used as she got comfortable. When Nash tried to mimic the sound, it made Mina laugh, and their daughter go sleep in another room.

Nash ignored the other sound. But on the third vibration, Powder got up and pushed her nose into Nash's. Even the dog worked harder than she wanted to.

Nash rolled over and looked at the screen. The name and time didn't make much sense, but then, it did.

Aware of the close quarters of the four people in the RV, she answered the phone quietly. "Yes?"

Mina paused. She was probably checking to make sure she had dialed the right number. "Oh. I forgot all about you bunking into tight accommodations. I have some information, but I'll text you the names and bank for you to ask Ms. Wright about in the morning. Good night sweety. Hug our daughter for me." The phone went silent.

Nash was almost drifting back to sleep when the text vibrated on her phone. She turned it over. The information dump was small but packed. It was going to be an interesting breakfast conversation.

18

WHAT'S IN A NAME?

THE IMMINENT DAWN drew Nash from the RV. She opened the door and then stepped back to grab the nearest jacket. It was tight on the shoulders, but it worked. It wasn't until Powder realized Nash wasn't coming back that she reluctantly left the warm bed in the back of the RV and succumbed to the call of nature.

Nash stood silently, stretching in the dark. She moved her arms in large, slow circles and, finally, massaged her one shoulder with her other hand as she moved her arm over her head from front to back.

The soft, deep voice rumbled from the dark. "Shoulder skin still binding up?"

She didn't flinch. She had expected Uncle would be up before her. The insomniac sitting in the dark like a large knot on a log.

She wasn't even sure where he was sitting. So, she didn't turn. "Some. But not much. Maybe it's the morning chill."

"You'll know soon enough, back there in D.C. when the snow is four feet deep, and you're shoveling your way out of your teepee."

She now knew he was to her right—along the side of the RV. She turned. "Snow removal is the job of the doorman. And even he's smart enough to shop the job out."

The harrumph was soft. "Coffee is over this way." He turned on a tiny red light. Nash knew it was one of the boy's night work lights. The color was the same as the battle station lighting. You could see, but it didn't burn the purple from your retina, allowing you to see at night.

The small table attached to the side of the RV. The compartment behind was just enough for the coffeemaker, coffee, and fixings. She snorted at the small bottle. "Who uses the pepper juice in their coffee?"

Uncle snorted. His smile glowed a soft red. "Felix. I think he has some Cajun in him. He likes roadkill too much. And, if there's sauce from tabasco... he's a cheerful boy."

She turned with her mug. In the dim red light, she could see the other chairs. "Did you park this way just so we got the dawn entertainment?"

"Felix parked this time. But he does have that unexplainable sense of direction."

Nash paused, her mug at her face. "The kid is a walking conundrum."

The door swung open. A leg cautiously felt for the step.

"Two steps Maggie."

The woman silently swung the door shut. "I wasn't sure. And I didn't want to go tumbling in the dark." She pointed at the red light. "Maybe the smart kid could rig something like that light to the door."

Uncle rumbled. "Good idea." He raised his mug. "Here's to smart women making our lives easier and less dangerous."

Maggie stopped with her hand outstretched toward the coffee carafe. She glared at Uncle.

Even Nash could feel the heat. "We haven't beaten him for the last week. We'll get back on that routine as soon as we get him back to the prison."

The woman faced Nash. Even with the woman's face in full shadow, Nash could feel the heat. "Honey attracts more appreciation than acerbic attempts at humor. But I appreciate the senti-ment." She returned to getting her coffee.

As she settled next to Nash, the sky turned from black to dun. The pinking would still be five or seven minutes more.

Nash pulled her phone out of her pocket and thumbed up the text from Mina. "Care to tell me about a Claudius Dubois?"

The woman stopped sipping on her coffee, lowering the mug gently to her chair's arm as she watched the sky.

"That was more than a lifetime ago."

Nash sipped on her coffee. She had taught classes on waiting out a question to get an answer.

"My brother was at a private school in Paris." She looked over. "That's in Texas. Right on the border with Oklahoma. A lot of oil money sent their sons there."

Uncle cleared his throat with a slight cough. "But your family wasn't in oil."

Maggie's head bobbed in the coming light. "Or wealthy. My father had been a schoolmaster. Now they call them principals or superintendents. One day, when I was very little, a policeman shot a woman stealing food from a grocery store. The city did nothing. She was a criminal and didn't stop. That she was stealing food to feed her children didn't make it right, but indigence never got a fair trial in city hall. So, my father spoke out."

Nash frowned. "Against the police? In the sixties?"

Maggie turned. "No. He wasn't stupid. But he had a big heart. He spoke out against poverty. The children came to his schools in rags held together with more rags, and he spoke out for them. There were large businesses, and he asked for their help. At one, the owner told him he wouldn't help because he was nothing more than a whining schoolmarm in pants."

"So, he ran for mayor?"

Maggie turned toward Uncle. "Why? A mayor is nothing more than a simpering snot-rag wringing hands looking for enough money to get reelected. No, he set his sights on the people who could bring a large company to its knees. He ran for the county supervisor job. And knocked on every door. He told people what the big company had called him and why he was running for office. The county controlled the water flowing into the man's factory. It was clean water. The factory turned it into a stinky gray goo. Then they pumped it back out into the river many people fished in. Or their children swam in. My mother told me he even carried a mason jar full of goo and would offer it to people to take a sip."

Nash nodded. "That could get some attention."

The woman nodded. "I guess people had never paid attention to who was in control and what they were turning a blind eye to. But that November, they had voted out every county board of supervisors and voted in new ones. My father included."

"So he had the money to send your brother to the school?"

She shook her head. "No, Wit came after daddy had quit politics and became a conductor for the railroad. It was there he met a wildcatter who was busting ground in Oklahoma. So he offered to give Wit a scholarship. And I'm sure it had some strings attached."

Uncle frowned. "Define wildcatter?"

She turned her head. "Standard Oil would be an oil company. They had crews, rigs, equipment, and everything they needed to sink hundreds of holes in the ground. Double D had a few trucks, a fast mouth, and a quick handshake. He might have a few guys help him, but he only had them as long as the money held out. So, he drilled on a promise, lived on prayer, and grew on a gusher. The company was as solid as his palm and profitable as his last successful well. For every company, there were two dozen Danforth Dubois sinking holed and praying for a gusher before their bank accounts ran dry."

Nash shifted. "And Claudius...?"

"Was his son. He was a year older than Wit and every bit his father's son. In his junior year, he had talked his way into being voted captain of the football team and quarterback. Wit brought him home for Thanksgiving. I was young and smitten. He returned for Christmas. Then there was Easter and summer. And by the next Christmas, I was pregnant, and the families were talking about marriage." She shrugged. "It was Oklahoma's summer of love... or lust."

Uncle stood and stepped to the coffee. "That's it? Well, case solved. I guess we can all go home now."

Nash rested her hand on Maggie's arm. "Horsewhip. We have a horsewhip. But back to pregnant and..."

Maggie shrugged. "Getting married at fifteen is still legal in many states. Hell, there are still arranged marriages where the girl is only nine or ten. In a few states, it's still legal. So, we got married. But it was an election year coming up, so they moved me to Claudius's aunt Dubois' home in El Paso. Supposedly, it was for my health. The drier weather and all. But we knew it was to keep the churchwomen from getting all aflutter with the vapors over a fifteen-year-old getting pregnant and having a shotgun marriage."

"And Claudius?"

"Still in his last year of school. Not a brilliant student, so he was finishing with Wit and a few other boys they had bonded with. And they ensconced me in El Paso with a nanny and other house staff to give me a life of leisure. With a newborn son, Nature Rustic Dubois. Rusty for short because of the reddish tinge to his hair until it got darker by the end of the year, and we ended with Nate."

"Nature Rustic?"

Nash snapped. "Shut up, Uncle. You and I are nobody to question unusual names. Besides, she already said it was the sixties."

Maggie touched her hand. "Keep up, dear. It's the seventies now. And I'm the wife of a man who is a squirt off the old gusher."

"Wildcatter and never home."

She rocked her body and head. "We saw him three or four times a year, and I took up painting to fight boredom. I saw the other women in the neighborhood. Bloody Mary for breakfast, gin fizzes for lunch, and martinis soon after five, even if it looked more like three. But I didn't spend much time with them. The slight improvement in my health was waning. So, the doctors sent us up to Los Cruces. The higher altitude, combined with the drier desert air, did wonders for my respiratory system and the scenery for my paintings. Soon, Nate and I happily wandered around the desert for a few years."

"Where's your son now?"

She stared down into her mug and weakly shrugged one shoulder. "I haven't a clue." She looked up. "Can I make breakfast now?"

The flap on the tan dome tent flipped back. Thomas's blond mop looked out. "Did someone say breakfast was ready?"

Nash growled at the interruption. "The chart says it's yours and Alex's turn to cook."

"I heard that." The red tent shook with the movement of the occupant.

Maggie stood. "I'll help." The sleeves of the oversized jacket slid down and covered half her hand. She held up her arm, looked at how large the coat was, and then pulled the unzipped body into a closer wrap.

Nash stood and peeled off the jacket she had grabbed in the dark. Then, noting the letters on the back, and the letters on the back of the other, she held it out to Maggie. "Here, I'll trade you Alex's jacket for mine. I'd offer Felix's, but that stick of skin and bones needs all the insulation he can get."

The RV door swung open. The subject of conversation stepped down wearing a thin tank top, tiny nylon marathon shorts, and shoes. He stretched his arms and pulled his knees up one at a time to his chest. "I heard breakfast was late today, so I'm going to grab a quick five and be back."

The five watched as he slowly jogged past other early-morning runners bundled in full sweats and ear mufflers. Maggie's demand broke into looks of amused awe. "Quick, give me his jacket. I want some of that energy. Hopefully, it's in the jacket."

THE PICNIC TABLE SAT CLUTTERED WITH THE REMAINS of breakfast. What had started with the suggestion of cold cereal had turned, through progressive recommendations, into pancakes, eggs, and bacon. Maggie's advice of using the strange can of lemon-lime soda instead of milk would change the future making of pancakes forever. Nash would later smile at the scrawled note of *LL SODA* on the unending shopping list stuck to the front of the fridge.

With one hand, Uncle set the two full carafes of coffee in the center of the table. "Just in case anyone needs more." Nash noticed his mug in the other hand was already full.

Alex pushed his finger over the cracked wood of the table. "So, they just took your son, and you never saw him again?"

The woman shook the mass of untethered gray curls. "No. At first, he came home for the holidays. But as he got older, the draw of the exciting world of his father drew him to wherever Claudius drilled that year. But only in the summer when it wasn't muddy and messy." She sipped on her coffee. "Even as a child, he was meticulous about himself, his clothes, and his surroundings. We never had to tell him to pick up his toys. They were always on their shelf or in the toy box. He would take them down, play for a bit, and put them back. By age five, he preferred reading. He would quietly sit at the table, his head leaning into his left hand, reading."

Uncle softly lowered his mug. "What did he read?"

"Everything. He would read the back of the cereal box or soup can if there wasn't a book or newspaper. By the time he was seven, he could tell you what all the ingredients were in any cereals he would no longer eat. Same for the cans of soup. If Josephina didn't make the soup in front of him so he could see all the contents, he wouldn't eat it. Breakfast boiled down to oatmeal or pancakes made from scratch."

Nash closed one eye and cocked her head sideways. "So, your Felix Unger didn't want to go get muddy anymore, but also wasn't coming home to Los Cruses... so where did he go?"

The still steaming body of the runner sprawled in the camp chair held up his index finger. "I object to that characterization."

Uncle and Alex laughed. "Own it kid. It was who they named you after, and it fits."

The head rolled forward with one closed eye as he tried to rumble a growl. "I'll never wear a suit."

Uncle leaned back. "Kid, your t-shirts, jeans, and boots are your uniform suit. Everything is perspective."

Nash's whistle was soft but sharp. "Getting back to the questions at hand. When did you lose track of him and Claudius?"

"About the end of high school. He was already studying law through the mail, and it would take too much time away from his studies to travel. So, Nate never came home anymore, and the few letters stopped. Claudius died in ninety-three, and he either never got word or decided not to come to the funeral. If I wasn't his wife, I think I would have stayed in Los Cruces as well. It was shortly after that when I bought the house in Taos."

Alex squinted slightly. "Maybe the move to Taos broke the connection? I mean... if he didn't know how to find you...?"

"He could have found me through Claudius or the company. Even in school, they issued him a nonvoting board member's stipend, the same as me. For many, it would have been enough to live on comfortably. For Nate, who knows? I never saw him spend any money. He never asked for any. And it wasn't like he was tearing up his clothes or living a wild and extravagant lifestyle." She thought with pursed lips. "A monk is more like it. Live in a cloister, dress modestly, and study all day."

"What about Claudius's company? Couldn't you track him through there?"

"Claudius and the rest of the Gang of Skulls..." She looked at the squints and frowns. "That was what the six boys had called themselves at school—or something as awful. They were thick as thieves and just as mischievous. All of them, except Wit, were living on stipends from home or company. But anyway, their getting together to get Wit into congress was probably their last hurrah. I heard that Lucius Pembrook and David Lassiter died on a small plane down in South America somewhere. Dupree, I never knew his first name. They always just called him Dupree. But someone mugged and killed him on the street in New Orleans." She looked over and pointed to Nash's phone. "Did you have the other guy on your phone? He was a Jeffry or Jefferson. A jealous husband or something like that killed him. It was shortly after they broke up their committee to get Wit elected."

Nash shook her head as she read through the shortlist. "No. He was the mystery person. His name never shows up in the incorporation documents. And he wasn't named in the dissolution decree either. There was just a notation about a sixth person. But how much do you know about the money they raised and where it went? The twenty-seven and a half seemed to strike a chord with you."

"Not a lot. But it was during one of my rare visits to Dallas when they drew it all up. I think they even got me to be one of the witness signers. I was only there to see my brother after several years. In those days, I still believed in family."

Uncle sipped and cleared his throat. "Then the PAC was only to get your brother elected?"

"I think the money was there to get him elected. But then also for him to use however he needed to get the oil pipeline dragged to the processing plant they wanted built in Illinois."

Nash scanned the brief document on her phone. "What can you tell us about where they sent the money offshore?"

Maggie put down her mug. "The only place I knew any of them went out of the country was to David Lassiter's vacation home in the Cayman Islands." She frowned. "Is Grand Cayman an island?"

Nash nodded. "But you don't know anything about the bank?"

The woman held Nash's look for longer than was comfortable. She put her hands on the table and stood. "I guess this isn't going to end unless I give you the information." She turned for the RV and then turned back toward Alex. "Is the potty in here okay to use?"

The man smiled. "Clean as a whistle and freshwater in the tanks. But if you're going to shower, I need to turn on the heater."

She pointed to the adobe-looking building down the lot. "The hot showers are down there."

Felix sat up and looked at the building. "Cool." He followed Maggie into the RV and, a second later, was running for the small building with a towel in his hand.

Nash watched the retreating young man. "Does he ever just walk anywhere?"

The three men shook their heads, and Thomas buzzed his lips.

Maggie returned and set her paint box on the table. Nash thought about the shape. In New York, it would pass for a very expensive briefcase.

They all watched as she pulled out two small paintbrushes. Near the hinge joint were two holes—one on each side. She turned the brushes and inserted the thin handles in the holes. A small mechanical click rewarded each insertion. She then took the clasps and turned the left counterclockwise and the right clockwise. They could hear something that had moved but couldn't see anything until she pulled on the handle. The front and bottom separated from the body of the box. Finally, she pulled out a thin sheaf of paper from the shallow hidden drawer.

Sitting, she scanned the one page.

"Dumont. Jefferson Dumont." She looked up at Nash. "In a family setting, we would talk about all the coon-asses in the group. How Cajan they were, I couldn't say. But I know they didn't appreciate the mana of Colorado. The fine flavors of the fire-roasted pueblo peppers are beyond their swamp-addled taste buds." She handed Nash the papers. "That is everything I know. And it's still thirty-some years out of date. But it might help."

19

BY THE NUMBERS

THE BEST PART of the morning was having the view of Taos Mountain out the window. Her first time driving through Taos had been short, and in the early morning, she hadn't noticed the large, timeworn mountain lording over the town. From the distance of the campsite, the mountain's mass was calming.

"The first numbers check out, but they're mostly the routing numbers and finding out which bank. For the deeper numbers, I'll reach out to the state department and see if they can give us some help. Otherwise, I'll work on my contacts at Interpol."

Nash sighed. "Thanks, Muna."

The young woman's face expanded as she leaned closer to the camera. "No. Seriously, Nash. What she gave us is huge. We now have all the names, and I can check death records. There should be a huge trail on the unraveling of the Political Action Committee, especially with it being less than ten years, which is what they're supposed to be for."

"Okay. When it comes to finding what we need, you're the magician. I need to go conference with Powder. She's trying to convince me she needs a long run, and I'm trying to tell her we're at altitude. But you know her attitude about runs..."

Muna looked at her other screen. The one Nash thought of as the computer that was never there.

"I'm having to find collections of their common tattoos." She moved back to the screen she was conferencing on, typed, and looked up. A side window appeared. The list ran from the Russian mafia to the Spetsnaz to the Aryan Nation.

Nash pointed at the list. "Are you sure about the Spetsnaz? That's a specific group and as old as Oz. Maybe you could ask him?"

"Did I hear my visage taken in vain?" The head of wild white hair lowered behind Muna. "Hi, Nash. And yes..." He poked at Muna's screens. "Show her."

The new window showed three similar tattoos. A gold laurel wreath circled a red star. The red flag on the flagpole in the center had a single word in Cyrillic. The CCCP banner on the bottom was recognizable, but not the word on the red flag.

"The flag says guards. It's still used today, yet slightly different. But it's still their elite military designation. So, it would be the source of the Spetsnaz units. Something tells me that in the world of shadows that these men lived in, one would not have this tattooed on their skins lightly."

Nash winced. "Are we talking about a Russian hit squad on a member of congress's family? On American soil?"

The man stood and cutting off his head and shoulders. Nash recognized that stance he would take in one of his teaching moments back in Quantico of the loose crossed arms.

"We only have three of the eight with the guard tattoo. But five have the neck tattoo of the Russian mafia. So, I would hazard a theory more like them being mercenaries with similar backgrounds. Mostly eastern European or Russian. All of them with a bent toward Aryan or White Caucasian superiority."

Muna took down the two windows and replaced them with tattoos with swords in a skull with the dead nutria. "The straight sword I traced to an ethnic cleansing group based in Serbia, and the curved sword one, is from a similar group in North Macedonia. Both groups are active in elite military training and renting out of what they call ambassadors."

Nash rested her face in her hands. "This just keeps getting better and better." She looked up. "Do you have any good news? Anything?"

Muna reached behind her neck and flipped her thick braid around. "I learned how to braid my hair by myself…" Nash had an image of a small child standing in a bathroom doorway with their pants and diaper around their ankles, proud they had gone to the bathroom alone.

She smiled as she realized this wasn't someone else's child but hers. During the training before, she wrapped her head in a scarf. "You're on your way. I can't wait to get back out there, and we can do a girls' night doing each other's hair and toenails."

They both laughed as Oz groaned and walked away. Nash waved for Muna to bring the braid closer. "Are you doing it damp out of the shower?"

"Oh, of course. Otherwise, it's four times thicker."

"Before you get out of the shower, rub a bunch of cream rinse into it. I like the horse stuff. It's made to leave in and isn't as expensive as some of the other ones. Besides, for us, it comes in quarts or gallon pump bottles."

Muna giggled. "Stop it. Nobody could use a gallon of…" Her face froze in horror. She realized how fast she was now going through shampoo and conditioner.

Nash snorted. "Bingo. And the penny drops. I'll send you information… girlfriend."

Nash closed the connection as Uncle stomped into the RV. "Your dog tried to kill me."

Nash frowned as Maggie entered. "He's just sore because a dog and old woman can walk five miles faster than he can."

Nash laughed. "Yeah, but can you sit on a wooden bar stool

twelve hours a day for thirty years?" She looked behind Maggie. "Where's Powder?"

The woman sat and waved her hand at the door. "She collapsed out in the yard. She's going to sleep well tonight."

———

MINA STOOD AT THE DESK. HER HEELS BROUGHT THE TOP of her wig to a few inches over six feet. The enhanced look on her face came from the subtle shadings of makeup she had perfected over the years. She called it her war paint, or time to kick someone's ass paint. The young intern had made three stabs at the intercom button while he kept a wary eye on the towering Asian woman leaning threateningly over his desk.

Mina finally reached over to the quivering blond and took his hand away from the phone. Placing it on his yellow pad marked up with bored doodles, she leaned closer. "Relax. I'll be back to release you for your potty break."

Turning, she strode to the door to the inner office. At the strained squeak, she turned and snapped her thumb and two fingers closed. If he had just wet himself, it wasn't her concern. She had no respect for whoever hired the intern. Paid or not.

Congressman Wright looked up angrily from his phone call. But seeing who had invaded his sanctuary, he cleared his face. "I need to talk to you later." They could both hear the screaming voice cut off by him cradling the phone as Mina settled in the chair.

He put his hands on the arm of his chair and then decided he was too late. "Ms. Lee, how—"

She cut him off. "It's Mrs. Running Bear, Wit. And if you want to work your way back up to congressman, you better have answers."

The man leaned back in his chair and steepled his fingers over his belly. "Nathan Donner was here this morning, finally bringing me up to speed on the reports. The shooting and the auto accident.

There were photos. And he had questions he wanted answered before he briefed me."

"The shooting." Mina carefully draped her right knee over her left. Her foot swung in agitation, leaving her face relaxed and passive.

"Someone came in the middle of the night and shot a lot of bullets through my sister's house. Evidently, extensive damage."

"That's all your best told you about it?"

The man's frown cascaded the wrinkles from his forehead and around his eyes and did nothing to enhance his jowls. "Was there more?"

"He intercepted the police report. You tell me. Just under eight thousand rounds of high-speed, fully jacketed armor-piercing bullets spread through the house and out into the desert. That was thousands. Spelled with a large capital T. If there had been a house within a few blocks, they would have done the same to it as well. Between knee level and chest high, the house is Swiss cheese. I understand the county is already talking about backing a garbage truck into one end to knock it over." She paused. "Eight. Thousand. Bullets. In under five minutes."

He sunk back into his chair. "Nathan wasn't so graphic. But he mentioned it was no longer habitable. I only assumed it would need extensive patching or something. Whatever they do with those mud homes out there."

Mina's right eyebrow raised. "You actually don't know. Do you? The iconic Greene brothers of the Arts and Craft movement in Pasadena designed the house. They built it as a retreat for one of their better clients. Not the Gambles, but a better client. It was the iconic 1906 lodge of its time. It is as replaceable as the White House is just another stone building in Washington."

"I never spoke to my sister about her home."

"No. You never spoke to your sister since she signed the documents to get you elected. After that, your career is all you care about until this threatened to end your time in office and any respect as a super-lobbyist after you're forced out." She cocked her head to the other side to change the subject. "The accident... as you so glibly put it."

"Nathan said Margaret was in the car with your wife, and there was an accident, totaling the car, but they were both okay..." His voice trailed off as he realized he was in for more.

Mina studied his face. The man was used to receiving information and never questioned its level of comprehensiveness or truthfulness. "And you hired this man. But, more importantly, you continue to employ him."

"He is a diligent worker, totally faithful to my service, and I've never had reason to doubt his word or work."

"Did he show you the collection of photos taken by the Colorado state troopers? Did he mention the other two vehicles? Or they're being armor-plated? Or the death of the eight-man death squad? Or the six hundred and ninety-four shell casing they found at the scene of the ambush? Because, yes, this was no accident. It was an ambush by eight highly trained foreign assassins. They were not there to scare your sister. They were there to kill your sister, my wife, and my daughter." She stood and leaned in. "Your lack of relationship with your sister, and the lack of competency of you and your staff, have put your sister and my family in the highest order of danger."

He held up his open hands to fend off her growing anger.

She leaned forward and knuckled her fists into the center of his leather desk pad. "Your complacent fat ass is only in that chair at my pleasure. I'm sure I can find someone in your party or the other who I can run as a lock in the next election. And you know I can do it. You thought the world finding out about twenty-seven and a half million dollars in a secret account in the Grand Caymans was a media nightmare... it will be nothing if one hair gets harmed on any of those three women. I'm taking a special liking toward your sister... and her not talking to you? I'm understanding."

He held his hands back to his chest, but the palms were still defensive. "Look. I'm—"

"No. You look. I might need your position and power to get something done. When I call, you will answer the phone in your left pocket. I won't waste my time calling here or with your official phone in your breast pocket. I'll use the one only your bookie and mistress use. And when I say jump… I expect to be talking to you in the air. Do I make myself clear?"

"Yes, ma'am."

"Good. Now my wife needs some help from the state department in the Cayman Islands. Who's in your pocket down there?"

The door burst open, and Nathan and two congressional police walked in.

The congressman held out his hand. "We're good here. Mrs. Running Bear and I were just wrapping up. Nathan, give us a couple of minutes, and then I'll need you."

Mina had never even flinched. She could hear the door close softly. Her voice through her teeth was low and feral. "Name."

2 0

MOVING ABOUT

THE DUNE BUGGY moved cautiously along the dark road. No lights and a quiet muffler. At barely over an idle, Nash almost wished for an electric car. But the sparse brush and stunted juniper trees didn't give back the muted sound. A bat played in the green cylinder of the tight beam infrared enhancement light. The helmet on Alex provided the rest of the vision.

From the right seat, Nash watched the offside. Not even a coyote stirred. The small rifle with the flash suppressor stood between her legs. Powder's front paws lay crossed on her left shoulder. Her warm breath washed over Nash's forehead above her starlight goggles.

Nash preferred the broader vision of the less complicated ambient light-gathering starlight than the high-tech heat-gathering monocular Alex was wearing. As she had once explained to a SEAL team that she had led in the sandbox, if your tech fails, you're blind. If the lower tech fails, you're still attuned to the dark and sounds. The starlight only enhances the ambient light but doesn't affect the purple in the eyes. They also provided a wider field of view. The only thing better was the hot breath on her shoulder.

They drove past the small driveway and turned around a hundred yards later. "Clear."

Two clicks sounded softly in her ear. Again, Felix's voice was smooth. "Back field clear."

Two more clicks. "Moving."

The Volkswagen casually approached on the road. If it had been dirt, the dust would be low and drop quickly. Thomas would take Maggie in to see if there was anything she wanted out of the house. Nobody doubted it would be a quick visit.

Nash pulled herself up to the turret harness. Standing, she watched to the sides and behind. Everywhere that wasn't the lights on the oncoming car. She knew Alex would shield his face and reception monocular. A light as bright as a car could night-blind him for several minutes. If anything were to happen, seconds could mean the difference between living or a coffin.

They listened to the small car stop and pull back into the short driveway. Thomas eased the rear up to the yellow plastic tape. The engine rattled into silence. One door gently squeaked open.

Uncle's voice hummed in all their ears. Even Maggie wore an earbud, so she quietly knew what was happening.

"Nash. Is Powder out on patrol?"

"No."

"Then we have a coyote passing by you, Thomas. Right to left."

Unfamiliar with the power of the earbuds, Maggie's voice was loud. "Well, it is his neighborhood, after all."

Three sets of double-clicks answered. Nash glared down at Alex's snickering.

The unoiled hinges of the passenger side door let everyone know Maggie was coming out.

Felix scanned the back of the house. "Clear to come."

Uncle cleared the front and surrounding areas with his night vision binoculars. "Espresso time. Keep it short."

Small gasps or soft whimpers punctuated the minutes as Maggie picked through the devastation of thirty years of her life. Nash flipped up her goggles and listened to the desert. The soft beams from the red flashlights in the house reached out through the broken windows to dissolve into the desert. Thin lines swung from the bullet holes.

"Is that a favorite pillow?"

"No. I just need the pillowcase to hold a few things. See if you can get this drawer open. It doesn't matter if you break it."

The sound of Thomas's boot kicking the bureau combined with his breathy "oof."

"These were my mothers. It's all I have left."

"Anything else?"

They could all feel the elderly woman surveying her now shattered life. A bedroom is one's sanctuary. It was now a charnel house.

"Let's look in the studio."

The sound of scraping and moving items and broken glass or pottery softly sounded in the four earbuds in the desert. The dune buggy engine was little more than a whisper in the desert air.

"Here. Lay those brushes in the bag. These have their own roll. They were handmade by a Navajo friend as a thank-you for teaching the children about painting the kachina dolls. The dancers they would become."

The quiet was cut by Thomas's soft question.

Maggie's soft reply held so much resolve and anguish. "No. No, we're good. There's nothing left here."

"Coming out."

"Front's clear."

Alex started rolling the buggy. As they passed the house, they could see Thomas had backed the bug into the driveway and was holding the door for Maggie. They continued to clear the road ahead.

"SHE'LL CALL THE COUNTY THIS MORNING AND GIVE them the go-ahead for knocking the house down. It's really a shame, but there are no bones left. I didn't even like her being inside last night."

"Was she able to salvage anything?" Nash could hear the honest concern in the deputy director's voice.

"A small pillowcase of some personal items. Things passed down from her mother. The sort of things you keep in your underwear drawer, along with a few dozen paintbrushes. Thomas said the cabinet where she kept her paint was bleeding technicolor. It affected him. He hasn't said a word this morning. Finally took Powder, and they went for a walk about an hour ago."

She could hear him grimace. He had never spent long in the field, but he was sensitive to what field agents went through.

"Where to now?"

"There's a place we can hook up the RV on the backside of one of the other pueblos southeast of town. She thinks we would be good for a week there. Have you heard anything from the Cayman Islands yet?"

"I think you probably need to check with the lead on that matter. She seems to have as many connections in the international community as you have with the alphabets."

Nash snorted softly. "The nerd community is a powerful agency all on its own. I'll check with her. Anything from the congressman?"

"Not since your wife paid him a personal visit. My sources tell me he hasn't even been up to the hill. He was lying extremely low yesterday. I don't doubt he will remain so until Mina lets him up."

"That's my girl. I'll check in when there's an update."

The screen went dark.

Nash punched in a new phone number and code. The computer pinged several times before the window blossomed into the full screen.

Nash chuckled at the tie-dyed short shorts over the metal legs.

Only the bottom few inches of the tie-dyed t-shirt were visible on the screen. "Is it casual Friday, Mike?"

He snorted. "We threw out office protocols and dress when Muna got caught in the shooting alleys dressed in tactical body armor over her Hello Kitty pajamas and bare feet. Oz is back to just black scrubs with skulls and blue scrubs with sailboats. After all, this is San Francisco."

"You kids need adult supervision."

The man laughed. "Are you offering to transfer and take the job?"

"Oh, hell no. Too many leather stores out there that want my money. Speaking of the shooting superstar…?"

The slender, dark arm elbowed Mike's hip out of the way. The plate held a sandwich that made Nash hungry. "Oh, my gosh. Is that a prosciutto and Swiss Monte Cristo?"

Muna picked up the sandwich quarter and took a bite. She chewed slowly and rolled her eyes closed in ecstasy. "No. Jamón and brie on egg sourdough, French fried and injected with strawberry preserves." She fluttered her eyes. "Why?"

Nash lowered her head and looked through the tops of her eyes as she growled. "I'm not moving to San Francisco."

The young woman tossed her head to one side as she rolled her eyes. "Your loss."

"The way you eat. I'd be three hundred pounds by Christmas. And that is not a good look in leather pants."

"But then I'd have someone to run with."

Nash laughed. "Powder runs with me. Where are we at with the Cayman bank?"

Muna leaned in and looked around conspiratorially. "That wife of yours can dig up shit for me any day. The bank was stonewalling me. So, I called the guy Mina dug up in the state department. I gave him the scoop, and he said he would handle it. By the time I got back from the toilet, the bank was calling me back."

"Is the money still there?"

Muna shook her head and pulled her braid over her shoulder. Her hands played with the end as she leaned back into the chair. "Long gone. And to a country who doesn't like to play nice with our state department since their independence."

Nash winced. "Venezuela or Columbia?"

Muna used the end of her braid like a pointer. "Worse. But somewhere, you seem to have friends. Barbados. But we do have names and numbers. Well... kind of."

"What do you mean, kind of?"

Muna flipped the end of her braid out of the way and leaned in. "When they gained independence from England, they shifted their banking codes from the old English system to the newer European system. But they should still have the conversions. We're down to one name but two numbered markers."

"I thought numbered accounts were in Switzerland."

Muna's head twitched to the side as she took a small bite of the sandwich. "Mope." She wiped at her mouth and swallowed. "Sorry. Nope. I've been running into it more and more. Even here in the states. People who have something to hide are doing it behind numbers."

Nash looked out the RV's window at the not-so-distant mountain. "Hmm, sounds familiar. Did you reach out to the bank in Barbados?"

Muna ballooned her lower lip and slowly nodded her head exaggeratedly as her eyes burned in a broad, maniacal way. "Reached out and hung up on. All three times." She reached over and dragged something with her mouse. "I figured it was time to call in the warrior."

A new small window blossomed on Nash's screen as her phone pinged. She pulled the phone out of her pocket. It was the same information. "Okay. Let me work on this." She glared back at the sandwich. "Next time I come out, there better be one of those waiting for me."

The young woman smiled. "I'll even make one for Powder. Give my niece a hug for me."

Nash stared at the blank screen and closed it. She enlarged the information box and thought about approaching the Barbadian bank. If the money was there, it would be almost the end of the game. But if it had only been a stopping point...

NASH HAD ONLY TOLERATED BEING HUNG UP ON THE second time. Sometimes diplomacy takes many forms.

She leaned back against the RV's side. The sun felt good on her face. "No, Jacob, I said they rudely just hung up on me. Twice."

"Did you explain who you were? And how important you are?"

She stiffened her lower lip before she spoke. "I had barely gotten out the FBI part when he shut me down from saying the United States' FBI had no jurisdiction in Barbados. And my state department says their hands are tied as well. The old ways under the British ended completely last year. It was as if it was a bad word—cooperation."

"I'm sorry you have experienced the worst we offer; when you two are the best your country has given us lately. When are you coming back? I'm not saying we are holding the captain's suite ready for you, but it's ready when you are. Maybe you come, and we will try to make some accommodations with the bank..."

Nash stretched her neck and wound her head. "But if they won't even talk to the state department, who there can put any pressure... er... I mean, persuade them to help in this matter?"

The man's voice oozed the smoothness of the soft sand and warm sun. "This is Barbados. The gemstone of the Caribbean. You come, bring the wife and the dog you promised, lay in the sun, walk on the sand, eat some great food, and let Jacob find a way."

"Jacob, you are the best advocate for your nation. Let me see what I can arrange."

"Of course. After all, why does your company have a nice airplane? It would be a waste to just let it sit in a field somewhere."

Nash laughed. "I don't think they'll let me borrow the jet, but I'll see what we can do."

21

OFFSHORE

"WE'LL KEEP MOVING. Thomas needs to get back home and attend to Harkin County. And Felix got a call to head up north. It's been a fun vacation, but the party needs to pare down and go lean. Time to think like a coyote instead of a pack of wolves."

Nash furled her lips as she thought about what Uncle was saying. She looked at Alex.

As he side-eyed Nash, Alex ran his fingers through his thick, curly hair. "Don't look at me. I think the ATF is happy I'm taking part of the twenty-seven weeks of personal time they owe me. Every time I talk to HR, the first words out of her mouth are, when are you going, and for how long? It's never: So good to hear from you, Alex. How have you been, Alex? Nope... It's always just go away. Or something to that effect."

Maggie snickered and patted the thespian on the knee. "Poor child. We'll take you in from the harsh winter storm." She looked at Nash with wide eyes and rolled them.

Nash slouched farther down into her director's chair. Her head rolled back toward Thomas. "Are the kids misbehaving back home?"

He sipped on the tall tumbler of iced tea. "Probably didn't even know I was gone. We got a new guy up from Modesto. He has that CDO thing."

Nash frowned. "OCD?"

His hand dropped, and the index finger pointed. "Yeah. Kind of like that, but in alphabetical order. And he rearranged the lobby to be more Fung Sassy."

Nash held up her hand to stop him. "I don't even want to know."

Uncle laughed. "It's what his five-year-old daughter calls it. But it makes the place more inviting. And the community information board works much better than stapling fliers to the trees. I think, come elections, Tommy might have to get serious about pressing some flesh and host a barbecue or three."

Nash snorted and sat up, coughing. She looked over at Thomas. "Is there enough roadkill to hold so many barbecues?"

Thomas rocked with wide eyes. "We're going to find out."

Maggie wobbled her head. "If I was just introduced to you five, I would think you were a comedy team instead of law enforcement. Well… except for Powder. She's all goofball."

Nash just leaned over and stroked the gray splattered back. Powder moaned and rolled over to present her stomach.

Uncle smiled warmly at the reservation dog, who made good. "Felix and I will trailer the buggy, and tomorrow morning, we'll drop you guys off at the airport. I hope they can handle the crush."

Nash held up her phone. "I think mine is first at ten-thirty. So, I'm good with nine or nine-thirty and our badges."

Felix looked at his watch. "I lift off at twelve-fifteen."

Thomas slumped down deeper in his chair. "I'm in first class, seat one-C at eleven-forty. My chauffeur will pick me up and whisk me away to the grand Shangri la overlooking the Pacific Ocean."

Nash snorted. "They're all first class, ass. And Muna said she might have to send Stinky to pick you up in the beater. Something about your federal permit expiring and because you haven't passed a qualifying shoot in the last five years... the Shangri la is off limits."

Thomas rolled his eyes. "Oh well. Uber and motel five and a half it is."

———

NASH LEANED ON THE RENTAL CAR COUNTER. "I DON'T suppose you have a Dodge Hellcat, do you?"

The woman's eyes got enormous with fear as she leaned back a few inches.

Mina rolled her eyes. "Ignore my wife. She thinks she's Dale Earnhardt. We only need a convertible."

The woman looked at her computer screen as she moved slightly closer to the tall Asian woman. "I have a Mustang or a Mini."

Mina smirked at her wife. "The Mustang, please. There's nothing mini about me or my wife. What color?"

"I have a silver and a red one."

The two wives harmonized. "Red," Mina added. "Please."

The woman laughed. "Who owns the red car at home?"

Mina pointed at Nash. "The Hellcat is red because our doorman chose it."

The woman hid her smile as she dipped her head and started typing. She grabbed the walkie-talkie and called the man in the lot. "Tony?"

"Tony, go."

"The red Mustang. And it best be washed, polished, and in perfect condition for my new bestie friends. Bring it up to the presentation. I will bring them out myself. And no funny business or I will tell your mother." She put down the walkie-talkie. "My sister's oldest. We're trying to make a human being out of him before he goes away to college."

Mina shrugged her face. "Which college?"

The woman rolled her eyes. "He got a football scholarship to

Oxford. But he's taking the math scholarship at Cambridge. He wants to be a computer engineer." She bounced her head around with a small smile. A proud aunt.

The top down had made the leisurely drive to Crane Beach a joy. The air and sun tempted Mina to remove her wig, but her oncologists had strongly stressed for her to limit her exposure to sunlight. The wig and a scarf had remained in place.

Jacob greeted them with open arms. To an outsider, it would have appeared as a family reunion. In a way, it was or an introduction to the new favored niece.

He dropped to his knees and put his hands out. Nash urged Powder to greet him. Soon, the rubs and scratches were everywhere under the harness Powder directed to his fingers.

"I can see how you took her into the family. She is adorable. And the staff all know she has the run of the estate. Even without her harness." He turned the harness and read the badge. "Oh… so very official." He looked up. "So, she goes to work with you?"

"Since she got her badge, it's been 'take your daughter to work and everywhere you go' day."

He smiled. "I would bring my pet, but she isn't as well-behaved as Powder."

Mina frowned briefly. The man had mentioned no pets before. "What kind do you have?"

He radiated a full mouth of teeth. "She will graduate to second form this June. I think you call them eighth graders. We just call them terrorists once we give in and grant them a cell phone."

Nash chuckled. "Bring her by. We can turn her training over to Powder. I'm sure her herd dog nature will have your daughter rounded up in no time."

He stood with pursed lips. "I'm sure her mother would have something to say about that. She calls Rebecca her Mini-Me."

Mina shied her head. "Sucks to be daddy."

The man softly laughed as his head rocked. "Here, let's get you settled in the captain's suite. It must have been a long flight, and I understand you have a busy day tomorrow."

Nash turned from the trunk. "We do?"

Jacob nodded. "They informed me you would have breakfast with Detective Hornblower from the Attorney General's office and banking affairs." He pointed at the entrance to the restaurant. "I assumed nine o'clock would be okay? The banks don't open until ten, and you wouldn't want to rush your morning run..." He reached for two of the bags.

* * *

THE WOMAN STOOD DRESSED IN A WHITE BLOUSE AND black dress. The badge hung from the dress at her right hip, in front of her weapon. She stepped forward. "Detective Mary Hornblower with the Attorney General's office. And no relationship to the fictional Horatio Hornblower. Obviously."

Nash shook her hand. "So good to meet you. Special Agent Nash Running Bear with Special Operations of the FBI." She turned. "And my wife—"

Mina stepped forward with her diplomatic smile and took the hand of the shorter woman. "Mina Running Bear. Just like the bird, but spelled like the hole in a mountain." She waved her hand down at Powder. "And our daughter and Nash's constant companion, Powder. Powder, shake hands with the gracious lady you need to work with."

Mary kneeled and held out her hand. "I have a chocolate retriever. Nice to meet you, Powder." They shook, and Powder took her paw back.

"A Labrador retriever is a good-sized dog."

Mary smiled. "No, I misspoke. Mop is milk chocolate. She's a King Charles and Corgi mix. She is a snuggle mop, and everyone is always retrieving her from wherever she is to come to snuggle or sleep with them. I have three children, including my husband."

Mina wiggled her eyebrows. "We don't share. Powder takes the middle of our king-sized bed. She's happiest when she can touch both of us at the same time. She also gets the middle of the couch. Shall we go for breakfast? I see Jacob is holding a table for us."

As they approached the uninterrupted expanse of floor-to-ceiling windows overlooking the mile of pink coral sand beach, Jacob bowed slightly, pulling out a chair. "You have the entire restaurant this morning. Our other guests are being treated to dining alfresco around the pool." He pushed in the detective's chair and pulled out the two across. "You can discuss anything you need to. I will be your only waiter today. Before I retired, I held a level four security clearance with the Royal Navy." He put his fingers to his mouth and pulled the zipper. "Now. What can I make for you three this morning?"

As Jacob later removed the dishes and refilled the coffee, Mary pulled her phone out of her purse and checked the ping. She turned it face down on the table. "I spoke to the bank president yesterday after I heard what you were after. Your state department is correct. The banking industry is not very cooperative with the United States since so many people who have stashed their savings..." She bounced her head softly from shoulder to shoulder. "Ill-gotten or not. But the United States has taken billions of dollars out of the Caribbean banking economy over the last twenty years. Barbados is not the island most think of, but we try to be the most secure."

She held up her hand as Nash opened her mouth. "I didn't say I wouldn't help. And I understand we are talking about funds reaching into British law. But strong-arming my uncle could leave a bit of a strained relation at the next family barbecue. So, you see, I need to be in a position where I have no choice."

"It wasn't our intent to force something—"

She smiled. "Which is not what I said or implied. I merely need to be in a position where I and the island are in your debt."

Mina rested her hand on Nash's arm. "Let me take over here.

She's talking my language, not yours." She smiled at the detective. "How can we arrange this?"

Mary picked up her purse and drew out a folded set of papers. "We have a delicate situation. And when I heard about your talented daughter..." She flattened out the papers.

Nash took the offered papers. She scanned and flipped through. "What am I looking at?"

"What you're looking at is an extremely wealthy and just as powerful person with a dual citizenship. And they aren't ours. They only bought their extended visa and clearance to own property. Not just a home, but large sections of land and buildings."

Mina muttered. "An oligarch."

"Yes, an oligarch."

Nash frowned. "How does someone get a Russian and United States dual citizenship?"

The detective leaned back in her chair. "In the nineties, Belarus was making nice-nice with the United States. Some power brokers made certain arrangements to guarantee sales of machinery and food for their country, which was at the time a breakaway from the former Soviet Union. Some arrangements allowed the Belarusian families to emigrate to the United States, and others negotiated dual citizenship in the US and Belarus but then lived in another country. Many moved to England. Some didn't want to live with other expatriates and moved to the Caribbean and South America." She held her hand out. "Which is how we inherited Mr. Romanov."

Nash set down the papers and then slid them over to the political expert. "How can we help?"

Mary leaned over and looked at the dog lying with her butt against Nash's feet, and her head on Mina's toes. "Rumor has it, she sniffed out bodies submerged in a river."

Nash froze. Mina looked up and realized Nash's eyes weren't seeing the woman in front of her. She stalled for time. "It wasn't bodies. They were skeletons. Over twenty of them spread over a mile. Some had been in the water for over five years."

Mary blinked as she frowned at Nash's paralysis and looked at Mina. "Is she okay?"

Mina rested her hand on Nash's arm and gently shook. "Honey? Are you with us?"

Nash blinked and then blinked again. "How many bodies did you say?"

Mary looked out the side of her eyes at Nash. "One. One we are certain of. Why?"

"How do we get into the house?"

"He's not due back until the end of next week. There is a work order for a new security system. Evidently, there was a problem during a gala event he hosted a few months ago. The same event a young woman attended, but was never seen leaving the estate. Her parents have reached out everywhere they could think of, but no luck."

Mina looked at Nash's stiff face but spoke to the detective. "But this isn't the first time…"

"No. It was before my time. They searched the residence, but nothing."

"And you think he buried them on the grounds?"

The detective nodded. "We have a small window of opportunity, and maybe someone who can help us solve a crime."

Mina sat back in her chair. "Which, with this crime, and this person, it would put you and the nation…"

The detective nodded. "In your debt."

2 2

DIGGING UP SECRETS

MINA STOPPED Nash at the car. "You did your thing again."

Nash frowned. "Bite my lip. I always do…"

Mina took Nash's chin between her thumb and fingers. "No. Where you freeze up and you're just not there. It's like you're somewhere else. But when I touched you… it took a second or two for you to get back. Mary noticed it too."

Nash's jaw firmed as her lower lip sucked into her teeth on the right side. "My mother used to touch something or sometimes for no reason at all, just see things." She turned her head to look at the people under the umbrellas at the pool with the ocean behind. "I didn't want to be my mother. I didn't want to be the strange woman who saw things."

Mina softly cupped Nash's jaw in her right hand. "When I was ten, someone called me a chink. All the way home, I cried. I didn't want to be Chinese anymore. I wanted to dye my hair blond, and have round eyes. For a couple of years, I laid out by the pool, played tennis in the skimpiest outfits I could. Anything to change my skin color. I even tried washing my hair with orange juice."

A small smile tugged at Nash's face. "Did it work?"

"The orange juice?" Mina laughed. "Mom showed me the ingredients in the stupid stuff. We bought real oranges, and I squeezed them fresh every morning from then on. I don't remember if I ever tried the real orange juice or not, but Mom took me out and we tried on wigs instead. Good wigs. Not Welch, but they were real hair in those days."

Nash started quietly laughing as her mouth pulled back into a strained neutral. "Did you ever find out it was lemon juice, not orange juice for lightening your hair?"

Mina rolled her eyes to one side and matched the toss with her head. "By then, it didn't matter. Our relationship changed. We became more friends and comrades in arms than the usual strata of child, nanny, parents. We even started shopping for clothes together. My closet became my personal space, and I learned more about our culture to understand it. By high school, I ran for Asian Student Body President, and won. And dove into the cesspool of politics."

Nash leaned in and hugged her wife. "And you still smell like a rose."

"Mm, there are no roses in China."

THE MANSION HAD ALL THE HALLMARKS OF GRAND living. The white of the façade was marble instead of stucco. Even the four tall carved multi-story Corinthian columns were solid marble. The wings of the building were expansive to impress anyone approaching up the long drive.

Mina pulled her Jackie O dark glasses down her nose. "Whoa. Even I'm impressed. If this was in Westchester, it would easily go for eight figures. Maybe even nine. When do you think they built it?"

Nash snorted. "We can ask, but we can't afford it."

The crushed shell driveway crackled quietly as they pulled in behind the other cars and vans. The fields of mowed lawns rolled away from the parking. At the far edge of the one field sat a white gazebo. It looked like it could hold an entire philharmonic orchestra. A true folly which was probably never used.

Nash stepped out of the car as she studied the giant front door. Everything to impress—and stop questions. As Powder stood on the seat, Nash kneeled and slowly scrunched at the dog's neck. "Let's go look for bodies first. Are you up for this?" Powder licked her nose.

As the three women wandered around the outside of the building, Powder ran, walked, and stalked through the garden beds.

"When was this built?"

Mary looked up at the windows as they turned the corner at the one end. She pointed. "Some of this, Romanov added. Most of this wing, you can see the vinyl windows. Some say they don't open because they are too thick. They aren't triple pane glass, but single bulletproof instead." She shrugged. "But the original estate dates to the sixteen hundreds. It was originally a sugarcane plantation. The slave ships dropped enslaved people here, took sugar to America, dropped more enslaved people there, replaced it with cotton and tobacco, and sailed back to England."

As they turned to the back of the building, they found Powder sitting on the grass, looking at a rose bush. Her head turned to look at Nash.

As they walked up, Nash held out her hand. "Powder says this is body number one."

Mina frowned at the well cared for perfectly formed rose bushes. "They didn't bury anything here."

Nash smiled. She enjoyed walking in her mother-in-law's award-winning rose garden.

The detective frowned. "So, the dog is wrong? I'm confused."

Mina turned. As she spoke, her hands and fingers spread. "Roses are sensitive. They spread their roots, and then they have micro roots. When the micro roots touch the other micro roots, it fixes each bush's boundaries. About six inches beyond the expanse of the bush's spread." She pointed between the two bushes. "See the distance between the stems? It's their natural distancing. If you dig in there to bury a body, you will destroy those roots. And the bush will react by dying on that side or dying altogether. Roses are amazingly hardy but also sensitive."

Nash leaned her head back proudly. "And this is why I keep her around. She knows a lot." She pointed to where Powder was still sitting. "On the other hand, grass has short roots, especially when it gets watered regularly. So, if you cut an area of about six feet wide and out to here and roll back the turf... you can dig and bury with no evidence. Scatter the extra dirt in the garden bed, and roll the turf back. By the next mowing, nobody would be the wiser."

The detective pointed at the lawn. "So, we dig here."

Nash shrugged her shoulder and face. "Only if you want a body or bones."

She pulled the walkie-talkie off her hip. "Rupert?"

The radio crackled. "Rupert here."

"Bring your digging crew to the southwest corner. We have our first body."

"Straight away, Mum."

She hung the radio back on her hip. And raised her eyebrows. "Next?"

Nash snapped her fingers and pointed out in the enormous expanse and pool. "Next one, girl."

As they watched Powder go back to work, Nash explained. "If they kill more than once, they kill and bury more and more. It solved their problem before, and soon they see all their problems need burying."

As the men came around the building, Powder sat down at the other end of the flower bed. The detective pointed to where she was standing. "To be safe, cut and roll back this turf about four meters by four meters. Then dig." She pointed at the dog. "And do the same where the dog is sitting. We believe she's sitting on another body."

"Certainly, Mum."

The man pointed at the spot for his crew. Pulling up his radio, he called for more workforce as he strode down to meet Powder.

Nash continued as they walked along the backside of the mansion. "I know many countries send various members of their police forces to take courses at Quantico. Maybe you can arrange for some time, and even time spent out at the body farm..." She turned her head to look at the detective's reactions. "If that interests you."

"Would I get to cheat on my exams and borrow Powder?"

Mina snickered. "Now there's a concept."

"Using Powder isn't cheating. Most of the dogs aren't even half as good. But then, Powder just makes it look easy."

Nash stopped and turned. She looked at where the crew was digging and where Powder was now sitting. There was a balance in the relationship to the wing of the mansion. With her heel, she marked a small line in the dirt.

The detective's face became darker. "What? What do you see?"

Nash turned and looked at the other wing. "It's..." She looked at the detective. "They have a lot of digging already. Let's look at the art gallery first."

"How did you know there's an art gallery?"

Nash debated what to tell. She glanced at Mina and winked. Spreading both of her arms, she chirped. "Why would you waste all this impressive building without having an even more impressive art collection to show off?"

The detective turned them toward the low fan of stairs to the back veranda. Nash quietly snapped her fingers at her leg, releasing Powder from marking the body.

From front to back, the grand entry filled the center of the building. Nash had followed her wife into the largest ballrooms of D.C., and this was larger. The mural-painted ceiling soared over forty feet or more. The returns of the stairways provided generous spaces on the landings of the twin curved stairways and the railing above.

Nash held up her finger. "First, where is his private office?"

The detective changed course. "This way. I thought you wanted to see the art?"

"No, just to watch Powder work. But first, she needs to get the scent of him. Or, to be more exact, his hand."

The office was not as grand as Nash had expected, but it was more lavish than the usual executive office of D.C. The deep colored paneling was common to the Caribbean, but exotic to the rest of the world. Nash and Powder walked around the desk. Powder stuck her nose close as she went. Nash assumed the staff had thoroughly wiped down the furniture using polish.

She studied the objects on the desk. The small gold mantel clock, an ostentatious fetish, would get wiped down as well. She leaned over and examined the pen in the walnut cup. The felt at the cup's bottom had an ink stain, but only in one small area. Only one person touched the pen.

She picked up the cup and held it down for Powder to smell the gold pen. Powder than sat. Nash looked up and smirked at the detective. "We've got him. Let's go see the gallery."

The thick drapes, puddling on the marble floor, all but shut out the light. As they entered the gallery, the indirect lighting grew brighter. Softly diffused, but more than enough to view and appreciate the brush strokes of the genius's handiworks. Some, Nash guessed, were forgeries. Other's probably not.

Nash kneeled and rubbed Powder under the back of her harness. "I want you to show us where the man touches."

She stood, and Powder started walking along the walls. Finally, at the large Pollock, she stopped and sat.

Mina snorted. "Jackson Pollock. Who would have guessed? I would have gone with the Kandinsky."

Nash pointed at the Kandinsky, four paintings further down the gallery. "The frame stops short of the mop board."

Mina wound her hand on Nash's arm and patted it with her other hand. "That's called a baseboard, dear."

Nash turned her face close to her wife's. "Not when we're talking about mopping up a crime scene."

Nash strode over to Powder. She kneeled and whispered. "Where does he touch?"

Powder stood and then rose onto her hind legs as her nose touched the wall and the back edge of the frame. Nash rubbed her back down and lavished some hugs and kisses as she whispered to the dog.

Nash stood. "Powder? You want to go find some more bodies outside?"

As they walked past the frowning detective and Mina, Nash smiled and quipped cheerfully. "Dead body time."

Detective Hornblower turned in horror to Mina. Mina shrugged and held her head back haughtily as she followed her family. Her voice was as perky as a high school cheerleader. "Dead body time. Care to join us?"

23

RATTLE THE BONES

NASH STOOD BACK from the two men in the hole. She had expected more like a three- or four-foot cover. But she also hadn't expected the body bag wrapped in thick Visqueen plastic and sealed with duct tape.

She turned as the other two approached. "How big was your missing girl?"

The detective cocked her head in confusion. "Twenty-one-year-old woman? About fifty-two kilos. One sixty-eight."

Nash looked at Mina. The woman had one eye closed. "About five foot six. Average height and weight."

Nash turned back to the two men, lifting the wrapped body out of the grave. "This one isn't her. If this one cracks five feet, she's wearing heels."

Detective Hornblower turned away as she pulled her phone out of her purse. All Nash and Mina picked up was her requesting a mobile autopsy unit come out for multiple bodies. As she turned to look back, Nash was sure she read the lips right as the woman asked for a sex crimes unit as well. The one missing person had turned into a hotbed of something else.

Mina stopped shoulder to shoulder. Her voice was just for them. "What do you think?"

Nash glanced over. "I think today will be extremely messy. A body here or a body there is usual, but spread over a year. I don't get the impression they have an understanding about dealing with a monster and serial killer." Nash nodded toward the detective. "She needs to understand how slippery this kind of guy is. If they don't lock him down securely, and have a judge who will throw away the key, his ninety-five lawyers will have their man on a private jet and somewhere nobody can touch him."

Mina nodded at the seven people involved in the diggings. "But if word gets out, he's never coming back."

"Like I said. These kids are on their own. They have my sympathy. This has thrust them into the deep end of the sleazy pool, but they are going to need to learn how to deal with the real world. As the safe places for the monsters become unsafe, they will invade the unsophisticated until they become not so naïve and drive them out. The best for the island and the world would be a well-placed bullet when the man walks through the door."

Mina's face reacted in horror. "You didn't say that."

"I did. And deep down, it is the honest truth. Anything less is my job and my personal decency as a human being. But, honey, we're not talking about a human." She glanced back at the detective, still on the phone. "Wait until we get to the cellar."

Mina examined the building. "There's a basement too?"

Nash turned, facing away from the men in the grave. "Sure. The seventeen hundreds? It's how they kept food stored and wine chilled." She stared down at Powder. "Come on, girl. Let's go find more bodies. Make mommy proud."

They strolled along the building as Nash texted to Muna. If Nash was going to need the island in her debt, she needed more than a few dead bodies and whatever was in the basement.

Powder sat. Nash marked a set of bracketing lines in the flower bed and waved the dog on. The game had gotten old, and Powder was slower, but all they had was time.

Nash was marking the third spot as the first crew came around the stairs. She stared at how close she was to the end of the building. Only if they didn't find the woman they were looking for would they come back and keep looking. She walked back and explained the marks and pointed at the other two sets of marks. The men silently groaned, but knew it was their job.

Detective Hornblower approached Nash and stood watching the new dig. Nash explained the three sites.

"What are the chances Powder missed one on the other side?"

Nash looked down at the grass and beat back her anger. Not at the woman, but at the situation. The woman had seen the dirty plastic taped tight around a body bag. The true nature of someone who kills several people, and buries them in their backyard, is only in fact revealed once they strip the plastic back and examine the killing floor.

Nash held up her hand to stop the woman from saying any more. Nash remembered a drill instructor who slowly took out his side weapon and methodically shot ten rounds into the sand. Holstered his piece, and then regarded the team. His face was passive. He wasn't mad. He had held his tongue and counted to ten in his own way. Nobody ever wanted to see the exhibition again.

Nash looked up. "I have two questions."

The detective nodded. "Okay."

"First, how many people know we are here, and what we are doing?"

The detective waved her hand at the digging crew. "And a few more back at the office."

"You need to call them. Tell them to go to lunch. Tell nobody. But, come here."

The woman shied her head to one side. "Why?"

"How long do you honestly think you can keep this all hidden from the media? How long before one of those guys posts a short video of the body dug up in an oligarch's backyard on TikTok or Instagram?" She scraped her lower lip under her teeth. "How long before the world media picks up how Romanov is a person of interest because of seven bodies found in his backyard?"

The detective counted on her fingers as she pointed at the graves. "Five."

Nash stepped a half step and leaned in. "Will you bet your career on that?"

A tick started at the corner of the woman's right eye. Nash knew it wouldn't go away for a longtime. "Are his billions here in a Barbados bank or four?"

"We hadn't examined that yet."

Nash stared across the swimming pool. "You have Powder. Let me know when you figure out how you want to use her to cheat. Because you needed to have the money and bank answer last week. If not years ago. If anyone is living here, and has more than a few million dollars, euros, Rubles, or even Rupees, you need to know if the money is here and how you can freeze the assets at a moment's notice."

Nash rested her index finger on her left little finger. "First, call in the others who know about this. Second, blow up the road leading to here. Make it a gas main or water main. Something big enough for a lot of work crews and to close the road. Nothing in and nothing out. The people here stay here. And no phones. Explain why. There needs to be nothing out there hinting of an investigation into Romanov. If he catches wind of this, you will never see or hear of him again."

The detective waved her hand at the house.

Nash shook her head. "It's worth nothing. It's stone, some paint, and furniture. Nothing. Nothing but evidence of who and what the man is. So now we're up to three. Now you work your uncle and find every dollar or Rupel or Euro this man has that you can, at the snap of your finger, control. When you have that all done, we'll be in the kitchen making sandwiches. Your men are going to be starving. With or without dead bodies."

Nash took a step and then rocked back. "How is your stomach?"

"How do you mean?"

"How many autopsies have you sat in on? More importantly, how many have you eaten lunch while you watch them?"

Her face lightened. "A few…"

Nash half smiled. "Eaten lunch?"

Her voice had a small stone in the throat. "No."

Nash nodded. "Don't eat with the others. Sip a little water. I don't know what we'll find downstairs, but it won't be pleasant."

"Downstairs? There's a cellar?"

Nash smiled. "Of course. Probably a few of them. But I'm merely talking about the dungeon."

IT TOOK NASH A FEW MINUTES TO FIND THE PIECE THAT felt wrong on the back of the picture frame. It was only a slight bump, but it didn't move. A latch should have some movement. And then she remembered Powder had touched her nose to the front and side of the frame. She put her finger on the bump and gripped the frame with her hand. The bump reduced. There were four soft clicks and the frame, painting, and door swung open—just as she had seen in her vision.

The stairwell was well lit and appeared secretly inviting. It was as if leading down into a more intimate gallery of maybe finer art treasures. Nash examined the inside of the secret door and then stepped down the stairs. Powder sat on the top landing and watched.

They had made the stairs of poured concrete and painted the walls. Utilitarian but tasteful. The passageway was wide enough to hold two people comfortably or to accommodate moving furniture. Nash noted the lower temperature inherent in a basement or cellar.

At the bottom of the long stairway was a solid wood door. As she opened it, she studied the thickness. Soundproof? Or just part of the castle motif of the room? The door swung open—into the large room.

A motion sensor triggered and increased the surrounding lighting in the new gallery. Hidden spotlights lit up the displays and sculptures. The sculptures ran from marble to bronze. The theme ran from ancient military combat to fantasy paramilitary or just raw muscle, lack of clothing, and savage use of weapons.

Weapons of all orders lined the walls. But almost all were cutting weapons. From stone knives to bronze artifacts, to rusted, dinged, and beaten steel blades. As well as many other weapons from the Dark Ages to Cavalier foils, sabers, and other ceremonial blades. It was a museum of man's violence against man. The testosterone was intense and hung in the air. But it wasn't what Nash expected.

Her voice was quiet. "Powder. I need you."

She could hear the nails clicking down the stairs. She felt the familiar pressure on her calf and knee.

"Where does he touch?"

She knew it may be futile. The man probably handled all the weapons much like a person fondles prayer beads.

She watched the dog walk around the room of displays. Occasionally, she rose on her hind legs to get a better sniff, but then continued.

Nash thought about the room, the displays, the sculptures... who cleaned this room?

Nash thought about the room. It was shorter than the gallery was upstairs. But not by much. Maybe only twelve or fifteen feet. The width was close to the same. But the shortness bothered her.

Powder stood on her hind legs, her front paws on the low stand of the bronze. A Roman Centurion, stepping back and pulling the man's head back by his hair so he could run his broadsword down through his foe's mouth and into his body. The sword was still in the dead man, with anguish on his face. The dead warrior's legs frogged beneath him.

Powder bounced to get closer to the sword, but it was too high. She finally gave up and continued around the last of the displays. Nash was about to say something, but the dog started over. Only a little faster this time. She ignored the center statues, but gave the wall displays a cursory glance or occasional sniff.

"Nash?"

She turned toward the stairs. "Yeah. We're down here." She listened for the footsteps on the concrete stairs.

"What in the...?"

Nash turned. "Upstairs is his gallery to impress the world. This is the gallery of his heart. The displays, if I remember my history of weapons, go back past the bronze age." She swept her hand along the gallery. "Through Greece, Rome, feudal times, the Dark Ages, Renaissance, French Cavalier, the golden age of Empires, and finally World War two, and the height of man's inhumanity to man, the Nazis."

The detective screwed up her face in confusion. "But no Russia?"

Nash shrugged. "Russia is about four hundred years old. Much of the time was under the Ottoman Empire. So even the brigades of their cavalry used thousand-year-old curved Saracen scimitars from the Holy Land. The lightweight, agile scimitar was the one sword that proved deadlier than the great sword or broadsword." She touched the hilt of the sword in the statue.

Her finger felt a slight movement.

She looked for Powder. "Powder?"

The detective turned to point. "She's right here."

Powder sat on the landing at the bottom of the stairs. Except she was almost leaning against the wall.

Nash stared back at the great sword in the sculpture. It wasn't a vision; it was a memory. The last class she took on the Roman

Empire was about the reasons behind the fall. She could hear the professor's dramatic lecture.

"The Huns swept in on horseback with their deadly scimitars outreaching the Roman short sword by a full foot. The Roman legions had ruled the known world for hundreds of years because of their superior military. But the shortness of their sword was their undoing when they scattered before the racing cavalry."

She turned to the sculpture of the quintessential Roman Centurion from his crested helmet and leather slatted shirt to his leather leg protection and high laced sandals. She looked at the long sword. "This is no Roman short sword."

24

MORE RATTLE, FEWER BONES, PLEASE

THE DETECTIVE LEANED IN. "But it's art…"

Nash growled. "Art is something which inspires and has meaning. This sword is a lie hiding in the guise of art portraying historical fact." She drew her finger along the Centurion's armor. "The artist paid attention to the proper length of the crest, and it being raised. The jowl guards aren't excessively done, as they were mostly ceremonial instead of armor. The human form on the boiled leather body armor isn't carved sharp and defined as if it was metal. They define the detail of the leather skirt and leg armor instead of just putting something there. They sculpted everything about this statue to actuality and true dimensions." She rested her finger on the top of the sword. "Except this sword doesn't come into existence for another four or five hundred years."

The woman scowled. "But how do you know it's not just artist… um… liberties?"

Nash tossed her head slightly. "Three things are wrong with this sword. The first is length. The Roman short sword was the length of a man's leg from his ankle to mid-thigh at the femoral artery. Both have mythological implications."

"But they buried half of the sword in the other guy's mouth."

Nash spread her hand and placed the tip of her small finger at the mouth of the dead foe, and the tip of the thumb resting on the hilt. She moved it to the Centurion's leg. The spread reached just past the knee. "Assuming there is still almost half still in his gut…" She laid her hand along the Centurion's upper arm. The thumb was at his shoulder as the little finger almost wrapped around the elbow. "The broadsword was the length of a knight's outstretched arm. About thirty-six inches."

"And second?"

Nash pointed at the hilt. "Roman's were proud of their fearlessness. If there was a hilt, it was only there to stop a blood-soaked hand from slipping forward in a thrust. This is a cross hilt. It was large, so a knight, with waning strength in a long battle, could grab this hilt with his second hand and deliver a blow with his whole body."

The detective leaned back on her heels and studied the entire sculpture. It was a lot to take in. "You said three."

Nash smiled. "Powder found this for me." She waved her hand around the general sculpture. "She didn't trigger on the legs or back or arms or head. Places one would expect would get touched. But instead, she nosed up as close to the handle of the sword as she could get."

Nash rested her index finger on the top of the sword. "Notice the sword in the mouth. It's not part of the casting." She applied pressure. The sword moved slightly.

Out of the corner of her eye, Nash saw Powder jerk and look at the wall beside her and behind the open door. "Shall we take the next secret door?" She held her hand out toward Powder.

"What door?"

Nash smiled as she moved the thick wooden door. "The hidden door here. Show us, girl. Powder, where does he touch?"

The dog pushed her nose against the wall, and it swung open. The lights came on beyond.

They stepped into an area the size of a large living room. Along one wall was a table and a couple of chairs. At the end of the wall was an international money counting and banding machine. Next to it was a shrink-wrapping machine. Nash had seen the same setup in the backroom of a large federal bank. What wasn't at the bank were the pallets of bundled money.

They banded bills in bundles of a hundred bills. If they are hundred-dollar bills, the band is ten thousand dollars. Then they stack the banded packets and shrink-wrapped in sets of twenty-five. Or two hundred and fifty thousand dollars and called it a football. A pallet usually holds forty footballs or ten million dollars. Romanov had stacked the pallets two high in each national currency: dollars, euros, pounds, rubles, and Saudi Arabia's Riyal. The values were substantial, but paled next to the nine pallets of gold bars and four pallets of bundled racks of gold coins.

The detective, trying to take it all in, leaned back against the object in the middle of the room. Nash grabbed her arm and stopped her. "Don't touch."

The detective turned, and her face furrowed. "Is that a...?"

"Exam table? Yes. The same kind you and I get our annual exams on. Only, we don't get strapped down." She pointed at the arm wings extending from the table. "We need gloves for this. And for a full forensic workup."

She looked at Nash. "I don't know what I expected to find down here, but it wasn't all this." She waved her hand around. "This doesn't make sense."

Nash rested her hand on the woman's shoulder. "More sense than you might imagine. Perverse, but sense." She pointed up. "I need to check in with my team. And you need to get your forensic people out here."

Nash had barely hit send on the text when the phone rang. The string of numbers was long, but she recognized the four-one-five area code for San Francisco. "Nash."

Muna's voice sounded panicked. "Where have you been? I've been trying to reach you for over an hour."

Nash glanced back at the thick walls of the estate. "Under a few metric tons of concrete, rebar, and stone. What's happened?"

"It's more like what is about to happen. I've been trying to track down Romanov. But the reason his phone isn't showing in Paris is because his plane landed twenty minutes ago at Grantley Adams International Airport. He's in Christchurch."

"Christchurch? As in Barbados Christchurch?"

Detective Hornblower lowered her phone and looked at Nash.

"Just a minute, Muna." She lowered her phone to talk to the detective. "Romanov landed twenty minutes ago at Christchurch. He'll be here any minute. We need to clear the front and ambush him inside."

The detective rushed off.

Nash slowly shook her head as she raised the phone. "Any other good news?"

"Geez, I wish. I found over nine hundred million stashed in three countries. I convinced England and Switzerland to freeze the accounts, but only Germany would confiscate the funds. But it's not nearly what the guy is supposedly worth."

Nash smiled as she leaned down to play with Powder's ears and head. "No, that's a good start. We found about that much here in his home. Along with five bodies. But reach out and see if we can find and attach anything in Saudi Arabia."

"I don't think we have a good relationship with them, but I'll see what I can do. What made you think of them?"

"Call it a hunch, but there's a stack of money footballs here as tall as you."

"Pallets?"

"Pallets."

"Ouch. That would buy a lot of napalm pork rinds. Oh, and Mike says hi. He wants a Caribbean t-shirt. Even though I told him Barbados is more England than England. He still thinks it's Jamaica."

Nash shook her head. "I'll see what I can do. Barbados is going to owe me for this." She looked at the two vans driving on the lawn around the building. Mary and her car followed. "Have you heard anything from the boys?"

"Uncle said they're doing something called dry camping. They're on a Navajo reservation. I can't locate them, so they must be in the middle of nowhere."

Nash watched the detective walking up with a hurried stride. "I'll check back later." She thumbed the phone and put it in her pocket. "What's up?"

"The front's clear. He's already at the roadblock, but he's going around with his four-wheel. So, he'll be here in about ten minutes. How do you want to do this?"

Nash thought for a moment. "How many of your people are armed and good at using deadly force?"

The detective shook her head with a shrug. "About a dozen."

"Okay, somehow, we need to circle the drive. There's nowhere to hide on the lawns unless your guys throw some of the sod over themselves. But we need to cut him off from getting back in their cars. So have them wait until he comes inside. I'll run down and close the secret doors, so we'll preserve the basement. But you and I are going to meet him in the entry. Powder's our backup."

The detective looked down at the calm dog.

Nash turned her toward the house. "Don't ask. She saved my life before. But we'll talk after."

As they crossed the grand entry, Mina came out of the side wing, licking her fingers.

Nash frowned at the unusual movement. "Where have you been?"

Mina smiled. "Well, you were working, so I found the kitchen and made me a snack. What's up?"

"Shit storm. Go back into the kitchen and stay there."

Mina spun on her heel and retreated.

Nash pointed at the front. "Get your team up to speed. I'll be right back."

Nash gave Powder the stay sign and ran down the secret stairs. She stopped at the still open hidden door of a wall. There wasn't an obvious switch or way to close the wall. She looked back at the statue.

She pushed on the sword. Nothing happened. She went back to the wall and searched all the edges. Still no switch.

She stood at the statue. Reaching over, she lifted the sword. The wall closed, but she also kept withdrawing the sword. It wasn't attached to the sculpture. She felt the edge. Other than Powder, she wasn't allowed to travel internationally with her pistol. She smirked. "If a buffoon in the Dark Ages can wield this, how hard can it be?"

She closed the wooden door and ran back upstairs. The trigger next to the opening back out to the main gallery was more obvious. The secret door glided silently shut.

Sword in hand, she stalked along the gallery of rare art. She thought about some of the art she saw as a young girl on pulp fiction fantasy books in the used bookstore. She swung the sword in an arch over her head, as she thought one of the Amazon women would have. The blade didn't sing or make even the described whoosh. But she felt the lightness of the held blade was completely different when it moved. She would need to ask Oz about the dynamics. Another time.

Detective Hornblower stood beside the sidelight, bracketing the front door. She frowned at the sword.

Nash closed one eye as she tossed her head. "Not exactly a concealed weapon, but it can do a hell of a job in the right fight."

The detective reached down and under her dress. She withdrew a PPK from her inner thigh. "Hopefully, we don't end up in an extended fire fight or we're both buggered." She handed Nash the extra pistol.

25

WELCOME HOME

MUNA SHIFTED from her usual computer to the sandbox computer, where she kept the dark web resident. Her connection was through a coded and dedicated line directly to a server in Virginia, which had no connections to the government or her. For all intents, she was squatting in a dark corner of a known arms trafficker. The man's computer traffic was heavy as he also ran several porn sites with extras if a customer could pay for the more personal treatments and were in the cities his contractors serviced. A friend of hers in college found it. She always thought of it as her bad girl room.

She smiled. It would horrify her mother. She thought of it as camping out in the alley behind a sleazy porn shop.

She heard Mike coming. She reached over and clicked a few keys on her official computer and pointed behind her. "Your report is now printing on Dewey. And if you would be so kind, would you grab the letter off Louie and give it to Oz. It's been there since lunch."

Mike looked at the three laser printers along the wall. There had always been confusion until Muna had labeled them. He snorted softly. It was always good to know Saturday morning cartoons were still alive and working in the top echelons of the FBI.

He turned from the printers with documents in his hands. "If you could, I'd really like a copy of—"

She pointed. "Huey should have it done in… now." The printer had fallen silent.

He leaned over and recognized the retyped and corrected notes for his lecture. "Thanks."

The hand waved above her head. "All part of the job."

He stopped at the door and turned back. "The transcription of my afternoon autopsy…"

She swung her chair around. "I'm good, but not psychic. First do the autopsy. Speak into the microphone. Use actual words I can understand and look up in a dictionary. Doohickey is not a medical term, so you can stop with punking the new kid. And then, and only then, will it magically appear in your files." She spun the chair back around. "Go. Do something. Learn things and teach."

She smiled as she leaned back into the sandbox. The records had only gone back to ninety-six. Before that, the man didn't exist. It was as if he was in witness protection. Except they confirmed they didn't have anyone in the city. It was as if the capitol of the nation was officially off limits for placing people under witness protection. Muna rolled her eyes. It was also the one city where everyone was used to all new faces about every four years.

"Okay, mister, let's go at this from another angle."

The bag of napalm encrusted pork rinds dropped on to the desk next to her hand and mouse. She jumped and then looked up.

Mike smiled. "Your addition to my lecture notes was brilliant. I don't know why I never explained the vivisection murders like that. It makes so much sense…" He turned and walked back to the lab. "Now."

Muna studied the information on the screen as she grabbed the bag of hot rinds. She pulled the bag open as she leaned back into the chair.

The first bite was always the best. Enough heat to take her breath away and leave a tear squeaking out of her one eye. The letters of the name blurred. She didn't move. She sat and thought. "What if... the letters in the name are close, but wrong?"

One of the old school trains of thought, but still taught, was aliases seemed to keep the same initials. Sometimes the same sounding name, but spelled differently. Or the same meaning, but from an unfamiliar language. The last name in England is Wright, but Whyte in Ireland, or Smyth in Scotland, which can come back to England as Smith.

She swiveled back to her FBI computer and started running other search programs. As she set up the search bots, she reduced their window, titled it, and stuck it to one side and started the next.

She hummed to herself. "A busy girl is a happy girl."

———————

THE MAN BARKED A COMMAND IN RUSSIAN TO THE MEN in the driveway as his personal bodyguard opened his front door. They walked through.

Romanov stopped as he suddenly saw a black woman in a white shirt and black dress coming toward him. She wasn't wearing a maid's outfit, and he didn't recognize her. He frowned and began to ask his bodyguard who she was.

"Confused, Sergei?"

He flared. "Who the hell are you and what are you doing in my home?"

Detective Hornblower smiled. "Ah, admission of ownership. Good, good. So, this is your home, and you own everything in it?"

His face was turning a reddish purple. "Of course." He turned to his man.

The bronze sword's tip rested at the man's carotid artery on his neck. Nash was just removing the Glock from the man's holster.

Nash smiled. "I believe you also have a pistol in the back of your pants." She pointed the Glock at Romanov. "Hands on top of your head while the good detective relieves you of the heavy load, please."

Romanov took a heavy breath.

Nash snorted and shook her head. "Your men outside were dead or face down the second the door closed. So, you can call them anything you want, but they're not coming to your rescue anymore. Now I asked you nice before... It would be a shame to get your man's blood all over this nice marble. By the time it's no longer a crime scene, the stain would be permanent and make the house unsellable." She twitched her chin upward, twice.

Slowly, the man complied as his eyes narrowed. "You won't get away with this. Do you know who I am?"

Detective Hornblower gently pulled the gun from his belt holster. "Of course we do, Sergei. We know everything there is to know about you. Right down to your little dungeon in the basement and the bodies buried in the backyard. The big question is, will we find your semen samples in them? And if so, were they delivered while the women were alive or after you had tortured them to death? Or was it in the throes of them dying when you got your jollies off? So many questions. So much money and gold to count."

She pulled out her handcuffs and ratcheted them onto his right wrist. Jerking it down, she shoved the extra gun in her waistband. She guided the left hand down roughly and ratcheted the other cuff on. "Sergei Romanov, you are under arrest for murder, torture, money laundering, having corporeal sexual intercourse with under-aged persons and necrophilia."

Nash tested the zip tie she had on the bodyguard. "Here, how about you sit down right over here?" She pushed him to sit on the floor next to a large marble-topped cabinet. The longer legs were perfect. She zip-tied his one wrist to the leg of the cabinet.

"Now be an obedient dog and stay." She turned. "Powder, make sure he doesn't move."

Nash rose. "Right now, Romanov, you are being neutered on five continents by my Interpol associates. Now, as you aren't a citizen of Barbados, you are currently a man without a country. So, we can send you anywhere we need. And there are many prisons suiting our needs, which you truly don't want to be in."

"You don't have anything to charge me with."

Detective Hornblower snorted. "Okay, but we will start with the five bodies in the flowerbeds. And we'll see where we go from there. As for the torture chamber downstairs, well, we haven't even begun to tear it apart." She pointed at the bronze sword. "But we have some good ideas about what we might find."

THE FOOD ON THE LARGE GRANITE ISLAND WAS remainders of what Detective Hornblower said was just rewards for her crew. Before she sent them back to digging. Someone had recently stocked the larder for the return of Romanov.

"Are you going to track down the staff and find out who cleaned the rooms downstairs?"

The detective nodded. "High on my list. How did you know the bodyguard would talk?"

"I didn't. But when you were describing the bodies of the women, he wasn't exactly stoic. We might even say he was a little green around the gills. I don't think he was allowed in for the tortures, just the carrying out of the trash. Those guys aren't always as loyal as their employer thinks they are."

"Experience?"

Mina blinked slowly. "On four continents."

Hornblower looked at the quiet Asian. "And you were?"

Mina smirked on one side of her face as she shook her head once. "Nowhere in the picture. I was still chasing undergrads at Georgetown."

Nash snorted and rocked. "That sounded as nasty as I could

think it." She turned to the detective. "She was the teacher's assistant from hell. In classes of four hundred or more, it's the TA's job to make the students study and turn in their work. Mina's babies all passed with top grades. The rest of the class... well, someone needs to make up the bloated belly of the bell curve."

"So you didn't go to college?"

It was Mina's turn to laugh. "Nash is what we call an over achiever. She piled all her bachelor's into two years."

The detective frowned at Nash. "How?"

"When I went down to Sacramento State at the end of my high school senior year, I learned that the week after I graduated, there were summer classes. The dorms were half price because the food sucked. So, I got a hot plate and cooked every class I could grab. They had transitioned to computers by then and so I dropped a class and added the two I needed. By the time fall came around, they knew me for making ramen noodles taste decent, and I was carrying thirty-three units."

"What's the usual?"

Mina harrumphed. "Twelve. Or sixteen if you're a brain. But at a state college where daddy's paying for you to go play? Six to nine."

Nash nodded. "You chose your classes wisely. No labs unless you must. The smaller the classes, the better. Get access to the genuine professors or teachers. TA's are assholes and the bane of an undergrad's existence." She held her hand out to Mina.

Mina bent over and kissed the fingertips.

Nash continued. "I had signed up for ROTC because I wanted the physical training. It wasn't until the end of the first quarter, I learned they would pick up my student debt if I ended up serving." She shrugged with a smile. "So, I ended up staying in shape and had a couple of serious study partners. I even got some guidance; I wouldn't have gotten any other way."

"Such as?"

"One professor who taught police science was former CIA. He suggested a few classes that helped me down the road. There was also an intensive living quarter he got me into. They only spoke Arab languages. Farsi and Urdu. Everyone there had their eye set on military intelligence, state department, or CIA. But more importantly, everyone there was looking to graduate in three years or less. I just upped everyone's game, and could cook ramen."

Detective Hornblower looked up at the man standing in the doorway. She nodded her head up. "Thanks Frank. I'll be down in five."

He turned and left.

She looked at Nash. "You sure you don't want to come watch?"

"Nope. Us three girls are going to go lay by the pool at Crane Beach for the next few days. When you're ready to talk to your uncle, come get us."

Hornblower stood with her hands on the island. "Well, today was more than I could have ever expected. So, if I need to get the president himself to come talk to my uncle…" She smiled around furled lips. "We'll get the sergeant to drive you back. And thank you again. It has been educational watching you and Powder work."

At the sound of her name, the dog rolled over, groaning.

26

A RAY OF SUNSHINE

POWDER ROLLED over on the chase lounge.

Mina lowered her sunglasses. "You know, Jacob, she's going to milk your kindness for as long as you'll sit there and massage her."

The man smiled as he chuckled. "Are you angry I'm spoiling my niece?"

Nash snorted as she sat up. "No. She's jealous she's not getting the massage."

The man fished his phone out of his pocket. "Oh, well, if that's all it takes. Let me see who can come out and give a massage or two this afternoon."

Nash looked at the childlike grin on the man's face. "She means a real massage. Not someone named Trixie or Yvette."

He held up his phone. "I have a Brunhilda. Or, no… I know… how about the twins? A and Bee. They do amazing things with their…" He snuck a peek at Mina. "You don't like Thai massage. They get all the knots out with the bamboo sticks, and then walk on your spine…"

Mina growled. "Are any of these people licensed massage therapists? Really trained in the therapeutic healing arts?"

He tossed his head back and forth. "My sister."

"How trained?"

"She's a physical therapist at the hospital."

Mina rolled over and pretended the shade of the enormous umbrella was sunshine. "No. Just a normal, wonderful massage. No kink. No doctors. Just massage."

He looked at his phone. All three of them recognized the ping of a text. "She wants to know if you mean Shiatzu or Swedish massage."

Mina rolled her head over and looked at the man. "If you're teasing me, I will pack us in twenty minutes, and I will write the worst review since I destroyed the George Trois in Paris."

He frowned. "There is no George Trois in Paris. It is the George Cinque."

She snorted a laugh. "Oh, sure. Now."

He put away his phone. "She's off in an hour. And she's bringing a friend." He held up his hands. "I don't know what she means."

DETECTIVE HORNBLOWER WALKED OUT ONTO THE private veranda. The massage tables were side by side. "Now I'm jealous. I've been slaving through mountains of paperwork. I didn't know massages on the veranda were in the offering."

Nash didn't move. "Detective Hornblower, this is Jade and Judith."

The detective nodded at the one. "Nice to finally meet you, Judith. I've heard good things around the department. And especially from Jimmy."

"How's his leg? Is he still walking every lunch?"

"I understand he walks to and from work on top of the kilometer at lunch. He even has a few joining him for the lunch walk."

Judith leaned her elbow into Nash's shoulder. "It's the only way he's going to keep that knee and get to retirement."

Nash moaned a little. "What can we do for you, detective?"

"My uncle wants to know if you have names or account numbers?"

Nash rolled over and drew the sheet across her chest. "He's going to cooperate with us?"

"He doesn't want to hear from the president. His wife was a strong, outspoken supporter of his opponent. Our island is small. We have a small intimate population. In any dozen people, three are cousins and one is in politics."

Nash smiled. "I have some information, but it's a few days old. When will he talk?"

"Over dinner tonight, at his house."

Nash nodded. "I'll get better intel. We just need an address."

"He'll send a car. I hope at least one of you likes wine. He owns a vineyard."

Mina shook her hand over her head. "I'll take the lead. What kind of wine?"

"Some Moscato, but his pride is his Pinot Grigio. And if he really likes you, he started experimenting with iced wine. His Pinot Grigio is close to a Riesling, but the icing takes it further into the fruit with a lot of apple." She looked at Nash for approval.

Nash pointed at the still waving hand. "I'm more the scotch drinker."

The detective snorted. "He's probably got a barrel or two lying around in the cave. Right past the rum."

THEY STROLLED DEEPER INTO THE CAVE. THE WINE barrels lay in racks stacked three layers deep. The cool of the underground was worth as much as the wine about them. He used most of what he got from his hundred acres in vines. His partners' microvineyards around the island provided the rest. One partner was joining them for dinner, but was most known for the food in his restaurant. So, he was busy at the open pit roasting the goat and lamb. As the man explained it, his vineyard was only a few acres around his house, so he made up in quantity with the quality of his cooking.

Mina and Nash had smelled the fresh herbs and hand-ground spices and were seeking refuge from drooling in the cave. Their usual order in food never smelled as seductive.

Mina kept her shoulder only a handsbreadth from the man's. She swirled her glass and sniffed the aroma. "How long do you keep the wine in the barrels, Peter?"

The man glowed in his cave. "Demand and lack of space have us down to mere months. We will turn out the barrels and bottle the wine after the crushing for the next season. Then the barrels are readied for the next season, and the year starts again. Pinot Grigio only ages to about two years at it's peak. One in the barrel and one in the bottles. This is when the restaurants on the islands want their supplies. Of course, making room for the next season's wine."

"And the Moscato?"

He shrugged. "We are playing with a Moscato that is somewhere between a Blanc and an Azul. We do it all in the large chill tanks. It still has wonderful fruit notes, but is dryer than the usual sweet wine. So, we bottle and sell to the cruise lines under their private labels."

They passed through a live stone wall into another cavern. He spread his arms wide. "And here is the finest of all. Rum on the left and scotch in the smaller barrels." He turned to Nash. "How refined is your taste?"

Nash shook her head. "I don't understand the question."

The man smiled. "How old do you prefer your scotch? Twelve, eighteen, twenty-five, fifty, two hundred and fifty?"

She snorted. "Oh, always the over two-hundred-year-old category."

The man smiled and crooked his finger. The five wandered down a narrow aisle bound by racked barrels with dates written on them.

"Tell me. Does your dog like scotch also?"

Mina huffed with a slight laugh. "She's not old enough?"

They stepped out into a small area around a center island bar. "This…" He turned with his hands out. "Is the inner sanctum. Many of these barrels were gifts from friends and enemies alike. But all are older than any of us. And a few are older than all of us combined."

Mina looked at two of the smaller barrels. A white, crusty substance coated both. "What is wrong with these barrels?"

He smiled. "What you think is wrong with these barrels is right with them. Both distilled over two-hundred-years ago and never tapped. Nor will they ever be."

"But the white crust…?"

"Is pure scotch. With the alcohol removed." He turned. "Nash?" He showed his two fingers and placed them in his mouth. Pulling them out, he petted the crust on the barrel and then put them back in his mouth. His eyes fluttered shut as he hummed.

Mina opened one eye wide as she studied her wife.

Nash snorted softly. She knelt and conferred with Powder. "Two barrels. Which one should I taste?"

Powder rose on her hind legs to sniff both barrels. She sat at the one the man had not touched.

Nash studied the barrels. There were no marks on the ends to give her any clues. She studied the crusts. As she looked, the crust back where it would be hard for a hand to reach between them, the barrel on the right had more crust. She licked her two fingers and then reached deep along the two barrels. She spread her fingers and dragged her hand along the bellies of both barrels.

She sucked on her index finger. The full body of a good scotch swelled in her mouth. She smiled at Peter. And then she stuck her middle finger in her mouth. The notes were subtle, but a slightly fuller body. Still sucking, she looked at Powder and knelt. The playing with the head and ears turned into a hug.

The man's head tipped as she stood. "Well?"

"The barrel on the right is older and a better scotch."

Peter glanced down at Powder. "And the dog knew this?"

"No. I only asked her which was better. But I also cheated by sampling both."

He pointed at the one he had petted. "This has more peat as they distilled it at the end of the glen near the sea. They distilled the other at the top of the glen and has less peat. Peat is a matter of taste, but you're right about the age. This one they brought to the Caribbean already a couple of centuries old. But we know it dates to the late seventeenth century. Where this one is from the early nineteenth century. Your dog has good taste."

Mina and Nash smirked. "And a better nose."

Detective Hornblower smiled at her uncle being beaten at his own game by a dog. "And you have another vote for her nose over here. I've seen it work when it counts."

The man playfully opened his eyes and face. "More than choosing a good scotch?"

She nodded. "Life and death. And we'll leave it there." She glanced at her watch.

He nodded. "Yes. Dinner should be close to ready." He turned to Nash. "As you liked the upper glen, let me tap you a glass of this one's much younger heir." He led them to one of the other barrels. "Same distillery, but about twelve generations later. But at thirty-five, still a good year."

As he turned the wooden spigot, he let the golden liquid slowly wander down into the snifter. "The aroma will be strong, so let it air and when we are at the table, it will be perfect."

As they walked out, Nash let Mina take her place at his shoulder. She and the detective brought up the rear with Powder. Nash sniffed at the glass. Her eyes danced as her mouth curled and jerked.

The detective chuckled. "As duplicitous as he is in his dealings, when it comes to his scotch, you can trust him."

Nash held the glass over for the woman to smell.

With one eye closed and her mouth cringed, she shook her

head. "It still smells like licorice dipped in paint thinner. But then, I'm more of a rum and chocolate kind of girl." She pantomimed with her hands in her explanation. "When I was a girl, there were little chocolate bottles, and they had maybe a few drops of liquor in them. They printed the wrappers with the liquor. It was my first taste of rum. But also, Peter has a dark rum with a lot of chocolate in with the caramelized cane sugar. He knows I won't drink and drive, so he'll send me home with a small bottle."

27

MORE NUMBERS

THE MAN'S office was decorated sparsely with a few photos, a couple of awards, and a restrained accenting of hand objects collected from travels. A bronze of the Eiffel Tower was the only paperweight on the desk. The shining rub marks suggested he commonly used it as a fetish for thinking and had much sentimental value.

The painting of a younger version of his wife dominated the wall across from the desk. Why have a small photo on your desk when you could have a large painting on the wall?

Mina pointed at the painting. "I should get one of these done and hang it in your office, Nash?"

Nash smirked. "Screwed to the ceiling over my laptop on the kitchen island? I don't think Chester would approve the Feng Shui."

Peter pinched the screen of Nash's phone. Larger. "Are you sure about these numbers?"

Nash stepped behind him and looked at the screen. "The numbers are from the early nineteen nineties when the money left the Caymans. Have they changed since then?"

He looked over his shoulder at her. "Our entire government has changed since then." He looked back at the screens. "I have a Jefferson Dumont with D&D Consulting. But there was a change in the mid-nineties. They restructured the estate to pay a dividend to an account in Switzerland. Later, a restructuring split the Swiss account into two accounts."

Nash narrowed her eyes as she tried to follow the scrolls of names and numbers. She couldn't see where he was getting the information. She thought about tracking footprints in sand and rocky terrain. The man sitting in front of her would have felt as lost as she felt now. It was about what environment you were used to. "Is there a name attached?"

Peter glanced back over his shoulder. "Switzerland is all numbered accounts. But I can reach out…"

Nash nodded.

The man pulled up his email account. He typed in the bank routing number and a name and bank email address automatically filled. The rest were formal greetings, inquiring as a professional courtesy, and with a personal salutation. He closed the email and returned to the screens of his bank as if what he just did was as easy as breathing.

Nash stared up at Mina. It was the same political chess she played in Washington, D.C.

She blinked slowly and gazed down at the computer screen. "You said the account for D&D Consulting was in your bank. Do you have the name for the second D?"

"Hold on. I'll need the signature card." He populated a small screen and input the information. The card appeared. He expanded the window to fill the monitor.

Nash read the names and then stood, rocking back on her heels. She locked eyes with Mina. "Nate Dubois."

Mina skeptically turned her head to the side. "Nature Dubois? Maggie's son?"

Peter glanced up with a furled forehead. "Is he the person you were looking for?"

Mina growled. "Yes, and no. Can you find his last banking movement?"

The man switched to another set of screens. This one made more sense to Nash. The columns were balances in the account, withdrawals or transfers, date, and remaining balances.

She pointed at the screen. "Wait, what year are we looking at here?"

He glanced back with a frown. "I went back to ninety-seven when the transfer to Switzerland started. Why?" His finger was on one transaction line.

"Which money is this showing in?"

He turned and seriously looked at her. "How much scotch did you have?" The smile crept into the side of his mouth.

"That's why I'm asking."

He glanced at Mina. "The lamb and goat were Barbadian. The vegetables are from my garden of fine Barbadian soil. Barbadian hands built the house you are standing in. We are looking at money in the bank of Barbados..."

Mina caught the meaning of Nash's query. "What's the exchange rate?"

Peter turned. "Two to your one. It's been as stable as your money."

Mina pushed her chin at her wife. "What are we looking at?"

Nash gently shook her head. "It's not twenty-seven and a half."

"But that was only a sixth share. So, we started with one sixty-five. And then there is compounding interest and time..."

Nash waved at the screen. "So, in ninety-eight, we're at four forty and change. So essentially two twenty in our dollars. What kind of interest rate does that?"

Peter leaned back and swung in his chair. His fingers steepled, and he had the look of a loan shark looking at an innocent old lady with a bag of money. "It is one reason people from around the world deposit sizable sums of money in the Caymans and about the Caribbean." He shrugged his face. "Even I have some money on deposit there. But you must understand, this is not the same interest you receive in your banks. That is only a small payment for lending the bank a small sum of money to invest with. You deposit, say, a hundred thousand. And someone borrows money to buy a house. They pay six percent interest, and the bank thanks you with a fifth."

Mina snorted. "Not anymore. Try a twentieth."

Peter held out one hand. "So, the bank makes more profit. But think what can be done with a million times of the hundred thousand? With this much money, we grant governments short construction loans with twenty-five percent interest."

Nash's face darkened in horror. "I think that's called usury. In less than four years, they would owe double what they borrowed."

The man bobbed his head slowly. "Yes. Which is why a long-term loan might run for maybe a month or three. Just long enough for the bonds issued to pay off the loan. But even then, I will have garnered at least ten percent. And even on a small hundred-million-dollar loan, the bank has ten million dollars of liquid asset to loan again. So, for you, I would reward you with, say, five percent on your hundred-million-dollars. Or five million dollars in that quarter alone. And then we have overnight loans that pay a flat five or ten percent. Those never run over twenty hours. They cover charges or checks while revenue clears."

Nash looked at Mina with an evil smile. "Do we have a hundred-million-dollars we can loan this man?"

Mina snorted. "Great minds." She looked at Peter. "How legal is our establishing an account down here?"

He held up his hands. "This is where you split the hairs of legal and ethics. Your country doesn't let you leave with over ten thousand cash. Which is a very nice vacation, but barely a pleasant start on an account I can do anything with. So, usually a bank says no. But it's also because most sizable sums of money are for tax dodging."

Mina narrowed one eye. "But it would produce income outside of the United States…"

"This would be a conversation you would seriously have with your tax solicitor."

She snorted softly at Nash. "He means Michael Crabtree, dear."

"He's a lawyer too?"

Mina smirked. "He was a lawyer for the IRS before he was our CPA. Where did you think I poached him from? A back alley?"

Nash leaned back against the heavy mahogany credenza. "So, all of this, at one point or another, is legal?"

Peter nodded in an extremely slow movement. "As far as the banking and transfers are concerned. Yes. They meet all the criteria for international banking. Yes."

"I hear a but in there."

His head rocked. "Taxes would be a United States or Swiss concern. But…" He swung back around. "The way I understand this characterization of the dividend, it is being paid tax free on investments."

"Those investments, being the money on deposit in your bank."

He leaned in as he scrolled through the column. "It would appear we are transferring a consistent two million Barbadian dollars to the two Swiss accounts every year. Or just under a million euros."

His scrolling stopped, and he made a notation on a notepad. "The splitting of the Swiss account was two thousand one. Many people took draws from their accounts after the attack on New York." He continued scrolling. Paused. Made another note and continued.

"Which brings us up to today." He swung around in the chair. "The last time Mr. Dubois moved any money was in two thousand nine. When he transferred a half million American to a bank in Arlington, Virginia. Which I believe is near your home." He looked at Mina. "Not what we would call a big spender."

Mina rocked as she thought. "But also, not Claudius Dubois either."

Nash looked at her wife. "So, who the heck is this Nate, and how does he fit in?"

Detective Hornblower cleared her throat. "And who is in Switzerland?" She looked at her uncle. "When might we expect something back from your friends in Switzerland?"

Peter reached over to his mouse and moved it to the time and date block. Upon clicking on it, a completely new bar appeared, stretching across the screen. It held the date and time of every major banking city in the world. "It's only three o'clock their time. So, I'll expect something when I wake up at seven. Maybe eight if they needed their coffee first." He glanced back at Nash. "If I have something…"

Nash looked at the pencil lines of her wife's eyes. "The princess decrees not before ten."

He nodded with a knowing pursed mouth. "I'll call you from the office."

Mina scratched Powder's ear. "I know. Your mommy needs to take you for a walk."

"OKAY, BUT IT ONLY EXPLAINS NATURE RUSTIC disappearing. But I still can't find a Nate Dubois."

Nash shook her head. "I don't know Muna. I was watching numbers looking more like the gross domestic product of small nations. But they're connected to individuals. Somewhere, there is a connection between them. Peter will call in the morning, and hopefully he has some better names for us to track down. But for now, this is all I have for you to work on. And before I forget, thank you for everything. And I mean everything. Romanov, Dubois, Mister Natural, everything."

Muna waved her hand across the screen. The connection made

the movement jerky. "It helps keep me busy." She leaned in. "I can see why this lab was only a two-person lab before. I've even been doing some remote work. Even for D.C. Which is fine with me. Just so the deputy director doesn't recall me. I'll push a broom out here before I want to go near D.C. again. Besides, Mike says having me upstairs in the dorm is an asset. So even the rent is right."

Nash laughed. "So, more breakfasts dressed in your Hello Kitty pajamas?"

Muna turned her face as she batted her eyelashes and drew out the word dramatically. "May... be..."

Nash looked across the pool at the man walking toward her. "Whatever happened to the waiter?"

Her face lit up. "Ali? The owner's son. Um... He's fine. We had lunch on Sunday. I met him over in Sausalito. He was there for a friend's art show at a gallery."

Nash gave her the best mommy's concerned or big sister spill the beans look she could muster. "And...?"

Muna shrugged her face. "It was nice. The art... not so much. But I liked the view along the bay. And Ali is nice. But I don't think there's anything serious there. At least not for me."

Nash gave her a wink. "Keep it there. Gotta go." She clicked on the delete and closed the laptop.

Nash looked up at the man in the usual white shirt and black slacks. "Yes?"

The man handed her a cell phone. "I think you left this in the restaurant this morning, miss."

Nash froze. She didn't recognize the man, and he left by the driveway. As a black car with tinted windows drove off, the phone rang.

She answered the phone but said nothing.

She recognized the voice. "I just thought I would let you know. I'm at the airport. My plane is leaving. I'm leaving. You think you've won, but I know who you are. You will hear from me again and again as I make your life hell." The metallic click was sharp in her ear.

People had threatened her before. "Not on this watch, Satan." She tossed the phone out into the pool.

She was dialing Hornblower on her phone as the black piece of metal and plastic sank to the bottom of the pool.

The detective answered her personal phone. "There was nothing we could do. We couldn't stop him. Wherever he's headed, he obviously doesn't need a passport."

Nash hung her head, looking at her knees through the mottled glass tabletop. "And he obviously had a lot of money stashed elsewhere where we couldn't find it." She sat back. "It was a good try. And at least you have one less monster on your island, and can clear some cases."

"I spoke to the commander this morning. We're flying in a ground X-ray machine today. I'm going to drive the bugger over every inch of his bloody land personally."

Nash drew in a long breath through her nose. "Document everything meticulously, Mary."

"We will. And thanks. I hope my uncle helped with yours."

"We're still working on it."

WHERE?

"IF YOU THREW A DART, blindfolded, at a spinning map of the United States, you might hit it."

Oz and Mike leaned in. "Is there anything in the town?"

Muna smiled as she slid another pork rind into her mouth. "In ninety-seven, there was a courthouse, and more importantly, the Dubois Bugle. And from what I can see, there were seven times more advertisements than there were articles of any news. Which includes the single birth announcement, two divorce announcements, one wedding announcement, and a reported death." She pointed at the obituary with a photo of the cat. "And a single name change."

Oz twitched his head. "When you're required by law to post a name change for six weeks, what better place than somewhere nobody looks or cares?"

Mike snorted. "Dubois Bugle in Dubois, Montana. No sense of irony there."

Muna started shooing the boys away. "Back to work now. Go earn your keep. The pizza doesn't get here for another hour. And I get first slice."

Muna spun back to her weapons of choice. To lighten the mood, she had imposed or decreed, depending on the view, Pizza Wednesday and first slice to the winner of coolness. By the second week, the new tie-dye shirt had become a non-starter, as had the Day of the Dead skulls on Oz's black scrubs. For two weeks, they had picked up their first slices together.

The Jefferson Dumont bots were still chasing leads down blind alleys in Texas, Oklahoma, and all points south. A small search robot she had running on the dark web was searching bank records in the rest of the Caribbean and Switzerland. She didn't hold out much hope in Switzerland. She also had a bot in the FBI computer searching through Interpol for any Dubois between the ages of forty and seventy. She had siphoned off several thousand before she locked out France and the Alps.

"Just for crazy..." She worked up another bot to do the same search, but for females with the sir name or maiden name of Dubois or Dumont. She held her finger over the *enter* key. She smiled and pressed. "Fly little robot butterfly, search for mommy Muna."

NASH GLANCED AT HER WATCH. THE PHONE CALL HAD never come. Instead, Mina and Nash watched the banker in his white pressed linen suit walk around the pool. He carried a thin briefcase in his left hand. His smile was warm but publican. Mina would have called it an inner beltway face. Never to offend, but not as cordial as it alluded to.

Nash closed her laptop as Mina moved from the chase lounge under the canopy to the table with the oversized umbrella. Powder followed. Nash reached across with her foot and pushed a chair out. Peter pulled it more and sat.

"I'm going to assume Mary called you already."

Nash pointed at the black blur at the bottom of the pool. "He had the nerve to messenger me the phone so he could gloat as he took off. The threat was more of the usual—goes with the job. And the bank?"

"Mm, cheeky bastard. But last night I couldn't sleep. Something nagged at the back of my mind and then I remembered why you were originally here." He dipped his head as he smiled. "So, I got up and went back to my office. I looked up all his accounts, and reverted them to English codes. He tried to run the bank at three this morning. Or I should say, someone was trying to clean us out at three this morning. I'm not sure, but I'm going to assume they will try again. But someone with the authority to do so would have to convert the numbers back to the Barbadian system."

Nash smiled at the man's sleight of hand. "I got a note from one of my team members. She was able to lock down or have confiscated over two-billion-dollars in seven countries. Interpol is celebrating an auspicious day today."

"And they will reward her... how?"

Nash held up her hand. "It's her job. We don't fight crime on commission. Besides, I already ordered a couple of cases of her favorite snack food. It's being delivered this afternoon."

His forehead furled. "Snack food? This is a reward?"

Mina snorted softly. "It's fried pigskins dipped in the hottest pepper you can think of."

"They have a Jamaican jerk spice called house on fire..."

Nash flattened her smile into the buzzing duck lips as she shook her head. "Children's stuff. This is more like powdered napalm. You only taste it once."

"And she snacks on this?"

Mina shrugged her face. "She's young and Muslim." As if it would explain everything.

Nash added to the confusion. "And she recently took off her hijab in solidarity with her sisters in Iran."

His face lit up, and he nodded in understanding. "The world is changing. The old guard needs to step down or lose. But pigskin..."

Nash tipped her head to one side—stretching her neck. "Isn't halal, but it is a conundrum." She nodded her chin at the briefcase. "But to more serious business…"

"I printed this out and brought it to you. Also, a few small bottles are being taken to your room. The unlabeled one I decanted this morning. Be gentle with it and remember, it needs to breathe." He drew out the papers and handed them to Nash.

The email was on top. Nash scanned the body and looked up. "You got this with the five second email you jotted off last night?"

He pushed his lower lip out as he rested his head on his shoulder. "The world comes to vacation in Barbados. As I told you last night, much of the scotch in my collection were gifts. There is a certain brinkmanship, which only comes from giving a better grade of barrel when the value is in the age or distillery and cost is not a concern."

Nash held up the email and glanced at the supporting pages. "But this… I would only expect after many days and phone calls with Interpol and maybe a court order."

He pursed his mouth. "Be we are talking about Switzerland here. A country which is accustomed to bribing with small gifts of chocolate. Which, I might add, comes from this part of the world."

Nash kept scanning through the pages. "Well… If I ever need something from a bank, I'll stop wasting my time with Interpol and just call you."

He reached over and patted her hand. "Give the kids a chance first. They get testy when they're shown up at their own game. But you have Mary's number."

Mina leaned in. "But I would still like your card. I have an appointment to talk to our tax lawyer."

He fished a card from his shirt pocket. "I thought you might. It would be a pleasure to help you. And, of course, you will need to visit your investment occasionally. And I will make sure Jacob keeps sufficiently stocked with your private reserve." The man stood. "Sadly, I must go straighten a few things out at the bank. Evidently, there were some accounting errors found this morning. A sizable sum of money seems to have been misplaced." He shook hands and left.

Mina watched the retreating man. "How do you think he keeps the suit from wrinkling?"

Nash looked up with a side-eye from reading the report. "It will just have to be your assignment for next time."

Mina stood and kissed her wife on the top of the head. "I'll leave you to work."

Nash smiled. "Enjoy your book."

Nash opened her laptop as she plugged in her earbuds and microphone.

The screen lit up with a view, looking toward the lab. The computer office was still dark. Nash glanced at her watch. Mina snorted a small laugh. "It's only seven o'clock in San Francisco. Muna is still punching holes in paper downstairs."

"Damn." Nash looked under the table. "Let's go for a run on the beach."

Powder rolled over. Thought about it and slowly stood up. Nash rolled her eyes. "Okay, we'll start with a walk and see where it goes from there."

MIKE PLACED THE SANDWICH ON THE DESK. "HOW DOES the dark underbelly of the world look?"

Muna didn't even flinch. "Do we need an MRAP and a mobile SCUD missile launcher? I found them cheap in Lebanon. The guy will even throw in a couple of crates of lightly used Russian AK-47s and a kilo or five of raw opium." She spun her chair around with wide eyes. "I think he was kidding about the opium, but there were pictures of the rest." She spied the sandwich and leered.

Mike waved his hand at the ravenous geek. He knew she did a lot of physical exercise before he had finished his first cup of coffee, but he still marveled at her calorie count and ability to maintain her pixie-like body.

"Anything further on the name tracking?"

"Effimae." She slapped her hand over her mouth and finished chewing. "Stephanie Anne Dumont. Her mother Bethanne passed away in 2012. I think there's something there, but I'm not sure it's discoverable through the internet. All I know is when Stephanie was three, Jefferson filed for divorce from Bethanne on the grounds of infidelity. Who she slept with wouldn't be named in the divorce papers, but if it went before a court…"

Mike rested his fist on the desk to stretch his right side. "Where was it filed?"

She looked back at the file in the window on her screen. "Um… Fort Worth, Texas. Eighty-six." She took a bite of the sandwich and looked back with a question on her face.

Mike's head shook. "Texas. Where the cattle roam and the women have fewer rights. It never even saw the courthouse steps. When a man in Texas says the wife cheated on him. The court clutches at their nether regions and pulls out their can of Hoppe's oil to clean their divorcing irons."

Muna looked up from biting her sandwich with her one eye. "Clutches their nether regions?"

Mike assumed an exaggerated southern accent. "Certainly, my dear. Where womenfolk have vapors and clutch their pearls, a man only has his… um… nether regions to grab."

Muna almost lost her mouthful of sandwich. She chewed and swallow with one eye closed. "So, all those rappers are actually clutching their pearls and having the vapors?"

Mike straightened, blinking. "I never thought of it like that. But a lot of them seem like they're getting a divorce by the language they use about their women."

Muna rolled her eyes. "Culture. And yes, I'm ashamed to be in not only the age group, but the color as well."

Mike swung his hand at the screen. "So, where is our mystery woman now?"

"That's it." Muna glanced back at the screen. "She's a mystery. I've got her in a private girl's school just outside Fort Worth. Lakeside School for Girls. But when I plug-in the address for today, it's now a children's strategic care hospital."

Mike closed his eyes and his head gently sewing machined through his memories and understandings of publicly used euphemism for delicate conditions and societies. "Call them. They may still have the records. We need to know what she was suffering from and if they ever released her."

"But it's not a school anymore."

"It never was. Well, in a way. They would have still provided some measure of education to meet the government standards. But it was always a hospital, or a delicately disguised sanitarium." He shifted his weight to the bionic leg.

"Back in the day of Oz..." He smirked as he waved his hand over his own graying head. "There were many types of schools for kids to be sent off to if the parents had money. If you were wealthy, the little woman was best to be seen at a local charity for the less fortunate than waiting in line to pick up the kids after school to schlep them to the soccer field or ballet classes. And if the child suffered any kind of medical deficiency, it was acceptable to send them to a school for those needs. Even if the need was an iron lung or wheelchair bound. This relieved the adults to work longer, hold gala events, and have affairs without having to deal with children or nannies."

Muna snorted. "Only just a wee bit misogynist, don't you think?"

He pursed his lips and dropped his head to the left. "After all, we are talking about Texas here." As he walked toward the lab, he finished. "Don't be surprised if it hasn't changed."

CHASING PAPER

"I SAW YOU CALLED EARLIER." Muna smiled as she swung in the swivel chair with the coffee mug clutched to her chest. "I was down punching paper. I didn't run today." She glanced at the rain-washed wall of windows.

Nash studied the way the young woman owned her space now. They had originally aligned the desks in the large office area for the light from the windows to fall on the workspace from the side. Muna had obviously moved the furniture to have her back to the lab. Nash could picture the view of the windows over and around the computer screens. If you didn't need natural light, and you're the only person using a large room...

"I scanned some documents and sent them." Nash felt the warm fur shift on her feet. "And your niece says hi."

Muna's face melted sweetly. "Aww. I miss the fur ball. And yes, I got the email about Switzerland and Stephanie Anne Dumont." She leaned forward and placed the mug out of the camera range.

Nash could tell she was looking at one of the other monitors and wondered how many monitors the junior agent was up to now. When Nash was last at the San Francisco office, she had noticed several window tabs open in a secondary tool bar on all three of the large monitors. Nash knew it would only be a matter of time before they would spawn children.

"I tracked down some shifty moves by our Nature Rustic Dubois as he transitioned to Nathan. He went up to Montana and, in all places, had it done in the tiny town of Dubois, Montana." Her eyes shifted, and she ended up looking at another monitor. "But before or during or whichever, he still had the documents to change the accounts. What has me confused is: why didn't he register the name change on the accounts in Barbados and Switzerland?"

"Look at what he did with the account." Nash pointed randomly at the screen and circled her finger in the air.

Muna shrugged. "That's the point. Almost nothing. He set up a quarterly draw to be sent to Switzerland and then nothing."

Nash shook her head. "No. There is a small draw going to the bank in Arlington. Judging by the time and where, I'd say he bought a house or condo. But yeah, other than that, there's only the money going to Switzerland. But even there, it got split into two accounts?"

"The one is in Stephanie's name, but the other is only a number."

Nash picked up the hard copy and looked at the last page. "The interesting part is, he didn't set up the second account. It started as a payment account from the Stephanie account, but the Stephanie account has basically become a flow-through account of the trust. This other dumps into a numbered account and disappears."

Muna nodded. "Nothing seems to happen in the Stephanie account, except this monthly charge for twenty-four thousand francs."

"Which is...?"

Muna held up her index finger. "I had to look it up. I would have thought they were on the Euro, but they aren't even part of the EU. But they are on a new franc system, and they tied it to the US dollar. So, parody with us. Twenty-four thousand dollars. Every month. Mike and Oz think she's in a sanatorium."

"Let's find the hospital and find out what condition she's in. If she was wasting away thirty years ago, what level of health is she in now? But for now, I need to be in Washington." Nash closed the connection.

Mina looked up from her book and removed her earbuds. "What's up?"

Nash stood. "We know who Nathan Donner is. And he's been a very bad boy."

Mina blinked as she slid her feet into her sandals. "Well, it was a nice vacation while it lasted."

"And you have some tasty wine waiting when you get home." Nash picked up the laptop and papers.

Mina bent over and scratched behind the ears. "Come on Powder, let's go earn some money."

———

"WHERE'S NATHAN?"

The congressman frowned. "He left yesterday. Said he needed some personal time."

"Where?"

Then man cowered in his chair as Mina leaned in. "I don't know. I didn't ask. I didn't think he ever took time off. I just assumed when we went on break… I just never asked."

Nash perched her one leg on the closest corner of his desk. The black leather pants weren't FBI uniform, but they gave the right impression. "Who would know? Who would make his travel arrangements?"

"He usually made mine… but I would assume there is some travel arrangements person for congressional sorties or such."

Mina perched on the other corner with matching leather. The man was highly aware of the dog's breath on his right hand. She picked up the phone. "Call another congress person's right hand."

He took the phone timidly and punched in some numbers. "Hi,

Celeste. Wit Wright here. Yes, thank you, but it's you I want to talk to."

Mina snapped her fingers and held out her hand. She took the offered phone. "Hi Celeste, Mina Lee here. Sorry to be in such a hurry, but we need to know who Nathan would have used to book travel arrangements with." She turned and wrote on the congressman's day planner. "Un, huh? Yes. Got it. Thank you and tell James I'll be by to see him soon. We need to discuss grazing rights on a super fund site he was supposed to clean up a decade ago. Yes, that one." She pushed the button for the next unused line and punched in the phone number.

She smirked at Nash. "Hi, Mina Lee, calling from Congressman Wright's office. Is Jackie in, please?" She rolled her eyes at the hold music. "Hi Jackie. Mina Lee, calling... Oh good, then you're up to speed. A few days ago, you made travel arrangements for Nathan, and we need to get a hold of him."

She turned and wrote the rest in the day planner. "Great, and the hotel?" She wrote more. "No, I don't think he remembered to get the Euro plan. It just goes to voice mail, and that isn't like him." She tossed her head back and forth as she listened to the other woman. "Right. Okay, well thank you. We'll reach out from here." She hung up and looked at Nash. "Does your connection go international to Geneva or just Barbados?"

Nash pulled out her phone and started texting. "We'll see."

They looked at Wit.

His voice was nine levels smaller than the blustering congressman. "Care to bring me up to speed?"

Mina looked for Nash's okay. Nash drew in a long, paced breath as she thought about what to tell the man. Letting it out through her nose, her nod was less than a blink. She rolled off the desk and walked Powder around the spacious office. With all the moving pieces, nothing was making sense yet.

She listened to Mina try to make sense of everything enough to explain it to a person who wasn't exactly detail-oriented.

"Wait. My sister had a son?" His face was a mass of confusion. "When?"

Mina slowed her speech. "Do you remember a schoolmate of yours named Claudius Dubois?"

"Yes, well, he was one of the PAC who put me in office. I think he died... I think he was the last to die. He lived out in Dallas somewhere. He took over his father's drilling company or something."

Mina nodded. "Great. Well, your sister and he were having an affair while you two were still in school. And a bastard child to a fifteen-year-old girl and your seventeen-year-old son aren't the most flattering of notices to hit the society pages in a backward state. So, they broke out a shotgun and quietly had a wedding. When she showed, they moved her to a relative in El Paso. Eventually, to New Mexico, but by that time, the boy had become estranged, and she lost track of him."

The man frowned. "But then, he would be a Dubois..." He looked up. "Unless he changed his name..."

Nash looked over as her phone pinged. She rolled her eyes wide at her wife. "Are all the crayons in the box as broken as this one, or is it just this one?" She looked at her phone. "He wants to know when."

"We're packed. We have our passports. However, he can get us there."

Mina leaned forward and patted Wit on the cheek. "To be continued. Just pray we don't have to shoot your nephew. Or throw him in a Swiss prison. I hear those can be as bad as Iraq."

The three strode past the receptionist. Mina paused and placed her finger on the corner of the desk. "Your job is safe... for now..." She smiled her simply inner belter smile and turned for the door and her family.

In the hall, Nash showed her the reservations. "We can leave the car here and catch a cab, or pay for parking at Reagan?"

Mina gave her a glare. "Reagan. I need to drive."

Nash smiled like a schoolgirl as she followed her two most favorite people out of the halls of political hell.

————————

"WELCOME ABOARD."

The flight protocols and tickets were not what Nash was used to. She showed her tickets for her and Powder to the flight attendant. "I'm sorry, but I'm new to this."

The woman smiled as she glanced at the ticket. She held her hand out down the forward aisle. "We moved you three. We thought you would like a little more room." The woman stopped them at the first pod. "As you can see, it is a couple's pod, but I think there is plenty of room for your service dog. Can I ask what kind of dog?"

Mina stopped Nash with a hand on her arm. "She sniffs for bombs and spare candy. Occasionally she helps me find a superb wine."

Nash rolled her eyes as Mina slid into the pod. "She's an extremely educated nose." She nodded at Mina. "She is partially right. She's also good at finding the best scotch whiskey. But she's even better at finding... well... things."

The woman looked down. "Is she socialized or a do not touch?"

Nash snorted. "She doesn't do the wild frat parties anymore, but friends around a nice campfire occasionally are more her speed. Her name is Powder. And, yes, you can pet."

The woman kneeled. "Hello Powder, my name is Natalia. I'll be your servant on this flight." She put her hand out and Powder sniffed and then extended a paw.

She stood. "It's an eight-hour flight and I'm the best cook on board. What would she like to eat?"

Nash stalled. Mina rolled her eyes and hung on her wife's shoulders. "She allergic to salads, but any meat and some vegetables would be good. Rice in a small measure, but she doesn't hold her wine very well, so just pass her share on to her mother." She pointed at her chest. "This mother."

"And your preference would be?"

"White, a Riesling is nice, or whatever is in the box."

Natalia pointed at Nash. "And the scotch on the rocks or neat?"

"Neat."

The rest of first class and business class were filing in, so she smiled and went back to work.

As Nash turned, she watched the captain or one of the flight crew approaching.

He stopped. "Good evening. I'm Captain Hans Gruber. You are Agent Bear?"

She stuck her hand out. "Agent Nash Running Bear."

He smiled. "I'm glad to meet you. I just wanted to let you know your service weapon is on board and in my personal lock box. If your state department makes it here before we take off, they will have your Interpol ID, and then I can release it to you for the flight... If you want."

Nash smiled and shook her head. "Captain, for the next eight hours, us three girls are on vacation. The plane is in expert hands."

He peeked over the wall of the pod. "Ah yes, I heard we had a Very Special Agent on board as well." He held up his cell phone. "Is a photo..."

"Our pleasure. Powder, come take a photo with the good captain."

He kneeled beside Powder. "My son Bjorn is going to be thrilled. He wants a dog."

Mina laid her chin on the top of the wall and smiled. "How old is your son?"

The man stood and held his hands about two feet apart. "Just turned two months." The man beamed.

Mina laughed. "Just the right age for a first dog. Right Powder?"

30

SWISS NEUTRALITY

GETTING a cab from the airport wasn't as easy as it should have been. The first several taxis in the queue refused to take a dog. Even a service dog. Mina watched Nash become redder and redder around the ears. She put her calming hand on her wife's hand and took the leash. Kneeling, she unhooked Powder. "Go find the right driver."

Powder walked along the line of taxis. The drivers were stoic and leaned against their cars with their arms folded across their chests. Near the last of the queue, a young man kneeled and kissed his lips at Powder, with his hands held out. Soon, the man was petting and playing with the dog's ears.

He looked up at the two women and their bags. "Yours?"

Mina smiled and pointed at the taxi. "Yours?"

He stood and opened the back door. "Oui."

"How much for the whole day?"

He thought. "At three hundred I break even…"

Nash tipped her head toward her left shoulder. "We have several places to go. How about five hundred?"

Mina bent to stroke Powder's head. "And if lunch provides our daughter a good meal as well, we'll cover your fuel and food as well."

He stuck his hand out. "René. Welcome to Geneva."

Nash smiled. Her wife and daughter had found a friend when they needed one. As usual.

———

HE TURNED AROUND AND FACED THEM. "SERIOUSLY? This is… Well, this is where my grandfather would bank."

Nash twitched her head sideways. "This is where the account is. So, this is where we're going. So, find a place to park and maybe you can go get some coffee over there and relax. We'll be out as soon as we can get some answers."

He pointed at Powder. "The dog…?"

Mina gave him a motherly smile. "Did you notice the badge on her chest? She goes anywhere Nash does."

The young man held up both hands. "I'll be over here having a coffee."

Nash pursed her lips. "Good idea, René."

The armed guard at the door pointed at the Powder. Nash flashed her badge. He looked at her identification and the match to Powder's badge and opened the door.

They stood in the middle of the bank. Mina had told Nash the trick to weeding out who is in charge and who isn't, is to make them come to you. The woman was all business. Nash narrowed one eye as she thought about watching old movies. The assassin in *From Russia with Love* came to mind. She made a note to stay away from the woman's shoes.

"Good morning. My name is Frau Müller, how may I help you?"

Mina touched Nash's elbow, and she moved closer. "I'm sorry, but they led us to believe we were meeting with the president of the bank. But I don't remember the name being Müller…"

"And you are...?" She looked down her nose at the unleased dog.

Nash handed her the two badge cases and kept her voice at a level other's could hear in the hushed bank. "Special Agent Nash Running Bear, Federal Bureau of Investigation, and envoy to Interpol. This is my K-9 support, Powder. We are here about a couple of numbered accounts tied to terrorist activities. Is the president in?"

She flipped the cases closed and handed them back. "The manager is in a meeting right now, but I am the assistant manager." She turned with her hand out. "If you would care to join me in my office, I'm sure I can help you with what you need."

Nash didn't remember her coming from an office. Specifically, she remembered her coming from a desk to their right. "I thought your desk is the one over there next to the break room."

The woman flushed. "I sit many places."

Mina leaned in. "But not in an office. So, you are the stooge they sent out here to stall or get rid of us." She pulled out her phone. "If you have called your police, I'll need to call our contacts in the Interpol, and the American Ambassador." She punched a number, and the ringing number was loud enough for all to hear.

The woman held up her hands. "Please. There was a misunderstanding."

The phone on speakerphone, answered. "Mina, how are you? What can I do for you?"

"Chester, we are here at the bank in Geneva. Is my uncle the ambassador handy? We seem to have a situation here."

The voice was deep and filled with unbending steel. "Certainly, my dear. I'm sure we can pull the ambassador out of his meeting with the Vice-Chancellor for his favorite niece."

The woman folded. "Please. Whatever you need, I can help you."

Mina took the phone off speaker as the few patrons continued to try not to be obvious about watching the drama. "Maybe there was a bit of a misunderstanding. I'll call you back if we need you."

"Anytime. We are always at your disposal." She clicked the phone off. "You were saying?"

The woman's tone was more servitude. "Please. Follow me and we can sort this all out."

NASH HELD HER FINGER ON THE LONG NUMBER ON THE screen. She checked it against the number in the file on her phone. "Right. That's the number. We need to know who they attached this number to."

Frau Müller leaned in. "This is an eight-seven-seven account. Highly restricted access. Those people pay dearly for their anonymity."

Mina pulled out her phone. "Yes, international terrorist usually do…"

The woman blanched. "Excuse me. This…"

Mina dipped her head and waved her open palm at the door.

As the door closed. Mina winked at Nash. "Now we will meet the man behind the curtain."

The man who finally opened the door was anything but the small, roly-poly Wizard of Oz. The blond going gray was slender and well over six feet.

"I'm sorry it took so long. I'm Herr Müller, the bank manager."

Nash smirked as she waved her finger back and forth from the man to the door. "And Frau…?"

He closed his eyes and shook his head. "Nine. No relation. But she mentioned your state department, Interpol, and…" He shrugged. "So, I took the liberty of speaking with Mrs. Judith Crist, your ambassador to Switzerland, and close friend. Maybe earlier it was a small faux pas…?"

Mina danced her head around. "In our family, we call it a fur paw." She pointed at Powder.

His face lit up as he sensed the path around the difficult situation. "Ah yes. Special Agent Powder, is it?"

Nash fished out their credentials. He reached out and then smiled as he waved them off. "No need." He walked around the desk and then thought better of it. He returned and drew up another chair and sat. "I also called Peter Fletcher in Barbados."

Nash leaned her head in with a raised eyebrow. "It seems Barbados owes you an enormous debt of gratitude. As do we." He pulled out his phone. "It would appear we have an account which was moments from disappearing if it hadn't been for a message passed to us by Interpol from, I believe, your office in San Francisco."

Nash nodded. "Special Agent Muna al-Faragi. She has helped to spearhead a couple of international problems for us. One involving Romanov and the one we flew here to investigate personally."

The man adjusted his shirt cuff in his suit sleeve. "Yes. Sergei Romanov. Your Agent al-Faragi wasn't the first to approach us, but she was the first to give us alarm and guidance. But as to the other account..."

Nash held up two fingers. "Two accounts."

"Yes. One, you have a name attached to the account, and the other you are looking for the name."

"Correct. We have Stephanie Dumont, but not where she is. So, if you can help us in that matter as well...?"

He reached into his shirt pocket and handed her a slip of paper. "For her first few years here, she was at a hospital for long-term care."

Mina nodded. "A sanitarium. Yes. But we don't know why."

The man blinked. "I was a young man when the unusual account came to my attention. The manager at the time asked me to take it into my collection of personal accounts." He waved his palm out to Mina. "You see, at the time, I was a personal banker. I personally knew many of the large depositors through my parents and grandparents, so it was a natural position for me to assume. Similar to Mr. Fletcher's situation, in Barbados."

Nash frowned, confused. "What makes the account unusual?"

"You are familiar with how much money is in play?"

Nash rocked her head. "A little less than a million dollars a year."

He dipped his head once. "A million dollars today is not what it was twenty years ago, but it is a substantial sum and one to pay attention to. Especially because it is a flow-through sum, as opposed to a static account."

He looked at his phone. "Originally, the money transferred from a bank on Grand Cayman. Then in the later nineties, the account moved to Barbados and eventually the recipient account split into two accounts. The arrangement with the hospital never changed. The monthly payment has grown, but so had the account. Each year, the hospital is now up to a quarter of a million francs." He looked up. "About the same as your dollars... plus or minus a few cents."

Mina smiled. "Peter briefed us..."

He turned his phone face down on his pant leg. "Oh... then you already know."

Nash held out her hand. "No. Only about how you are on a franc and it's parity with the dollar. Not anything concerning distributing the funds or the whereabout of Stephanie. None of it. Please, continue."

He held his phone out and pointed at the line. "I won't even pretend to understand what this means. I think the joke is, I don't even play a doctor on television. But I never even dressed up as one for Halloween."

Nash read it four times. She turned to Mina and held up her two hands with the index fingers wide apart. "It's a group of words this long." She shook her head and turned back to the man. "So, what does it mean? Her. Personally?"

He sighed. "Years ago, she could speak. She even recognized me when I would visit. I'm not sure she understood who I was, but she would smile, which was enough for me."

"But now?"

He shook his head. "I'm sure you will go to see for yourself, but don't expect much. The doctors take care of her and think she will live a long life. Just... not a productive life."

Mina's pragmatic side kicked in. "And the account?"

"I've crunched the numbers. The account will take her until she is about seventy-four. If she is still alive, the money coming from Barbados will need to be increased. But I don't know who has control over the accounts there. Here, it is in a trust with the bank administering the payout. But as I said, there is only so much we can do."

Nash bobbed her head. "Hopefully, our investigation can shed light on the account and get it all adjusted. But the other account?"

"Is not so simple. Or maybe I should say, it's complicated, but only from my end. You see, here, at this bank, it is a number account, nothing more. In twenty-oh-two, the primary account was split. But it wasn't the account itself, which accounts for the sizable, accrued sum. But it was the deposit which became split. All the matching documentation was certified, and the account was re-characterized into the two accounts."

Nash narrowed her eyes as she turned her head. "So, what is going on with the account? I mean, a number doesn't just walk into a bank and make a withdrawal. So, what happens?"

He smiled. "That is exactly what happens. And like Ms. Dumont's account paying out to the care facilities, the other account compiles the accrual, and pays out to demand notices as international transfers."

Nash groaned. "More international."

He held up his hand, halting her. "Only from where we sit right now."

She lowered one eyelid. "Where?"

He smiled. "To the exotic foreign city of Denton, Texas."

31

STEPHANIE

MINA RELAXED in the back with Powder. They watched the rows of white buildings slide by. She placed her thumb between the dog's eyes and slowly drew it back. She could feel the eyebrows soften with each stroke. It was as close to the dog mother licking her pups as Mina would get. A thumb is as good as her tongue. Her voice was softly forlorn. "All the cities look closely the same. Even if they are four hundred years old. Nothing has character like a large stand of trees. Eh Powder?"

René glanced back. "Does she need to stop? There's a park a few blocks away…"

Nash didn't know if he sounded helpful or scared a dog might take care of business in his car. "Probably a good idea. It was a long time in the bank. And we appreciate your patience with all this."

René pursed his lips and tossed his head in a statement of cavalier. "What is this patience you speak of? I am spending the day with two lovely women and a wonderful dog. What more can a young man want on this beautiful day?"

Nash looked at the hovering thin layer of soft high clouds. "For the snow to hold off for a while?"

He peeked over and shook his head as he turned right. "No snow until Sunday. Tonight, will be a light rain shortly after a wonderful dinner. But no snow."

He drew up next to a sprawling park. The center field looked like it could hold several soccer games at once. A well-attended forest of evergreen and leafless trees encircled the field. Powder didn't hesitate.

As Nash watched her family wander with the driver, she drew the vibrating phone from her pocket. She notice the caller as she answered. "Deputy Director. What a pleasant surprise. I'm assuming it is after four thirty in the morning there?"

He chuckled. "It's shortly past eight. I expect the children... er... agents to be filing in soon. What's this bank?"

"It is the bank where whoever is connected to the account is getting a half million dollars a year. They hacked the Swiss bank account back in oh-two, or before, and have been siphoning off money since then. My guess is, find the person running the account and we have our domestic terrorist."

"Did you want to run this part?"

Nash watched as René waved his one arm, pointing out something about the field. She guessed he had played soccer on the field at one time. Mina looked entertained by something that wasn't politics or power. "No. I can turn over the reins on this part. However, I would suggest, once you have found the name or names, turn them over to Agent al-Faragi and let her coordinate with some of the other computer squints. They can run the usual searches through the person's past and social media. But I think, she's the top when it comes to the black arts of the darker side."

He cleared his throat. "With anyone else, I would have expected a humbler opinion. But based on your team's past performance, I'll let her know of her position in the research command structure and let her choose her own team. Any other insights?"

"Probably, when you go for a take-down, figure more than a

squad. And I would pull in Homeland, SWAT, ATF, and anyone else you can fill holes with. Denton doesn't appear large and sophisticated, but remember what we left on the highway in Colorado. And Muna should have better details about whom those mercenaries were."

"She filed her provisional final report yesterday. I haven't had time to go over it in detail, but it looks like they are a mix of elite white supremacists from many countries. So no, I wouldn't send a small squad to question them. This isn't a shoe salesman molesting children after school. But then, we, as a country, passed out of those simpler times a long time ago."

Nash rocked in agreement as the other three approached. "The entire world has lost its innocence, sir. Keep me posted. And thank you for hearing me out."

She slipped the phone back into her black leather pants pocket. "Did we have fun?"

Mina pointed back over her shoulder. "René played soccer on the field in school. It's really an extensive field. Famous as well. The new Swiss army guards for the Vatican practice their ceremonial marching out there. Maybe we could take a brief vacation when they're doing it and come watch?"

"Sounds fun." Nash opened the back door of the car.

———

Nash and Mina had been expecting some large, neo-gothic edifice dripping with carved stone gargoyles and heavy, fluted columns. The hospital would pass for a school built at the end of the twentieth century. The columns were four-inch-thick pipes holding up the entrance portico. Although the windows didn't look like energy-efficient double pane glass, they also weren't iron casement windows either. All hopes of a romantic building disappeared at the reception desk fully banked with state-of-the-art computers. Nash leaned in for only Mina to hear. "Muna would kill for a desk like this."

Nash stepped up to the receptionist and produced her credentials. "Good afternoon. I'm Nash Running Bear with the FBI and Interpol. We are here to see Stephanie Dumont."

The woman standing at one end of the desk looked up. The receptionist looked at her.

Putting the chart down on the desk, she approached. "Yes. Herr Müller called. I'm Doktor Holster. I'm the doctor in charge of her care." She extended her hand.

"Nash Running Bear, and Mina Lee."

"And your interest in Ms. Dumont would be...?"

"It's extraordinarily twisted and complicated, but she is a piece of a puzzle to an investigation involving international terrorists, much money, and grift at an international level."

The smile was small but there. "And you believe she may be involved somehow?"

Nash could sense being led down a garden path to a cesspool at worst, or a parking lot at best. "As I said, she is a small piece of a much larger puzzle. Even her existence is a mystery which only recently came to light."

The doctor looked down and then back up with her head cocked. "So, you know nothing about her?"

"We only know she had been in... um... your care for the last thirty years."

"But her condition...?"

Nash pulled out her phone and found the document. She turned her phone and expanded the page to make the type readable. She held it out. "I'm not a doctor. I'm a policeman. I don't even presume to know what this means. I know when I stub my toe. When I get shot, I have holes in my body distressing my wife and dog. But this...? This, I rely on someone like you to fill me in. But I am standing here being interrogated. They always led me to believe the Swiss had good chocolate and were hospitable. I still have hopes for the chocolate; because my wife loves her chocolate."

The staring match was a test of wills. Germanic pragmatism against the stoic patience of a California Paiute. Years before, the mountain herdsmen in Afghanistan had learned the hard way. Don't ever bet against the woman who could wait for days in a deer blind, while the world froze around her.

The pale blue eyes finally slid to look at the less threatening face. "Rue du Rhône, any taxi driver can take you there. Don't go to the Lindt. You can buy that in America. But the Rue du Rhône has truffles that will steal your soul." She turned and spoke over her shoulder. "Also, fruit jellies. Come along, agents. You are about to get your education."

Several tables stood about the large room, softly lit from the large north-facing windows. The single occupant sat in a wheelchair facing the windows. Shear drapes hung over most of the windows, except where the woman was. A blanket of snow or ice would eventually drape the denuded trees. The entire landscape seemed to hold its breath in anticipation of the next act.

The doctor nodded. "Stephanie Dumont. I think you will find she is not the terrorist you are searching for." She gave an inch of bow. "I'll be up front in my office when you are ready."

Powder walked around the woman twice and then stopped where the woman could see her. There was no reaction.

Nash pulled up a chair and sat. The woman's gray hair was thin but brushed. The pale gray blue nightgown was a soft flannel with tiny darker blue flowers dotting the fabric. Nash thought it was the kind her mother would have bought to remind her spring was only a long winter's nap away. The milk skin hands rested peacefully in her lap. The eyes blinked a few times a minute. If they saw, Nash couldn't tell what.

"Stephanie? My name is Nash. I'm with the FBI."

"She can't hear you."

Nash and Mina turned. The man stood leaning against the large doorjamb. His right supported his left arm. The left hand gently tugged at the salt and pepper cowlick. The sleeves of the starched white shirt hung gracefully rolled to mid-arm. Only the way the slacks hung told of the days without care. Only half of the crease still showed on the lower right. Sitting and wear had pressed out the details days before.

"She stopped hearing anything from this world when she came here. Any joy, or music, or laughter is inside her head. We only get the pulse from her heart and the sound of her breathing. Anything else..." His left hand fell from his hair and hung impotent in the air.

Nash stood. "Nathan, I presume. Or is it still Nature?"

The slight grinding of his head back and forth matched the slow close of his eyes. "It was a silly name. From a sillier time. But then, they were only kids." He uncrossed his legs and stood. His lips furled and then he passed his upper lip across his lower teeth.

He strode forward. "I don't have all the answers, but I can fill in what I do know." He held out his hand. "Nathan Donner. But then, you already knew that."

Nash held her hand out to another chair. "Please."

His sitting was of exhaust, having carried a heavy burden for a long time. He sighed and looked up. "Where to start?"

Nash held her hand out toward the woman in the wheelchair. "Let's start here."

"Stephanie... Stephanie was the closest I ever had to a sister."

"But she was a Dumont, not a Dubois."

He nodded as he wistfully looked over. "Well Dumont and Wright. So, in a perverse sort of way, she is my cousin."

Nash's forehead crushed into lines. "Wait. What? How do you get Wright out of it?"

Mina held up her hands and stood. "Is there any coffee around here? Because I think I'm going to need a lot of coffee for this."

He held his finger back toward the door. "Just tell them at the desk. Afternoon service for three. They already know I prefer tea. But they'll also put on some finger foods."

Mina took a deep breath and let it out with enormous eyes. "I'll be back."

"Maybe take Powder...?"

Mina pointed at Nathan. "Don't you dare start without me."

32

TEXAS TWO-STEP

THE HOSPITAL FARE did not disappoint. The finger food, as Nathan described it, rivaled more than a few five-star hotel's tries at putting on a British high tea. A small plate appeared at Mina's left hand. She looked up at the doctor's small, pursed smile.

"Your driver is also being entertained in our commissary. I have advised him where he needs to take you for chocolate." She pointed at the small confections. "These are just a preview."

Mina blushed slightly. "Thank you." She hadn't thought about René.

The doctor touched Mina lightly on the shoulder. "It is but a small thing. Many of our clients have drivers they seem to forget about. I'll leave you in Monsieur Dumont's apt hands. Enjoy."

Nash turned her narrowed eye on Nathan. "Dumont? Shouldn't that be duplicity?"

"The only person who could sign the contracts for Stephanie was a relative, or an agent of the family. To engage a solicitor would've led to many more complications. It was easier to have forged documents made to secure her place and then destroy them."

Nash lowered her head slightly. "And Jefferson, Jeffrey, whichever Dumont?"

"Was never in the picture. By the time we had to move Stephanie, he had passed away."

Mina burped a short laugh. "Define passed away…"

"He died of lead poisoning… in the bed of his head driller's wife."

Nash smirked. "Texas is a regular Peyton Place. But you said we had to move Stephanie."

"Bethanne, Stephanie's mother, and I. She lived for another couple of years after, but was the end of the dynasties. Good riddance."

"Dynasties?"

The man chewed on the small nibble of a tea sandwich. He dabbed at his mouth with his folded napkin as he bowed his head. "The skull and oil five. All were basically wildcat drilling companies who aspired to be large. When the wells gushed, they splurged in the grand. Never believing they would ever be back living on a dirt tract. The only permanent endeavor they ever engaged in was getting Congressman Wright elected. Even the refinery fell on hard times and became sold." He looked through the raised eyebrows. "It's hard to go bankrupt in American oil, but it happens."

Mina waved her hand at him and the silent woman in the wheelchair. "So why you? I know it wasn't because the father died and suddenly you stepped up to take over the care of a distant cousin…"

He pushed his small plate an inch forward. Looking over at the statue of a woman, he leaned back in his chair. "Like I said, our fathers were wildcatters. They chased oil or the hint of oil under barren land. They were more at home living in a sand blown tent on the west Texas plains than in a house.

"More than once I heard the creak of a bed being gotten into, only to be followed by an angry voice. And then the sound of heavy boots dropped on the floor. They forgot the fineries they grew up with as they wallowed down into the styes of their chosen addiction. To walk into the front door and smell oil and filth was to know the man was home."

Mina cocked her head as she pointed at Stephanie. "Her father…"

Nathan nodded. "Let me start over."

Nash held out her hand. "Please do, because this sounds like it gets sticky."

He grimaced and shook his small finger in his ear as if clearing water. "Somewhat, yes. But not where you think. More like slippery."

He poured more coffee and sat back. "When I was first sent off to boarding school, it was a grand adventure. Which rapidly became tedious. The trip from Paris, Texas, to El Paso, even today, takes all day to drive. On the bus, it is even longer. I would board shortly before lunch, and the bus would stop in Dallas for dinner. It was usually an hour and a half as the driver also would have the bus refueled as well. By eight at night, we were back on the road headed for Austin."

Nash frowned. "But your mother was living in El Paso…"

He held up his hand. "Shortly before midnight, they would change drivers in San Antonio, and I would change buses. My bus would stop for a snack or lunch at Fort Stockton. For years, I kept a book of matches from the Fort Stockton café. I don't know what I was considering, but I was ready if I needed a match. In El Paso, mother's driver would pick me up and I would arrive home in time for lunch."

Mina rolled her eyes. "And you were, how old?"

He smirked wanly. "It started when I was five."

Nash closed one eye. "Unaccompanied…?"

He looked at her blandly. "We were more resilient then. And we trusted strangers. I was in the care of the bus driver. Whether or not he was drunk was never in question. But when I was seven, I knew riding in the car to Dallas and the Dumonts was a better choice than the bus to and from El Paso. So, I only went to see my mother for Christmas. Until Stephanie was born. And by then, my mother had moved again to Los Cruses. The choice, for me, was obvious."

"So, the Dumont's had Stephanie. How does it make her a cousin?"

He smiled. "I didn't say the Dumonts had a child. I said Stephanie was born. There is a fine line of difference."

Nash closed her eyes as she took a breath. "Okay, explain the difference."

"When I went to the Dumonts, I was usually riding in Wit Wrights Buick. He was attending college at the University of Tulsa. It was a straight shot down the three-seventy-five to Paris and then over to Dallas. So, every holiday he would pick me up on the way down to be with Bethanne and if he was there, Jefferson."

Mina's finger went up as her eyes slid sideways. "So not to share old times with his school chum... but to have an affair with his school chum's wife."

Nash winced. "And you were just the distraction he was transporting out of the goodness of his heart. Ouch."

Nathan jogged his eyebrows. "Yes. How do you think I felt?"

"Something on the bottom of a shoe comes to mind." Nash rolled her eyes closed. "And this makes Stephanie the congressman's love child? Do you have proof?"

He shrugged. "Nowadays we can do a DNA test. But as I said, the floors and walls are depression era paper-thin. You can not only hear the boots drop and words spoken, but you can also hear bare feet on the floor and a nightgown being placed on the chair across the room." He lowered his head and looked through the top of his eyes. "As well as who isn't too drunk to make the bedsprings squeak and the headboard pound the wall. Need I continue?"

Nash and Mina both held up their hands.

Nash crossed her leg and rested her arm over the back of her chair. "So, Stephanie is born... is Jefferson happy or..."

He ran his finger along the grain of the table. But spoke flatly.

"Over the moon. Ecstatic. Jumping for joy. Even bought a new truck. He had not one well come in, but two." His face never changed as he looked up and pantomimed the man. "Oh, we had a child. Is dinner ready?"

"Did he ever know?"

Nathan shrugged. "What happened at home never seemed to matter. I was there, or I wasn't there. It only mattered to Bethanne and Stephanie. But when she was six, the business and government were changing. Drilling was becoming a game of permits and regulations, and Jefferson would rail against Washington and their do-nothing friend they had bribed into office." He held up his hand. "His words. Not mine. But it's where I first learned of the money they had raised but never spent. His drinking never seemed to cease in those days. He would arrive home reeking of whiskey, always had a bottle nearby, and would drive off back to west Texas already more than a few shots into breakfast."

Mina looked down at the last truffle—debating. "And at home?"

"We had already noticed the changes in Stephanie. The fall here, a stumble there. Words didn't always come out right. Her teacher at the private school suggested a doctor. The doctor suggested another doctor in Oklahoma City, and he referred Bethanne to a specialist in Chicago. I learned to drive, and by the end of the summer I had probably twenty thousand miles under my belt." His face winced on the left. "It was also the year I decided to become a lawyer and sue inept doctors. Nobody had an answer, just referrals to more and more expensive specialists."

Nash waved her hand at Stephanie. "Until..."

"It was a neurosurgeon in Baltimore. The man sat Bethanne down while I entertained Stephanie in the outer office. He didn't sugarcoat anything. He told her what was wrong and the prognosis. There was no surgery, no magic pill, no anything. The only sunshine was also the worst possible curse—she would progress to this, and then just grow old." He held his hand out. "In its own way, Alzheimer's is more of a blessing. At least it has a definite ending. Not pleasant, but it does finally end. With this…" He looked toward the hall. "There is a man here who is in his nineties…" His head sagged.

Nash moved both of her arms back to the table as she leaned in. "I hate to bring us back to work… But what are you doing here? Now?"

He looked at her. "I was afraid. If you found the money, I was afraid you would confiscate it, which would stop the payments to here. And there's nowhere for her to go. The United States only has warehouses. When any government allowance runs out, they would simply withhold her nutrition and let nature take her." He looked down at his hands and then back up. "But why are you here?"

Nash smiled and glanced back over her shoulder. "To meet Stephanie. To get an understanding of what was going on. The banks can only tell us so much. Even the hospital might only share a bit more. But it would be nothing compared to what you just told us. But also, tell me about the mercenaries in Taos and in Colorado."

"Not much. The bank account here, somehow, got split. Someone used Jefferson Dumont's access, even though he never had it. But Bethanne did. And as modern as Texas is, it is also as backward as it was before the Civil War. A woman is still little more than chattel. What she has, her husband owns as well. And his rights supersede hers. It is to keep a woman from divorcing a man and taking his life savings." He held out his hands. "It's not right, but it is how it is. So, someone, somehow, found out about the account and hacked it. But when they did, it also locked me out."

"Which is why you haven't changed anything since then."

"Correct. I knew if things didn't change soon, the money for her care won't be there. Which is why I came. To plead her case."

"The bank?"

He shivered his head. "To them, I am just another John Doe. Even though I showed the woman the records and name change and my being the executor of her estate. Nothing got her past showing me the door."

Nash and Mina looked at each other and rolled them in unison. "Frau Müller."

"Who?"

Nash turned. "Frau Müller."

"No. It was a Miss Stevens. She's the attendant to American accounts." His voice faded off. "Or so I was told."

Mina snorted softly as she confided to Nash. "Washington bureaucrats are so easily hoodwinked."

They looked up at the sound of a footstep. The nurse held out her hand. "Please. Stay. It is time for Stephanie's nutrition."

Nash glanced out the window at the gathering gloom. There was no rain yet, but also no snow. "We need to go soon, too. So, there's no connection between the split off account and the original."

"None. The only thing I have ever done with the original account was to move it to Barbados, took a draw to buy a condo in Arlington, and set up the account to take care of Stephanie. But that got hacked and what should have cared for her well past her turning a hundred… Well now…"

Mina smiled as she leaned back in the chair. "I think we can help you with that. So often the money thrown at politics ends up in pockets already lined with slime. At least with this, something good can come of some of it."

They stood. Nash leaned down and spoke to Powder. "Yes. We'll go outside and let you use the grass." She straightened. "Do you have plans for dinner?"

33

STRATEGIES

RENÉ PROMISED the bistro was over three hundred years old. The walnut paneling on the walls appeared older than most of America. The smells were subtle and enticing. Mina turned to Nash as they both named the same restaurant in Paris. "Tour d'Agent."

René laughed. "Ah, yes, Gustav's Ratatouille."

Mina enfolded her hand in a frowning Nathan's arm. "There was an amusing cartoon movie made about a rat who cooked at the Tour d'Agent in Paris. It is the oldest restaurant still in the same family. The duck is to die for, and with your newfound freedom, you will need to go spend some time in Paris."

He looked at her with caution. "My... freedom?"

Mina patted his arm. "Certainly, my dear. You didn't think all this would happen and you still have a job, did you?"

"But... what did I do wrong?"

They followed the troupe. "You? No... You were perfect. They entrusted you with a secret and you kept it. They entrusted you with the welfare of your cousin, and you cared for her better than anyone could have expected. No. You were perfect. But your boss, on the other hand. After he finds out he had a love child, he has not only not acknowledged, but ignored as she wastes away in a foreign country... No. He will step down to spend time with his newfound family. And to reacquaint with his sister." She lowered her head to his shoulder and growled. "Or I will smear his name until he emigrates out of defense."

She laughed at his shocked face. "Oh, calm down. It will be great. Someone on cable will make a docudrama and Texans will watch it in sleazy by-the-hour motels on the side of old highways. They will eat nacho flavored lard chips and cheer for the underdog wearing stars and strip boxer shorts. It will be great and win many awards and become a cult classic. Who knows, maybe it will bring back VCR and Blockbuster." They stopped at the table. "Or Wit will be a good boy and simply retire next week."

Nathan sat with a frown. "But there's the budget vote coming up..."

"And his successor will be great." She stared over at René. "What is the chef serving us tonight?"

René smiled and held out his hands to the person behind Mina.

"Good evening. I am Gerda, but if it makes you feel better..." She placed her hand on Mina's shoulder. "You may call me Chef. What would you like tonight?"

Nash smiled at Mina, getting caught out. She licked her lips and beamed. "My only request is for meat and vegetables mixed in a bowl for my dog. She's starving. Beyond that, we are in your hands. René guarantees it is the best in Switzerland, so that is all we are expecting."

Chef scowled at René. "I knew I should have held out for the French prince instead of settling for your uncle." She laughed and spun on her heel. "The meat. Raw or cooked?"

Nash glanced at Powder and thought about Uncle. "Probably either way, but let's go with cooked."

Gerda nodded her head to one side with a wink and spun on her heel. "Dinner for five, coming up."

The young waitress pursed her mouth to keep from laughing at René's blush. As she got around to his side of the table, she bumped his shoulder with her hip. The table laughed, and it was her turn to blush.

"I take it this is all family?"

René turned to Mina. "The barman isn't. But I played soccer with his younger brother in secondary."

As the festivities wound down and the meat and cheeses on the wooden trenchers disappeared, Nathan turned back to Mina. "When we get back…"

She popped a small piece of cheese in her mouth and chewed. "I'll handle Wit. But he will need to do the right thing and step down. He won't have to say why, but just let it be about family."

"And do what?"

"He needs to face his consequences. Maybe even use some of the wealth he has massed to shore up the account and look after his daughter."

He looked around the table. "He…" He furled his lips. "Without politics…" His body collapsed in on itself and he slowly deflated back to the chair.

Mina gently squeezed his arm. "He will need to learn how to be a regular human being. You too. When was the last time you went out on a date?"

He shook his head weakly.

"You don't remember? It's been so long?"

He looked at her. The wet glazed his eyes. "Never."

She glanced at Nash and looked back. "Did you ever want to? Was there someone…"

His eyes wandered along the table and to the side. "Years ago. There was an intern. But she was…"

"Out of your league? So much more than you? A goddess on a pedestal?"

The nod was small.

Mina pointed at Nash. "The first time I saw my Indian princess, she was playing mud baseball. It was drizzling, and the CIA refused to concede the game to the FBI. The red clay covered everyone and everything. You could barely tell who was who. They had tied the score at two to two, for five innings. There was a runner on second and first, and Nash was at bat."

His voice was only a shade of snarky. "Did she hit a home run and save the day?"

Nash looked up and started laughing. "Is she telling you about the baseball game of the decade?"

He nodded.

René frowned, and Nash leaned back and pointed at Mina.

"The runners were halfway off the plates. The pitcher wound up and just before he threw, the catcher called Nash an easy-out floozy."

René snorted. "Oh, shit." The man was used to competitive trash talking.

Mina nodded. "Nash caught the ball in her right hand. Turned on the catcher just as he was going to stand up. She ripped the mask off him and beat his face and nose with the ball. Broke his nose. Well, the umpire was so shocked he stepped back out of the way and never called the play dead. The two runners didn't know what was going on, but the ball had been pitched, so they were running. The score was four to two. Last inning, and Nash was the pitcher. First up to bat was their catcher, who could barely see where the home plate was; much less the ball to hit."

Nathan is now snickering, and René is holding his sides as Nash is smiling at the ceiling.

"Nash throws a missile underhand like she did throughout high school and the Marines. The ball was easily over ninety-miles-per-hour. Straight to the guy's ribs. Everyone could hear them crack. And then Nash yells out. Who's next?"

Nathan laughed. "But how did you ever meet? I mean, you're not CIA or FBI..."

Nash held out her hand as René leaned, laughing into her shoulder. "Tell him."

Mina blushed. "When she barked out who's next, I just raised my hand. I don't know why, I just did. Not much, but it was a movement in the small bleachers. She walked over and called me out."

"Did you bat?"

Mina pushed her fist into the man's shoulder. "I run my mouth. I jog people's memories, and I peddle ideas. There was no way I was ever getting out there in front of a bullet of a hardball and sweat."

"So, what happened?"

Mina looked over at Nash and blushed. "I hadn't dated for several years, so it was scary for many reasons. But I knew I wanted to meet this person."

The penny dropped for René. "Mon du. You did not know if she was..."

Mina shrugged her shoulder and face, shyly. "At the moment, it didn't matter. Dinner is dinner. Asking someone to bed is a different matter. Nes pa?"

The man gently cocked his head. "Oui...?"

Nash held her hand out at the remains of the meal. "Did we just have dinner?"

He pointed at the table. "Oui."

Mina pushed her lower lip out as she bobbed her head around. "Two men and two women... is there a difference? We didn't ask about your sexual appetite or nature. We only asked about dinner."

Nathan rolled his finger in the air. "So, you asked her out."

Nash chuckled. "She didn't even ask my name. She just asked if she could take me to dinner that night."

Mina laughed. "And she asked if she had to cook me breakfast in the morning, or could she just take us out?" She rolled her head and looked at Nathan with a single fluttering eye. "I peeked. There were only a couple of bottles of water in her refrigerator."

Nash leaned in, still laughing. "So, the answer is, always ask.

The answer can always be no. But if you don't ask, you'll never know if it might have been yes."

He leaned back. "But to date for the first time at fifty-six…"

René held his hand on Nash's arm to block her. He leaned over, man-to-man. "It is better to ask and strike out at fifty-six, than to die at eighty-nine and having never asked."

Mina tapped Nathan's arm and pointed at the other man. "Listen to him. That's the wise advice from a worldly man. Besides, you have a lot going for you. Steady employment for a full career. Your own house. And you are ready to explore the world. You will always find it is better to share a pleasant trip, with or without sex, than take a glorious trip and have no one to talk to."

He thought quietly and then his face became sober. "All fun aside. What happens now?"

Nash pulled her phone out of her pocket. She thumbed it open and touched the text message. "Funny you should ask. It would appear my other daughter is going to get her big girl pants next week." She smiled over at Mina. "Muna will lead the Incident Command Structure next week in Denton, Texas. She's going to be running herd on the whole alphabet. She wants to know if I want in." She stuck out her tongue and shook her head. "I've been there, done that, and have the holes in the neck to prove it." She leaned over and scratched Powder around the ears. The entire table could hear the groan.

Nathan's forehead creased above his nose.

Nash waved her hand. "It was another case. Powder and I were both shot." Then she realized it wasn't his confusion. "The other person in your account. They are about to get a rude awakening."

He looked from Nash to Mina and back. "What should I do?"

Mina's eyes turned to slits as she glanced at Nash. "I think we need three tickets to a certain island. There is something needing the attention of a good uncle."

Nash nodded and pulled up her phone. "On it."

Mina leaned toward Nathan. "Do you drink wine, scotch, or rum?"

"Um… scotch?"

Nash smiled as she kept typing her text to Magic Rick and his talent of all things travel.

34
NEW LIFE

A FEW GALLONS of blood poured into certain parts of the ocean is a recipe for water foaming from a feast of sharks, ripping at any movement, and biting whatever comes before their mouths. The marble-sized brains aren't engaged as much as the smell of a wounded creature. Turn on some powerful, flesh-searing lights, fill the space with pheromones of fight, flight, and fear. Stir in an overload of testosterone, and you have a press meeting during a slow news cycle.

Spice it up with a member of Congress who most of the news crews had to look up, and cameras will be live an hour before the official time as everyone speculates. Great white sharks are lightweight rookies compared to the battle honed press corps of the capitol.

Every reporter knew a three o'clock press meeting was explicitly timed to limit questions, and still make the evening news cycle. By the late night, it could be yesterday's or last-years news. The evening news was king, and blood out ruled any announcement about announcing a new bill or the usual blah blah blah of a Wednesday press brief by the junior whips of each party.

A man, who some reporters tried to remember if they had seen him before, stepped to the lectern. Someone snickered softly about makeup and hair, having missed a cowlick of hair at the side of his head.

"Good afternoon and thank you for coming. Congressman Wit Wright has faithfully, and selflessly, served this body, this nation, his state, and his constituents for over thirty years. It therefore comes with a heavy heart, and only after much concerted thought that as of this morning he has stepped down from his office. He has informed the governor, and they are selecting his replacement to serve out his term."

Nathan looked up. "I'll take a few questions at this time." He smiled and pointed at the woman in the red blazer holding the large, ostentatious advertisement microphone. Mina had all but guaranteed she would be in that spot.

"Where is Congressman Wright now?" The fluffy question he was told to expect from her.

Nathan nodded. "He is on his way to be with family. Next?" Ignoring the woman's open mouth.

He pointed to the older man with the camera crew behind him.

"Congressman Wright isn't a household name. What could have happened so suddenly for him to vacate his office in such a manner?"

Nathan smiled at the hours of prepping under the artful hand of Mina. "Just because you haven't been paying attention, don't assume this has happened overnight. To assume such does a disservice to the congressman, his long service to this nation, and your viewers. Last question?" He pointed at a friendly face he had only met the night before.

"Will the congressman be returning to his home state soon, or will he remain abroad for a while?"

Nathan smiled as the host of shocked faces turned to the newest member of their cadre. She had been languishing as a fluff reporter at one of the lesser stations. Watched by only a few, like Nathan. Mina had called her the day before. The foursome for lunch had also included the producer of the most watched evening news in the D.C. area.

Mina had promised the producer the reporter would ask the most insightful question, obviously scooping the rest of the news corps. Their cameraman had positioned himself to catch her in the center of the news corps, and the reaction from the other reporters. If three reporters turned their heads at the question, she had a ninety-day probation. If five turned, she had a one-year contract and a quiet dinner with the congressman's former top aide.

Nathan waited for the faces to point back his way. "I believe, as a private citizen, Mister Wright's visa is good for two years. But after today, I will no longer work for him. So, I'm no longer privy to his intentions. Thank you everyone. That's all the time we have." He nodded and walked back up the stairs into the capitol.

The two women and dog stood a small distance away. Nash leaned into her wife. "I would say this was the press conference to make a career."

Mina smiled. "I did some snooping. She started as one of the weather crew standing in two feet of floodwaters as the rain hammered her and the city of Houston. The next story was with a microphone held by a national guardsman as they were loading her into an ambulance."

Nash snorted softly. "Is she the one who went swimming, and they pulled her out like a mile away?"

Mina held up her two fingers. "Ready for dinner duty?"

Nash chuffed. "Some duty. Three helipad hops and we get free dinner for two and our dog."

Mina smirked as they turned toward the street. "The political paparazzi will go nuts this evening trying to find Nathan."

"How much will he be divulging?"

"The daughter kept secret because of health issues. The short-lived secret marriage because of mental health issues. And then, of course, the: *We kept them out of the spotlight to give them the calm life they needed*." She looked over with a smile. "The usual Washington bull-shit line ends discussions and speculations."

Nash opened the front and back doors of the red car. "Do you think he'll go over?"

Mina slid in and kissed Powder, now stationed with her front paws on the center consol. "He said in about a week or so, after he spends a bit of time with his mother. He wanted to give Wit some personal time to get comfortable with the situation and maybe take off the tie he's been wearing for fifty years. What about you?"

Nash slid into the driver's seat and started the car. She smiled at the deep rumble and rolled her head toward the dog. "I think I have some paperwork at the office. I know the deputy director will want a luncheon debriefing. So, about a week and then I'll go track down the kids."

THE BIRD WAS CATCHING ITS BREATH. THE USUAL LUNCH crowd inflated with last-minute add-ons to reservations. Immune to the needs of the usual wave of Belters, Nash and the deputy director had taken the table just out of the window, but not in the dog and pony show center. Their nearest patron was the service end of the bar. In effect, they hid in a corner nobody looked at. It was the deputy director's favorite table. Nobody had ever interrupted him, and the bartender was the server. Always busy and under attentive, as well as a former agent.

"I take it Agent al-Faragi filled you in on all the details?"

Nash smiled in her napkin and then sobered. She knew the official file had been brief and dry. "Oh yes. Her new body armor was a step up with the special fitting. She also took the new SIG Sauer. She had worried about the size and her smaller hand, but it seems there is a custom weapon shop there in San Francisco who made her thinner grips. And she was already used to the nine-millimeter rounds."

He watched her across the top of his coffee cup.

She twitched as if she had just remembered what he had been asking about. Powder rolled over with a short groan at her boot. "Oh yes. The operation in Denton, Texas. Turns out he was a known commodity to the local office there in Dallas, but because they never saw or heard anything, they had no reason to investigate. He belonged to a few of the white supremacy groups, but never strolled around in tactical gear or open carried. He had the lawn signs during the elections, and made donations to local campaigns, but never anything large or overt."

The deputy director leaned back in his chair with his coffee cup. His silverware lay gathered at the five o'clock. "But online...?"

"Very little on Facebook, or the usual social media. He was more known for grilling tips or posting pictures of his dog and barbecue dinners than anything political."

He put down his empty coffee cup as the bartender approach to clear his plate. "But in the black?"

Nash gathered her silverware and held up her plate. "Thanks, Denny."

The man dipped his head. "Certainly. Deserts today?"

She shook her head. "I have an obstacle course tomorrow. Just coffee."

He looked at the deputy director for the nod. Coffee it was.

Nash dabbed at her mouth with the napkin. "Muna found his fingerprints in many places. But the worst was the mercenary site. For a man showing the IRS an income of less than a hundred and fifty thousand, he has some serious explaining to do. He's been brokering several international and domestic training sites, gun ranges, gun swap meets, and what he titled as *parties* or *meet-ups*."

"And the raid?"

Nash winced. "I guess I should have taken Powder." She took a sip of the fresh coffee. "If it hadn't been for a radio squawk, they would have never known the house had a basement. They couldn't find any secret panels, so they cut a hole in the living room floor and dropped into the basement. The underground explained the enormous concrete patio in the backyard. The detached garage had an access elevator for receiving crates. The house access was through the pantry and another through the closet in the second bedroom.

"The armory looked more like the storage at Fort Sill. He was ready to arm a few companies up to and maybe including a nuclear dirty bomb. They had racks of hazmat suits, cases of iodine pills, injection pens from inflections to bee stings, to drug overdoses. And the list of weapons ran from every kind of hand weapon you could think of to RPGs, stingers, and even a couple of armed drones."

"So why the ransom? Where's the connection?"

Nash rolled her eyes wide as she picked up her coffee. She held up her index finger backward. "One the PAC. The original hack of the account was through the old account. Two, when the first account, in Paris, Texas, closed, and the funds transferred out of the country, the names connected were Wit Wright, Jefferson Dumont, Claudius Dubois, Nate Dubois, and Maggie Wright. Which was where he aimed his shenanigans."

The deputy director frowned. "Why was Maggie on the list?"

"We think maybe someone figured out she might outlive Claudius."

"So, how did Nathan get on the list?"

Nash leaned back in her chair. "In his youth, he had some smarts and a lot of spunk. He sent papers originally used for him to help Bethanne access the money in their bank. The notarized letter gave Nate Dubois, power of attorney, to all of Jefferson Dumont's banking."

"Why would he do that?"

Nash snorted softly. "Because he was living in a misogynist state and mind-set. At one time, not too long ago, like the early seventies, woman weren't allowed to own a home, a business, or do banking in their own names. A male member of their family had to co-sign. Even going to their gynecologist, they had to have a male member with them. If it meant dragging a five-year-old nephew into an annual checkup, the kid grew up real fast."

He winced for all the males in a position of power. "Power of attorney in hand, and he moves everything to Barbados."

"And removed everyone else from the new account. Except Stephanie. But, because Maggie was originally on the previous account, and with our friend's help, we split the old account and established the two new accounts."

He pushed his finger along the tablecloth. "Which will be for…"

"One, Nathan has the access, but it also has a part to increase the allowance for Stephanie's care and if anything should happen to Nathan, the estate rests entirely for her care."

"And upon her death?"

Nash's head rocked. "By that time Maggie may also be gone, but it would all go to whatever Maggie will set up for her estate. My guess is it will continue her work of education and clean water and living in the pueblos."

He looked at the ping from his phone. "It would appear we can only hold the world at arm's length for so long. You fly out…?"

"Tonight. Straight to Albuquerque this time. Felix, the young Homeland agent, stayed with the cleanup down in Texas. I'm hoping he knows how to find Uncle and Maggie."

The deputy director bobbed his head as they stood. "New Mexico is a large area to just rely on Powder's nose."

"As Uncle would say, never count out an Indian dog or General Paiute Sense."

ALSO BY BAER CHARLTON

The Very Littlest Dragon: NEW Editions
(All-new full-color ebook, a paperback with
coloring pages, and a full-color Collector's Edition hardback)

Stoneheart — Pulitzer Nominee 2015
Angel Flights
What About Marsha?
Pirate's Patch
Flat Surf

I Drink Coffee and Make Shit Up
One Writer's Journey Without Signposts

JOLIE "ROCKET" ROBERTS SERIES
Dry Bridge of Vengeance – Book One
Dry Ridge of Redemption – Book Two

THORNY WALLACE SERIES
Death in the Valley – Book One
Light to Light – Book Two

SOUTHSIDE HOOKER SERIES
Death on a Dime – Book One
Night Vision – Book Two
Unbidden Garden – Book Three
Boomtown – Book Four
One Day Under the Grass – Book Five
Southside Hooker Series: Books 1–5 Box Set

(Collector's Edition hardback & ebook available)

<u>Nash Ruunning Bear Mysteries</u>
A Skeleton in Bone Creek – Book One
Double-time Out of Taos – Book Two
Three Crows East of Empty – Book Three

<u>Coming 2023</u>
Four-corner Spread – Book Four
Cinco d' Mojave – Book Five

BAER CHARLTON

ABOUT THE AUTHOR

Bestselling author Baer Charlton graduated from UC Irvine with a degree in Social Anthropology, monkeyed around for a while, and then proceeded onward with a life of global travel, multi-disciplinary adventure, and meeting the memorable array of characters he would come to describe in his writing. He has ridden things with gears, engines, and sails, and made things with wood, leather, and metal. He has been stitched back together more times than the average hockey team; his long-suffering wife and an assortment of cats and dogs have nursed him back to health after each surgery.

Baer knows a lot about many things in this world. History flows through his veins and pours out of him at the slightest provocation. Do not ask him what you may think is a simple question unless you have the time to hear a fascinating story.

You can find more at
www.mordantmedia.com